"Don't look like that, my love,"

Worth murmured and brushed an errant lock of hair off her temple. His dark eyes gleamed, and he bent over to nibble her earlobe, then whispered, "Don't you realize that we *must* stop? Unless you wish that I seduce you right here, prey to the curious eyes of anyone who might enter the study?"

Hastily Olivia scrambled to her knees, ran her fingers through her disheveled curls, then stood up and tugged at her bodice and skirt. "Of course I don't wish *that*," she said gruffly.

Fabiàn chuckled softly and got up unhurriedly to help her straighten her sleeves. Olivia darted an incredulous glance at him, then hastily lowered her lashes to hide her confusion and dismay. He was laughing at her! There was no mistaking the glint of his eyes or the quiver of his lips, however quickly he surpressed them.

"What is it you *don't* wish, my sweet delight?" he asked. "Be seduced, or be caught at being seduced?"

Also by Karla Hocker

A Bid for Independence

Published by
WARNER BOOKS

～A～
MADCAP SCHEME
Karla Hocker

WARNER BOOKS

A Warner Communications Company

WARNER BOOKS EDITION

Copyright © 1987 by Karla Hocker
All rights reserved.

Cover art by Don Case

Warner Books, Inc.
666 Fifth Avenue
New York, N.Y. 10103

 A Warner Communications Company

Printed in the United States of America

First Printing: February, 1987

10 9 8 7 6 5 4 3 2 1

To my husband Jim
who encouraged me to write

CHAPTER 1

"My dearest, sweetest Merrie! Say you will help me."
Olivia Fenshawe looked imploringly at her old governess.
It was not absolutely essential to have Miss Merriweather's
assistance in this daring plot, but it would make her feel less
guilty, less scandalous, were Merrie to approve of the
scheme, at least in deed if not in spirit.

"It's outrageous and foolish beyond belief, Olivia! How
can you even think of it? I'll not help you to certain ruin,
child!"

"You may believe me foolhardy, but admit, Merrie, it's
the *only* way to safeguard the position for Tony!"

Olivia tugged a length of starched muslin from the depth
of her cloak bag and shook it with a flourish under Merrie's
bespectacled nose.

A pained expression crossed Miss Merriweather's disci-
plined countenance as she regarded the tall young lady
towering above her with arms akimbo in a challenging
stance. Olivia was clad only in skintight hose of ecru knit
and a man's shirt of snowy lawn with frills of lace down the
front and around the wrists and collar. Long, disheveled

locks of a very dark nut brown with reddish highlights framed her face, softening the lines of her stubborn chin and high cheekbones.

"Olivia, you'll be disgraced if you're found out! I cannot permit you to do it!"

Olivia's hazel eyes twinkled with golden specks of mischief. "You forget, dearest, that I'm in your charge no longer. I've passed my twenty-second birthday; I'm my own mistress and need ask permission of no one—and I shan't be coaxed out of this either!"

Miss Merriweather drew herself up and sat ramrod straight in her chair, the only chair for that matter in the minuscule second bedroom of her Hans Town flat. "I have *never* during my forty years of teaching and governessing resorted to coaxing!"

"Except when you were dealing with Tony." With loving tenderness, Olivia placed her hand against the old lady's still smooth and rosy cheek. She smiled. "You coaxed him out of his dark moods, and you even cajoled my stubborn little brother into attending his books."

"And see where it got us! Anthony should have learned by now that he cannot run away from his responsibilities. I should have punished him with bread and water in his room instead of sweet-talking him out of the old barn whenever he hid there in a fit of the sullens. I spoilt him!"

"It wasn't your fault alone," Olivia said consolingly as she draped the muslin cravat around her slender neck. With her chin pushed toward the ceiling and inexperienced fingers laboring at her throat in an effort to tie some kind of acceptable knot, her voice sounded strained and weak. "I have my share of blame to carry, and so does everyone at Fenshawe Court, from the butler to the boot boy—except for *dear* brother Richard and his wife."

When the feat of tying the cravat was finally accomplished, Olivia pressed her chin down against the painstakingly arranged folds and added more forcefully, "And if Richard and Harriet had waited to let *me* speak to Tony instead of browbeating him, he would not have felt so insulted; he would be installed tomorrow in the very lucrative post as secretary to the Earl of Worth!''

''That looks more like a Belcher kerchief than a cravat,'' muttered Miss Merriweather with a judicious glance at Olivia's handiwork.

''You do it, Merrie dearest,'' said Olivia in a coaxing voice.

''I'll have no hand in this, young lady! Do not waste your wiles on me.''

For a few moments quiet reigned in the small chamber while Olivia removed the offending article and tossed it onto the narrow bed under the window. She rummaged in her cloak bag again and removed a pair of well-worn tan corduroy breeches. With a shudder Miss Merriweather closed her eyes when Olivia donned the male garment and did not open them until a very unladylike exclamation from her young guest's lips compelled her to take notice.

''Thunder and turf!'' muttered Olivia, again busily at work with the cravat. ''It's like trying to tie a knot in a slithering snake.''

''Not that way, child! And pray don't swear! It's not befitting a lady of quality.'' Miss Merriweather came to her feet and, with few economical movements, tied a fair imitation of the Waterfall.

''Thank you, Merrie.'' A dimple peeped beside an infinitesimal, heart-shaped mole at the left corner of Olivia's mouth.

''Humph! And why, pray tell, did Tony not jump at the opportunity to work for Lord Worth? He's been champing at the bit ever since Sir Richard called him down from Cambridge, and now he's botched the perfect opportunity to get away from Fenshawe Court and stand on his own two feet. Let him face the consequences and confront Lord Worth with his excuses for showing up late for the post. Let him grow up and be a man!''

''Merrie! I can't believe you are speaking so harshly of Tony. He's young yet and will learn, but what would he do if Lord Worth employed some other young man in the meantime? Tony has no other prospects and he may never receive an offer like this one again—he *needs* this position!"

"He could have had other offers of employment," countered Miss Merriweather fiercely, "had not Sir Richard deprived him of a valuable education!"

"But Richard did, and that's why I must help Tony now. He'll come around, you'll see. He's miffed now because he learned that Richard had *gambled* away Fenshawe Court after Mama and Papa's carriage accident."

Miss Merriweather nodded, causing her steel-rimmed spectacles to bounce to the tip of her slender nose. Impatiently she pushed them back. "Yes, that would throw Tony in a pelter."

"You knew?" Olivia blinked in surprise. "Even to me the information came as a shock."

"Servants will talk, child. Not to you, of course—you were too young at the time—but they confided in me. After your parents' death, while Sir Richard continued on his jolly way in London and you were hounded by bill collectors from sunrise till dark, the staff at Fenshawe Court lived in constant fear of being turned off. That coat is too large, dear. You look puny and undernourished with all that material flapping around your shoulders. What we need is a bit of buckram padding. Take it off!"

Olivia perched on the hard bedstead while Miss Merriweather bore off the coat to her sitting room, where she kept a well-stocked sewing basket near her favorite wing chair. An impish smile flitted briefly across Olivia's face—Merrie was more than half won over to the scheme, whether she realized it or not.

Tony had feared that working for Lord Worth would prove a dead bore, but Olivia hoped she'd have—at the very least—some stimulating experiences at Worth House. The earl was actively involved in government affairs; his name cropped up in *The Times* with predictable regularity. She might meet Lord Liverpool or Lord Castlereagh, might she not?

Even if her work would only be concerned with dreary

estate matters, she should be able to derive some entertainment from her extraordinary position. Surely it was impossible that in the guise of Tony her life would continue along the usual, humdrum path she'd been treading for so long. But what if she were discovered? Pricks of apprehension raced up and down her spine.

It *was* rather daring of her, wanting to fool the Earl of Worth! She must succeed, or Tony would be in dire straits. Their sister-in-law Harriet would see to it that Tony would never again be welcomed at Fenshawe Court.

Quickly Olivia banished the timid voice of doubt and assumed a carefree attitude, hugging her knees to her chest when she heard Merrie's busy steps approach the door. Actually, it felt comfortable to be wearing breeches again. Years ago, when she and Tony had gone riding, she'd worn breeches and again when Tony had appointed himself her fencing master. Initially Tony had merely wanted to kick up a lark, perhaps ruffle Merrie's feathers a bit by introducing his sister to the manly art of fencing; but Olivia had shown herself an apt pupil, and they had continued with the lessons until she'd approached her eighteenth year. Then Merrie had put a firm halt to such scandalous proceedings, and Olivia and Tony had had to sneak out in the dead of night to continue their fencing practice.

"Here it is." Miss Merriweather carried the coat between two fingers and dropped it in Olivia's lap. "The only thing I never understood is why on earth the earl did not claim his winnings," she mused.

"I don't suppose he'd have gained much had he demanded that we leave. After all, the Court was heavily mortgaged and the bank owned most of the estate," replied Olivia. "It was poetic justice, don't you think? No man should take another's home in a game of cards!" She slipped into the coat and pirouetted before the cheval glass. "Apparently Lord Worth redeemed the mortgage, then he ordered Richard to marry an heiress—"

"Harriet."

Olivia bowed before the mirror. "Yes, our inestimable

Harriet, whose dowry paid for improvements on the lands and the tenants' farms, and enabled Richard to get a start on repaying his debt to Lord Worth."

Olivia practiced several more bows, some low and respectful, some curt and haughty.

Miss Merriweather, watching Olivia's antics, raised a brow and muttered, "I wonder, do you really undertake this masquerade for Tony's sake, or is it for your own edification?"

And who could blame the poor child, she thought when Olivia stared at her in surprise. When Sir Richard had returned from London a pauper, he'd been embittered and cruel, lashing out at Olivia and Tony with cutting words *and the whip!* Olivia, a child of fifteen, had tried to mother young Tony and protect him from Sir Richard's fury. There had been no help from Sir Richard's new bride, who had resented living at Fenshawe Court at the mercy of the Earl of Worth. On the contrary, Harriet had delighted in making Olivia's life more miserable than it was already. She had tried, but without success, to quash the young girl's joie de vivre and her adventuresome spirit. Not even a come-out had been arranged for Olivia!

Miss Merriweather shook off these oppressing memories and addressed Olivia, who still stared frowning into space. "I must say, Olivia, it was quite generous of Lord Worth not to insist on instant payment of the debt. Now he's trying to help further by offering Anthony employment."

Olivia swallowed a bitter retort, then substituted a milder version of her thoughts on the earl's "generosity," her husky voice tight with suppressed anger. "More likely it was expediency which governed his actions. What could he do with a mortgaged estate, except throw good money after bad? And when he was in need of a secretary, *voilà*, there was the younger Fenshawe who could help out. Probably Lord Worth cannot employ anyone else because he overworks his staff and word has gotten out so that no one will apply!"

"Olivia!" admonished Miss Merriweather. "What a mean-spirited thing to say! You are jumping to a conclusion without knowledge of all the facts. Besides, if you really believed that, why do you feel you must masquerade as Tony?''

Olivia's cheeks flamed crimson at the reprimand, and she lowered her eyes in shame. In a gentler voice Miss Merriweather continued, ''Try to curb that trait, dear. I do not like the hardness and cynicism you've developed. I wish Sir Richard had not insisted on my leaving when you reached your twentieth birthday.''

''Oh, I wish so, too!'' Olivia enveloped the slight old lady in a warm hug. ''But it was best for you. I know you hated living with Richard and Harriet, and you had stayed so long only for Tony's and my sake.''

Miss Merriweather cleared her throat and then asked, ''When did Lord Worth offer the post to Tony?''

''He stopped at the Court in June, ostensibly on his way to Bath, although I never saw him or heard tell of him there. I was in Bath at the time—Grandmama had sent for me to give me another lecture on the perils of being left on the shelf!''

The two women exchanged speaking looks, and Olivia continued, ''The earl stayed only a few moments to speak to Richard; he didn't confer with Tony, or even ask to meet him. Tony just happened to cross the courtyard when Lord Worth was climbing back into his curricle, and the earl called out to him, 'I shall expect you on the first of September, Fenshawe. Do not fail me!' ''

''Indeed,'' said Miss Merriweather dryly.

Olivia chuckled. ''Yes, indeed! Tony was furious when he learned that Richard had committed him behind his back. Time and again Tony asked Richard for a commission in a cavalry regiment or to be allowed to breed horses instead of being condemned to a life of drudgery.''

Miss Merriweather shook her head sadly. ''Tony tends to dramatize his own situation. 'Life of drudgery!' Pshaw! But I did hope he'd matured enough not to run off.''

''I do not think he would have had Richard kept a better rein on his temper.'' Olivia assumed her older brother's stance, hands clasped behind her back and rocking to and fro on the balls of her feet. "Lord Worth and I between us have housed and fed you for years," she blustered in a fair imitation of Richard's gruff voice. "The least you can give in return is an honest day's work!"

"I get the general drift of that edifying conversation." Miss Merriweather nodded knowingly.

"Well, and to top it all, that very same afternoon Harriet insisted that Tony return a vastly becoming vest he'd ordered from his tailor. She wasn't going to pay for another item of his clothing until he started working for Lord Worth!" Olivia's face crumbled. With the back of her hand she dashed away the tear that threatened to drop from her long lashes.

"Tony did return the vest to the shop in Bath, but then he simply vanished with Thunder. That was two weeks ago," she said quietly.

Miss Merriweather sighed. "I need not ask whether he's staying with your grandmama. She'd never take in such a rambunctious youngster. But at least he has Thunder," she said to comfort Olivia. "Sometimes a good horse proves a better companion to a disillusioned young man than any friend of the human species could be."

"You are quite right, Merrie." With more force than necessary Olivia pulled on her boots, then paraded through the bedroom, determined to overcome her tearful mood. "See, Merrie? Don't I look complete to a shade?"

"Mercy, child! Where do you pick up those expletives and cant expressions? From Richard and Tony, no doubt." She answered her own question and immediately fired off another query. "How ever will you explain your prolonged absence to Richard and Harriet?"

Fully aware that Miss Merriweather was just as averse to fibs as she was to expletives, Olivia confessed with a mutinous scowl, "I told them I'd be staying with Grandmama indefinitely . . . until Tony would return. They'll never dare check on me *there*."

Contrary to her expectation, she received no scolding on

account of that bouncer. Miss Merriweather only stated complacently, "You'll never carry it off, you know. How could you possibly hide your hair? You cannot wear a hat or a cap in the house. And the earl, don't forget, has met Tony!"

"For thirty seconds, over two months ago!" cried Olivia. "With my hair cropped, Tony and I will be as two peas in a pod."

"Cut off your hair!" Miss Merriweather stared in horror as Olivia brandished a pair of scissors and started cutting away. A long brown curl gleamed softly with a hint of chestnut in the candlelight, then dropped to the floor.

"You are butchering it! Stop!" With this anguished cry, Miss Merriweather rushed to Olivia's side and snatched the scissors from her hands. "Thank goodness," she muttered, "Tony wears his hair rather long; we need not make you look bald." With great caution she ventured a snip here and there.

Olivia passed her a brush. "Try to arrange it sort of wild and mussed up all over. Tony calls it the Windswept."

The governess sniffed disdainfully. "I've seen young gentlemen strutting about with a mop of hair like that, only I thought they'd forgotten to groom themselves."

Olivia chuckled and relaxed. With Merrie putting on the finishing touches, she'd have the best disguise she could hope for.

"If only I need not go to my niece's just now," Miss Merriweather declared. "Why in heaven's name did the wretched girl choose to have her first confinement this September? How long do you plan to keep up this masquerade, Olivia?"

"Only until Tony comes to his senses and returns. I have to prevent the earl from engaging some other young man, for Tony's bound to realize soon that this position is just right for him. Why, he could save enough money within a twelvemonth to buy himself a cornetcy or a share in an Irish stud!"

Miss Merriweather bit her lip in indecision, then took the

plunge courageously. "Good luck, child. I shall have a second key for my flat made tomorrow and have it delivered to you. If anything goes amiss, leave Worth House at once and stay here! Promise, Olivia!"

Olivia nodded her head and hugged her good friend, who promptly pushed her away to removed her spectacles and wipe her eyes. "I shall be returning by the end of November latest," said Miss Merriweather gruffly and restored her glasses to submit Olivia to a final, careful inspection.

The old lady shook her head mournfully. "You look more like a man than many of the fops promenading in St. James's and Hyde Park." A last stroke of the hairbrush was applied to the short curls, a final twitch given to the cravat, and then she pronounced,

"*Now* you look complete to a shade, my dear."

"Fenshawe, there's no reason to overdo it. I won't be giving that speech until next week, you know."

The deep voice, with it's lazy, amused drawl, drove the color into Olivia's cheeks. This was her third day working for Lord Worth, but each time he addressed her—be it as "Fenshawe" or "Tony"—she jumped guiltily.

Olivia placed her pen in the inkwell and rose to stand behind her small escritoire wedged between the window and the earl's impressive mahogany desk. Straightening her cravat and buttoning her dark blue coat, she focused tired eyes on her employer, who stood tall and imposing in the shadowy doorway. She could not distinguish much of his person beyond his dark head, the fiery glint of a ruby in the folds of his snowy cravat, and another one on his left hand resting against the doorjamb.

"Come, put away the papers; it's past eleven. I'm off to White's—won't you join me for an hour or two?" The earl strode farther into the candle-lit study, providing her ample opportunity to admire the elegant, midnight-blue evening coat molded to broad shoulders and hugging his trim waist. An immaculate white shirt, a pearl-gray vest, and pantaloons of a darker shade of gray completed his attire.

Envy raised its ugly head in Olivia's breast. If only Tony had aspired to such understated elegance, she need not now sport a checkered waistcoat or striped pantaloons to add variety to her meager wardrobe. But, more pressing than the lack of appropriate clothing for a visit to the exclusive club was the necessity to remain hidden from public view as much as possible to make Tony's entry into the fashionable world later on a smooth one. She shook her head, declining Lord Worth's second casual invitation to White's.

"No, thank you, my lord. I'll line up a few more arguments to convince your colleagues that Lord Wellington's request for speedier delivery of adequate supplies and provisions warrants immediate action, and then I'll retire if you have no further orders for me."

Dark brows snapped together over equally dark eyes. "You make me sound a veritable slave driver. If I have any orders for you at all, it's to *ask* you to quit for the night." He flicked a finger against some papers on his cluttered desk, then looked at her sharply. "Why won't you accompany me?" he demanded. "You must wish to taste some of the town life after your long seclusion in the country."

"I appreciate your concern, my lord, but I've no hankering for a fashionable life."

"More of a mind to see the sporting events, eh? Horses, sparring, cockfighting?" Lord Worth nodded understandingly. "Let me introduce you to a few knowing young chaps who can take you under their wings. You'd much better trust me to find companions for you than go about on your own, a pigeon ripe for the plucking by some Captain Sharp."

Although her insides had heaved in a most squeamish manner at the mention of cockfighting, Olivia drew herself up to her full five feet six inches and retorted haughtily, "I'm no green youth to be taken in easily!"

"Oh?" The charcoal eyes gleamed mockingly. "And how old are you, o ancient one?"

"I'm twenty-t . . ." A paroxysm of coughing shook her as she tried to swallow the "two," for Tony, of course, was barely twenty years old. ". . . Too old to be plucked," she finished lamely. "Besides, I don't like White's, or Brooks's, or Watier's!"

There was a moment of silence, during which the earl regarded her intently. Gone was the sleepy, bored look he was wont to show the world. Olivia had to force herself not to squirm under that all-observant stare.

"Ah, yes," he finally drawled. "The lamentable excesses of the inestimable Sir Richard have left their mark. But, for your information, bantling," his voice sharpened to steel, "you *need not* gamble at the clubs. There's good company to be found over a bottle of Burgundy, or even some smuggled cognac."

Olivia felt the heat mount in her cheeks again and berated herself for her lack of composure. Her lips tightened and her eyes sparked dangerously, but she said nothing, merely bowed her head in acknowledgment of the subtle reprimand.

"Very well, suit yourself." The earl dismissed her stubborn refusal with a wave of his hand. "Don't forget, tomorrow morning I want you to accompany me to Tattersall's. Sir Richard informed me you're beyond compare as a judge of horseflesh."

Without waiting for a reply, Lord Worth turned on his heel and strode from the room.

Slowly Olivia expelled her pent-up breath and unclenched her fists. She must not let the earl get under her skin like this! She'd been here only a few days and already she felt skittish in his presence. She'd come quite unprepared for Lord Worth's many-faceted personality. Richard had described him as saturnine and aloof; he'd given no warning of the earl's magnetism or the dynamic force he employed to sweep aside obstacles. The first time Lord Worth had invited her to White's, she'd almost succumbed to her curiosity about that famous club, so charmingly had he spoken and cajoled. This time, thank goodness, he'd tried to browbeat her—and he was much easier to withstand when she could feel anger at his arrogance well up within her.

Olivia tugged at her cravat and groped for the gold chain around her neck from which the key to Merrie's tiny flat hung suspended between her breasts. It was there, safe and secure. She might have to make use of it sooner than anticipated, if only to get away from Worth House for a few hours to sort out her confusion.

Olivia had come here with only loathing in her heart for the Earl of Worth. He had accepted Fenshawe Court as the stake in a game of cards when, most likely, Richard had been too drunk to know what he was about. She'd thought of Lord Worth as a despicable cad who would mistreat his servants, lead a life of dissipation, and display manners fit only for the barnyard or the cockpit. But she'd been wrong on at least *two* counts—she could not judge on the life of dissipation as yet.

I still detest him. Unfortunately, since her image of the earl had proven cracked and incomplete, she could not put any force behind that statement. Since she'd met Lord Worth, she could not but wonder what his version of the fateful card game seven years ago would be. . . .

Olivia tossed her head and kicked in frustration against the carved mantel of the fireplace. Two wickedly elegant rapiers hanging crosswise above the mantel clanged softly, and she quickly reached up to still the sound. With a sigh for her sore toe and the wayward Tony, she resumed her seat at the small desk and immersed herself again in the preparation of the speech Lord Worth planned to make in the House of Lords.

Engrossed in fiery arguments which the earl would inevitably reduce to ashes—she could not picture him emotional about anything, even the dearth of supplies to Wellington's hard-pressed army in Spain—Olivia was alerted to the arrival of a late visitor only by the opening of the study door and a nasal, masculine voice addressing the butler in disdainful accents.

"There's no need for you to follow me about, Robinson. I won't make off with the family silver, even to spite you, you old doom croaker!"

A vision of male elegance minced into the room and took Olivia's breath away. Her eyes popped wide open, then she blinked rapidly as she took in the dazzling magnificence of a daffodil-yellow coat worn open to display a white satin waistcoat embroidered lavishly with strutting peacocks, and sea-green pantaloons strapped over high-heeled evening pumps. Besides a quizzing glass, this tulip of fashion sported no less than half a dozen fobs and seals suspended from silver chains. His chin and long, pomaded locks disappeared inside a cravat and collar so high and stiff as to make any movement of the head impossible, which was why he hadn't seen her yet.

The slight young man, not much taller than she, headed in the opposite direction from her, to the credenza where decanters and glasses were invitingly arrayed on a silver tray, and poured himself a generous measure of brandy. As he raised the glass to his lips, it occurred to Olivia that she should make her presence known.

"May I be of assistance, sir?"

Her polite words had a startling effect. His hand jerked, sending a stream of amber liquid trickling down his chin and exquisite attire. Since he could not turn his head, he spun around to face her at a half crouch as though ready to pounce on an enemy.

"Damn you, imbecile! You've ruined my new vest! Who are you?"

Olivia bowed. "Anthony Fenshawe, sir, Lord Worth's new secretary."

"Get out then! I require no assistance. Know my way about Worth House better than you, I dare say."

But Olivia had no intention of leaving this rude stranger to his own devices, not, at least, in the study where the mahogany desk was littered with the earl's papers. She walked toward the fireplace and would have tugged the bellpull had the young dandy not rushed over and caught her arm.

"I told you to make yourself scarce!" he hissed. "How dare you ignore me! Apologize this instant!"

"Sir, I merely planned to ring for a footman to conduct you to another room and to fetch a cloth and water. That brandy will leave a stain if it's not removed immediately. Satin is nigh impossible to clean," she pointed out reasonably.

His color rose and his dark eyes, very like Lord Worth's, narrowed to slits. "How dare you patronize me, you dunce! What do you know about satin anyway?" he spluttered.

Olivia bit her lip. What *would* Tony know about the laundering of satins? She must take care not to blunder like this again. Looking down her nose at him, she attempted to brazen it out. "Anyone who is not an absolute featherbrain would know—"

"I'd not be caught dead with a checkered cloth vest like yours," he interrupted, then sniffed and cast a disparaging look over her attire.

"And I wouldn't be caught dead with a soiled vest like yours!" she countered.

Unfortunately, this reminded the young man of his grievance. "Why, you upstart! First you destroy my waistcoat, then you ignore my orders, and now you want to mock me! Apologize, I say!"

He glowered at her for a moment or two, and when she remained mute, he shouted in his annoying, nasal voice, "If you won't apologize, I demand satisfaction! Name your seconds, sirrah!"

Olivia, feeling as if she had somehow blundered into a play without having been informed of the plot or her role, raised her brows at the irate dandy. "I beg your pardon?"

"Too lily-livered to give me satisfaction, eh?" he asked with a smirk. "It's too late now to beg my pardon."

"Well, since I hadn't meant it that way in any case, we should both be satisfied. Now, sir, if you've come to see Lord Worth, which for your sake I hope you haven't, you must return at some other time; he's left for White's. Or, if you must, you may join him there."

She tried to steer him discreetly toward the door, but he spun around and slapped her face. "Now you'll have to meet me," he said calmly.

Shocked, Olivia let go of his shoulder and stared at him while he began the difficult struggle of extricating himself from his tight coat. Her eyes widened, and when he tossed aside his shoes as well, she retreated cautiously behind her desk.

A madman! If only she were closer to the bellpull—but now he was approaching the fireplace, still with that smirk on his face.

He'd snatched down the earl's dueling swords!

Understanding hit her like lightning, and she bit down a smile. Well, she would show that hothead a neat little trick or two with the foil! When he tossed one of the rapiers toward her, she caught it by the hilt and automatically tested its weight. A mite heavier than she was used to, but still quite manageable.

The young man with the glittering dark eyes raised his foil. *My God!* There was no protective button on the blade's tip, nor was there one on the sword in her own hand. He was planning to *duel* with her! The feeling of participating in a strange play gave way to the certain knowledge of living in a nightmare. She could not possibly duel with this . . . lunatic!

"Sir—" Even to her own ears her voice sounded croaky and hollow. *Tarnation!* But she would not appear a coward before this dandified popinjay. She was Tony Fenshawe, daredevil par excellence! Tony would rise to the challenge. She could not make a laughingstock of him now by cowering under the desk, or her young brother would never be able to hold his head up again once he'd taken over the post here.

Olivia clenched her jaw and her chin jutted in determination as she slowly edged out of her tight corner into the spacious area in front of Lord Worth's huge desk.

"En garde!" exulted the stranger. Greedy anticipation and enjoyment of the sport to come emanated from him.

The blades barely touched in a brief salute before he leaped to attack—but Tony had taught Olivia well. Her technique was good and her defense was well executed. However, the weight of the foil soon tired her wrist, and the absence of buttons was disconcerting and inhibiting.

If she scored a hit—or if he did—blood would flow!

Great beads of sweat gathered on her forehead, slowly trickled lower, and slid annoyingly into her eyes.

"Lionel! Tony!"

At the sound of the deep voice, the blades froze in midair, only the vibration of the points giving evidence of the force which had thrust them forward seconds earlier.

Lord Worth, followed closely by his friend Lord Charles Baxter, strode into the study and twisted the rapier from Lionel's hand, but when he turned to repeat the harsh procedure, he noted with grim satisfaction that the sword had already slipped from his secretary's nerveless fingers. He picked it up and rounded on Lionel again.

"You don't have a particle of honor in you, have you, cousin? Fighting a stripling in *my study*—and with nary a second present! Take yourself home!"

"There's nowhere else I'd care to go in a soiled vest," muttered Lionel sullenly. "Just look what that paperskull did to me! Ruined my favorite design!"

The earl threw his cousin a disgusted look, then tossed coat and shoes at him and pointed to the door.

Lionel scowled, but, obedient to the authority behind his cousin's gesture, donned his clothing and stalked off. At the door he turned back and snarled at Olivia, "You haven't heard the last of this affair yet!"

With trembling knees, Olivia edged over to her chair and sank down, unable to carry her own weight a moment longer. The earl, after a dark look in her direction, turned his back on her. He affixed the swords back on the wall above the mantel, then busied himself watching the dying embers in the hearth.

Lord Charles, however, strolled over to the credenza, filled a glass, and carried it to Olivia. When she took no notice, he waved it under her nose until the powerful bouquet drifted into her nostrils and lifted some of the haziness from her mind.

"Drink up, Tony," he commanded.

Meekly she complied and felt the fiery liquid burn down her throat, then hit her stomach with the force of a grenade.

It wiped all mistiness from her mind as a wet cloth would lift soot and grime off a windowpane.

"Thank you, Lord Charles." She looked up at the tall, blond man and smiled hesitantly in response to his boyish grin and the amused twinkle in his gray eyes.

"What the deuce possessed you, Fenshawe," demanded Lord Worth, perching himself on the corner of his desk, "to get yourself embroiled in a row with my ramshackle cousin?"

Stung by the scathing tone of his voice, Olivia swiveled around and flared at him. "You didn't warn me, my lord, that a cousin of yours would be released from Bedlam tonight to pay you a visit, else I'd have taken every care not to be caught on the premises!"

Reluctantly the black brows smoothed. There was no aggression in his voice when he admitted, "Lionel *is* the black sheep of the family. He's not exactly mad, but spoilt beyond salvation by his mother."

"He's a firebrand and a demmed nuisance," interspersed Lord Charles. "Forever walking in here as if he's master of Worth House and Worthing Court, just because he believes himself to be your heir."

"Well, he is—at the moment."

"Don't talk fustian! You ain't living with a foot in your grave yet; you've dozens of years left to beget scores of heirs."

"Not without a wife," Olivia pointed out.

Lord Charles grinned. "Quite right, Tony. Worth, like his sainted pater, is too honorable to beget bastards. There was only one Worthing who liked to surround himself with hordes of his by-blows, and that was the Fifth Earl's younger brother, the honorable Frederick Worthing. He broke his neck a day after Lionel's birth, celebrating the arrival of his only legitimate son, no doubt."

Ignoring the blushing confusion his words had inexplicably caused in the young secretary, Lord Charles took the empty glass from Olivia's hands and refilled it, then poured out generous measures for himself and Lord Worth.

"To the future Lady Worth!"

Fabian Worthing, Sixth Earl of Worth, ignored his friend's toast and frowned darkly at his glass. Charles's words about his late uncle's by-blows had disturbed him. Some vague memory was niggling at his brain. . . . The countryside around Fielding, Lionel's small estate, was littered with Frederick Worthing's natural offspring, causing his wife, Lydia, no little discomfort. They all had the Worthings' dark eyes, and one or two of the young men looked sufficiently like Lionel that Lydia had once, to her horror and everlasting shame, addressed one of them as her son.

Yes, now he recalled. . . . About two months ago he'd seen Lionel with a new groom, and that new groom was undoubtedly one of his late uncle's offspring. It might bear looking into.

With a proficiency acquired through years of practice, Fabian swirled the cognac around in his glass before sniffing the bouquet, and only then did he take a small sip. When Charles repeated his toast, Fabian finally looked up.

"Do you know, Charles," he said thoughtfully, "on those rare occasions when I do think of a future Lady Worth, I have the direst forebodings—a goose walking over my grave, you might say."

Slowly Fabian lifted his glass in a salute, then drank deeply.

_____CHAPTER 2_____

Impatiently, Olivia tossed the crumpled length of muslin onto the floor. She should have watched more carefully how Merrie had tied the cravat; this business was taking her forever with no results to boast of but a pile of discarded cravats at her booted feet—and she wasn't even trying to rival Beau Brummell.

The marquetry clock in the corridor boomed out eight times. Olivia's fingers fumbled frantically. Lord Worth would be sitting down to breakfast now, and in an hour he expected her to go to Tattersall's with him. Of course she could tell a sound horse from a showy hack, could even discern the finer points of a "good 'un"—but choose among several thoroughbreds? *Tony* could do that. Horses were his passion, and horse-breeding was in his blood. Why did Richard have to brag about Tony's talent to the earl? Usually Richard did everything he could to belittle his younger brother's ability. Well, probably the earl would do his own choosing; he was not a man to rely on anyone's judgment but his own.

Olivia practiced drooping her eyelids. Since Merrie had cropped her hair to cluster in short, tight curls about her head, her eyes appeared to have grown larger, which might be all right for a girl, but not for Tony Fenshawe! And her lashes, perhaps she should trim them. But, no, Tony's were just as long. She pushed her chin out to make it look more like her brother's prominent jaw—but she could not banish a vague feeling of apprehension.

She had not expected her position as Tony's substitute to be an easy one, but neither had she imagined it would prove quite so trying. Why, she'd worried she might feel bored! Now, on top of all her small troubles, there would soon be the test of fire at Tattersall's. Yesterday it had been a duel with the earl's deranged cousin!

At the memory of that hair-raising episode, Olivia started to shake again and gave up on the cravat; it simply would have to do. Perhaps Merrie had been in the right when she'd warned that this was an impossible scheme to carry off, but then even Merrie could not have foreseen the arrival of a madman on the scene. Aside from that disastrous interval, the new secretary had so far proven "himself" equal to any task Lord Worth had set before "him." Would she be able to hold out for a couple of weeks or a month?

Surely Tony would not require longer to simmer down and reconsider his actions. He'd come hotfoot to Worth House, ask to see the earl to beg for the position, and would meet instead his loving sister, ready to hand him the post on a silver platter.

Olivia shook herself out of her daydream. Tony was not here yet and she must get to work. She snatched Tony's riding coat from the wardrobe and slipped it on. It was a good fit: not so loose that it was obviously a borrowed item, but not tight enough to give her away; Merrie had done marvels with the buckram padding. The breeches, however, were a different matter. They clung so tightly to her hips and thighs as to drive a tidal wave of color into her face each time she thought about them. Best not to look down!

With Tony's hat clutched under her arm, whistling a catchy little tune painstakingly taught her by the stable boy at Fenshawe Court, she ran down the two flights of stairs to the breakfast parlor.

At her entrance Lord Worth looked up from his copy of *The Times*. The greeting he was about to utter died on his lips as he stared in fascination at her cravat. Well, so much for her efforts.

"My dear boy, tomorrow I shall send Alders to assist you with your toilette, but in the meantime, permit me—" With three long strides he towered before her, reaching for the offending article.

Olivia backed away and groped for the doorknob. "I can do it!" she said hastily. "Just give me five minutes."

"Tony, stand still."

The words were spoken softly, yet unmistakably a command, leaving her no choice but to obey.

"For three days I've said nothing," Lord Worth continued, and deftly untied the cravat, "not wishing to offend your sensibilities. But this . . . creation tops everything." He shook the muslin in an effort to remove some of the creases, but with no noticeable result.

An irritated frown drew his strong brows together; his

long, tanned fingers beat a rapid tattoo on the table as he contemplated the recalcitrant muslin.

Of course, he *could* send her upstairs to fetch another cravat, mused Olivia, but it would be Lombard Street to a China orange he wouldn't even consider the possibility; he must come out of this "encounter" victorious.

As if on cue, the earl propped one foot onto an elegant, chintz-covered chair and slid the length of cloth rapidly back and forth across his knee. "There now," he muttered. "That'll do."

There was laughter lurking in his dark eyes when he leaned forward to drape the snowy material around her neck. "Were you trying to set a new fashion? In that case you were going about it the wrong way. *That* attempt of yours could only have been called the Futile."

Olivia stared at his face as it came closer. As if seeing him for the first time, she studied his features—the straight nose, the sensitive mouth which could tighten so ominously in disapproval or disdain, but was relaxed and shapely now with just a hint of a smile lifting the corners; a distinctive cleft was hewn in his masterful chin, and his cheeks were lean under rather prominent cheekbones and showed dark shadows although he must have shaved but an hour or two ago.

His fingers moved at her throat, touching her skin fleetingly, yet leaving a burn like a piece of glowing coal. Her chest felt tight as breathing became difficult.

Peagoose! Don't act as though you've never stood close to a man before. Well, she hadn't, at least not this close that she could smell the scent of his skin.

The cravat was tied, she suddenly realized, but Lord Worth was still too close, with his hand under her chin, looking at her as intently as she must have looked at him. Again she could feel the infuriating color mount in her cheeks, but forced herself to meet his inquisitive gaze. He was so annoyingly perceptive.

"Why did you—and Richard—lie to me?" he asked in a voice as soft as silk.

Her heart skipped several beats, and the roar of a thousand waterfalls droned deafeningly in her ears. This must be the warning signals preceding a dead faint, she thought in despair, then held tenaciously on to awareness as she caught his next words.

"Your cheeks have yet to submit to a razor for the first time—you *cannot* be twenty years old." His thumb touched briefly against her cheek, then he stepped back abruptly. "I abhor deceit," he stated quietly, conveying disgust and threat through that very casualness.

"I am . . . not quite . . . twenty yet," stammered Olivia, trying frantically to gather her wits. He had *not* realized the full scope of her deception, but of a certainty he would if she did not tread carefully.

"And it has long been an embarrassment to me," she blustered, "that I need not shave. There's no call for you to rub it in!" Attack was the best defense—somebody cleverer that she must have said that at some point in time. "A defect . . . a malfunction of the nervous system, that's what the physician told me. There's some slight chance that time might cure this particular ailment. Yes," she nodded for emphasis, and crossed her fingers, "that's what he said!"

One dark brow was raised skeptically. "Indeed."

His eyes once more roamed over the delicate face, noting the high color, then traveled slowly over the slender figure encased in a rather ample riding coat and tight breeches. He shook his head and turned back to the table. "Sit down, Tony, and have some breakfast. I plan to leave in fifteen minutes."

"We are not driving in your curricle, my lord?" Disappointment was writ plainly on Olivia's features as Lord Worth walked past the mews and continued along South Audley Street.

"No, but I'll be taking out my grays this afternoon. I'm planning a drive to Hendon and wouldn't mind some company—might even let you handle the ribbons. You have driven a four-in-hand?"

Olivia nodded and flushed with pleasure. To be allowed to drive the earl's priceless team of matched grays was a treat she'd coveted since she'd seen him tooling off with Lord Charles Baxter at his side on the day of her arrival at Worth House.

"Thank you, my lord." She quickened her pace to keep up with his long stride and started to whistle again. What unrestricted, wonderfully exciting lives gentlemen lived! No such offer would have been forthcoming had he met her as a female.

Fabian slanted a glance at his young secretary. Gad, to be so young that a drive to Hendon could inspire such enthusiasm! What a refreshingly unspoilt young cub he was.

He?

Fabian's brows snapped together as once again the dreadful suspicion crossed his mind. *Malfunction of the nervous system—what a taradiddle!* He scrutinized the smooth cheeks showing a disarming dimple at the corner of the full lips. Furthermore, Fenshawe had very slender hands, now hidden inside a pair of serviceable York tan gloves, but which he knew to be soft skinned with long fingers and oval nails.

Yet the youth's long stride was free and jaunty as a man's, and young Fenshawe's capabilities as a secretary were those of a very well-educated gentleman. That speech he'd written yesterday, for instance, was a masterpiece of powerful arguments and persuasive logic. He'd lay odds those weren't a woman's syllogistics.

But what an uproar it would cause if this stripling were indeed a girl! Damnation! What was he to do? If Tony *was* a young man, albeit an effeminate one, he'd only hurt his feelings by questioning his masculinity. On the other hand, if a young woman lived under his roof—unchaperoned— he'd never live to hear the end of it! Irritated now with the young cawker beside him, Fabian walked faster, swung around the corner of Curzon Street, and fairly raced down Park Lane, noting grimly that his secretary was all but running to keep up with him.

The clatter of hooves and the rumble of carriage wheels

penetrated through his anger. The sounds came from some distance behind them, but the fast-increasing racket warned of the approaching vehicle's breakneck speed. Fabian veered closer to the building beside him and shouted, "Get out of the street, Tony!"

But Tony appeared deaf and dumb, having stopped in his tracks to stare over his shoulder at the runaway team and monstrous traveling chaise bearing down on him.

With a muttered imprecation, Fabian reached for Tony's shoulders to draw him to safety, but his clutching fingers encountered a wad of buckram padding under the material of the riding jacket, and his powerful jerk half ripped the coat off Tony's back.

Then events happened so fast that Fabian was hard pressed to remain calm. A shot was fired from the carriage as it drew abreast, causing the team of six horses to back and plunge like mad creatures, and Tony stumbled backward, landing heavily against Fabian's chest.

Fabian grunted, wondering for an instant if he'd been hit by the gunshot or kicked by one of the terrified horses before he realized that he'd been winded merely by a knock in the stomach from Tony's elbow.

Drat the boy! He was like a dead weight. Why wouldn't he stand on his own two feet?

While Fabian struggled to right his secretary, he noticed from the corner of his eye that a gun barrel still protruded through a slit in the curtained coach window. He was close enough to see a charcoal-black eye narrow and the gun rise slightly to aim with deadly accuracy at his own head.

Even while he threw himself to the ground with young Fenshawe still clutched in his grip and braced himself for the second shot, the cloaked and muffled coachman on the box finally brought his team under control and swung his whip to set the chaise in motion again.

The shot went wide, burying itself in the cracked bark of an old oak standing sentinel between two large mansions. Fabian took a deep breath and mopped his moist forehead with the sleeve of his coat. With a quelling look at excitedly gabbing bystanders who now rushed closer for a better view of the happenings, he hoisted himself up to dust off his once immaculate breeches.

Young Fenshawe had not moved—still lay sprawled face-down on the cobbles.

"Tony!" Fabian dropped to his knees and carefully rolled the limp young man onto his back. At the sight of the boy's waxen face, his stomach tightened. Had he knocked the stripling out when he'd dragged him to the ground? Then Fabian saw the dark stain spreading ominously on Tony's left shoulder.

With calm and precision born on the bloody battlefields of Portugal and Spain, Fabian removed Tony's and his own cravat and folded one into a neat pad which he slipped under Tony's riding coat.

Fabian's hand jerked back as if stung.

Ye gads, what a bumblebroth!

This was unmistakably a young woman! His mind raced. What to do? Take her somewhere where he wasn't known? Fabian rejected the fleeting, cowardly thought immediately. She needed a physician and care, and he'd see that she received both. Worth House was the best place for her—at least for the moment.

Without wasting a glance at the gaping crowd, he ordered, "Someone get a carriage!" and proceeded to fasten the makeshift pad with the second cravat.

"Worth! What happened?" asked an elegant dandy. He minced a few steps closer, but hastily averted his eyes from the sickening bloodstain on the ocher riding coat. "Be glad to put my curricle at your disposal, Worth." He did not look at Fabian, who was leaning over the lifeless figure on the ground, but concentrated on the content of his snuffbox, which he'd opened with an expert flick of his wrist.

"Much obliged, Petersham." Fabian glanced up briefly and explained, "It's my secretary; he's been shot. Can you give me a hand?"

Lord Petersham retreated a step. "Sorry, old boy. Be glad to drive you, but look at the blood I will not. Can't stomach the sight, don't you know. Here, my tiger will help you carry the fellow.''

''Never mind.'' Fabian eased his arms under the prone form, scooped up his burden—amazingly light—and stepped into Lord Petersham's curricle. When he propped the young woman's head and shoulders securely against his chest, he noticed a slight movement of her eyelids and a tightening of the white lips. So she was coming to—and about time!

''Any preference which surgeon will dig out the bullet?'' called Lord Petersham from the box.

Fabian dragged his attention away from the long, fluttering lashes. ''Sorry. What did you say, Petersham?''

''Which physician should I drive to? There's a competent fellow in Clifford Street. Epswich used him a month ago after his duel with Bigsby.''

''No. Take us to Worth House,'' replied Fabian with another long look at the girl's pale, delicate features. ''It's closer, and I can send for Sir Whitewater.''

''As you wish.''

For a while they bowled along in silence, then Lord Petersham risked a peek over his shoulder. ''Did you see who fired the shot?'' he asked.

''It was fired from the traveling chaise.''

''That much I could see for myself, Worth! I meant, who was inside the chaise? Looked to me like it was the carriage Mrs. Lydia Worthing uses when she comes to town on her annual visit.''

''My aunt would hardly take potshots at anyone,'' said Fabian mildly and shook his head at the girl who'd opened pain-dilated eyes and looked as if she was about to speak. ''Besides, Aunt Lydia's at Fielding. She never comes to town at this time.''

''Don't be daft, Worth. You know I'm talking about that wild cousin of yours. I wouldn't put anything past him!''

''Lionel's at Fielding as well,'' replied Fabian without hesitation. ''Besides, he'd have no cause to shoot at my secretary.''

''He might have been shooting at *you*.''

"Lionel's a dead shot. He'd not have hit my secretary if he'd meant to aim at me."

"Be that as it may. But perhaps you ought to know that Lionel's been spouting off, about being your heir I mean. You may remember, I already warned you a month or so ago when you were waylaid and Lionel stood by and watched you being clubbed because an 'injured' wrist prevented him from coming to your aid."

Fabian vouchsafed no reply, and Lord Petersham lapsed into silence as well until he pulled up before Worth House. "Well," he said, "I can understand if you don't wish to rattle the family skeletons, Worth, but if I were you, I'd do something about that firebrand cousin of yours."

"I will deal with Lionel if I must. Now be a friend, Petersham, and keep your suspicions to yourself—and ask your tiger to knock on the door."

Lord Petersham grinned. "I'll be a friend and do it myself," he said and tossed the reins to his tiger. As soon as Robinson had flung the door open, however, Lord Petersham tipped his hat and departed hastily.

"Quick, Robinson!" commanded Fabian. "Tell Alders to come with his bag and send someone for Sir Whitewater. Young Fenshawe's been shot."

The butler paled. "And *you*, my lord, are you unhurt?" he asked in a quavering voice.

"Quite unharmed, Robinson. Don't waste time worrying about me; our prime concern must be Master Tony's injury. He's lost quite a bit of blood."

"Yes, my lord. I'll see to everything."

Fabian nodded and carried his burden upstairs. The girl might be a featherweight, but after cushioning her head and torso with his arm to prevent any jolting of her injured shoulder during the ride in the curricle, and after two flights of stairs, his arms were nevertheless beginning to protest against the strain. With a sigh of relief, he eased her onto the bed in Tony's room.

The girl had passed out again, he noted with a worried frown. He'd best fetch the bottle of cognac from his study. She'd need it for the surgeon's visit.

Now he must think of an explanation for the servants, and it had better be a good one. Why on earth would a girl want to masquerade as his secretary?

A pungent, vaguely familiar aroma alerted Olivia's brain before the fiery liquid rolled down her throat and forced her back to consciousness. Along with the bracing burn of the potation came awareness of a fierce pain in her shoulder. Her eyes flew open and met narrowed charcoal ones clouded with concern. Lord Worth was bending over her, a glass of cognac in his hand, ready to administer another dose if necessary.

"How are you feeling?" he asked softly and placed the cognac glass on the bedside table.

"Simply wonderful," she gasped. "Fit and raring to dance a jig." What a daft question when he must see that she was in pain—and what was he doing in *her* bedchamber?

Lord Worth said nothing, but his lips twitched infuriatingly. The fiend was laughing at her! She tried to sit up, but immediately he pounced on her and pressed her down again—but she needed no encouragement. She'd realized instantly that it was impossible for her to move without being consumed by red-hot flames of agony and a Stygian wall of darkness closing in.

"Drink some more cognac," recommended Lord Worth.

Olivia's stomach heaved, but she couldn't shake her head for fear of pain, or tell him no, because already he had the glass at her lips again and started to force its contents past the barrier of her teeth. He stopped only when a rivulet of cognac flowed down her chin and she coughed after breathing in a few drops.

"Dammit! I'm not trying to get you drunk! I just want to spare you some of the pain." So much for his bedside manner. He certainly did not have any patience to speak of in dealing with recalcitrant invalids.

Olivia frowned. "What happened? Did the horses run me down after all?"

"No." He looked at her consideringly, weighing whether she could handle a truthful answer. "You were shot," he added brusquely. "And, unfortunately, the bullet is lodged in your shoulder."

"Shot—" That would, of course, explain why her shoulder burned as though it had served as the target for a firing squad. If only he'd go away so she could slip into oblivion again. But he stayed, and reluctantly her mind set to work on the difficult process of going back in time. Slowly, painfully, she came to a logical conclusion.

"Your Bedlamite cousin shot me!"

"What?" The earl towered over her, his scowling face not two inches from her own. "How can you be so sure?"

"Let it be for now, my lord," advised a gruff voice.

Neither one of them had heard Alders enter, but there he was, a wiry little man, treading purposefully toward the four-poster with a beat-up black leather bag in his hand. The valet pulled a table closer, opened his bag, and spread some wicked-looking instruments on a snowy napkin. Without actually coming in contact with the earl's powerful frame, Alders seemed to shoulder him aside, and suddenly it was he who loomed over Olivia with a pair of scissors glinting in his hand. He inserted the scissors in her sleeve and started to cut the riding coat off her shoulder.

"No!" she choked.

The clammy moisture on her forehead and upper lip multiplied until the cold sweat trickled in great, salty beads into her eyes and mouth. Lord Worth bent over her from the head of the bed and gently dabbed her face, while Alders proceeded with his task. The coat had been peeled off, and he attacked the sleeve of her shirt.

"Stop! I want to leave!" she protested. "Just call me a hackney, and I won't be any bother—my own physician will take care of me."

Keen dark eyes bored into hers. "The one who diagnosed a disorder of your nervous system? I believe Alders will do much better in this instance. He was my batman in Portugal and Spain and helped scores of wounded men, including me. Unfortunately, surgeons were few and far between on the battlefields.''

"But don't you understand—" She knew her protest was as soft as a breath and that, even had they heard her, they wouldn't pay any heed.

For he *did* understand. His eyes told her so.

This time, when the glass was tilted to her lips, she drank obediently. Would that it knocked her out completely. At least he couldn't expect her to answer any questions while she was foxed or unconscious. Already a whirling fog was descending on her mind, and still the cognac rolled down her throat. It tasted smoother with every sip.

The intoxicating beverage was finally withdrawn when Alders admonished, "That will be quite enough now, my lord! We may still have to resort to laudanum. The lad— Blimey! My lord, it's a lass!"

"Yes, Alders. I began to wonder if you'd ever catch on."

The pain in her shoulder now felt as if it belonged to someone else, and Olivia wanted to giggle. She could picture Alders's craggy features puckering up in disbelief, and Lord Worth's quizzical look at his valet; but only a hiccough escaped her dry lips—and it was again *her* shoulder sending screaming messages of agony to her numbed brain.

A knock on the door sounded as though it had been administered through a layer of cotton lint; then the earl called, startlingly close to her, "Who is it?" and the muffled reply, "Jenkins, my lord."

Someone opened the door, and the footman's voice came a trifle clearer. ". . . Sir Whitewater is from home . . . urgent message with the housekeeper . . . attend your lordship as soon as possible."

"Thank you, Jenkins, that will be all."

Footsteps approached the bed, but she had not the strength or sufficient willpower to open her eyes. The last words she heard were,

"You know what to do, Alders. Let's get on with it."

A powerful force was dragging her slowly but inexorably toward consciousness. Olivia struggled against awareness, knowing instinctively that it would mean excruciating pain and bitter humiliation. She raised her lids a fraction and encountered a clear order, *not* to pass out again, from a pair of dark, threatening eyes.

"Lie still, you little fool," muttered a familiar deep voice. "You'll only tear off the bandage." His hand, astonishingly gentle in contrast to the biting words, wiped her forehead with a cool, wet cloth.

Olivia pried her heavy lids fully open and stared resentfully at the earl ensconced in a deep armchair by her bedside. The room was steeped in darkness save for a pool of soft light radiating from a small lamp on the nightstand.

"Why did you wake me up?" she groaned. "If you want to play nursemaid, you must learn not to shout or douse the invalid with ice-cold water."

He rose and lit the candleabrum on the dresser between the windows. The flames flickered and shot up as though fanned by a gentle breeze. "I didn't shout—I've no need to resort to such a vulgar display to make myself understood—and I didn't douse you. That was a cold compress to keep your temperature down. You are developing a fever."

So that's why she felt hot and sticky; she'd assumed there was a roaring fire in the hearth. "Open the window," she fretted. "That'll cool me soon enough."

"It is open." He was losing patience with this cranky waif. Instead of gratitude for his concern and forebearance, she showed nothing but peevishness.

Lord Worth busied himself at the bedside table. He sloshed a bit of water into a glass, then carefully measured and mixed drops from a spouted medicine bottle into the water. All the tales of horror Merrie had told her of ladies who'd become dependent on laudanum came back to Olivia with a vengeance.

"No!" She put up both hands to ward off the evil mixture, but the immediate, cruel reaction of her left shoulder triggered a violent lurch in her stomach and caused dark patches and stars to dance before her eyes. Trembling, she let her hands drop back on the coverlet. Tears of pain and frustration smarted her eyes, and she gasped. "If you give me laudanum, most likely I'll cast up my accounts.''

"Balderdash! You are a lady, even if your speech is that of a guttersnipe.''

Olivia glowered. Did he actually believe ladies could control their stomachs at will? He'd soon learn the fallacy of that notion.

The earl sat down again, still holding the glass, and studied her for a long moment as though he'd read her mutinous thoughts and was trying to find a way to outwit her.

"Listen, child. You are straining my patience to the utmost.'' He gave a long-suffering sigh. "This small bottle contains a distillate of Peruvian bark. Added to water, in the exact dosage prescribed by Sir Whitewater, it makes up a draught which may keep the fever down. You will now drink it and prepare yourself to answer a few questions— unless you wish to be turned out into the street. Sir Whitewater also prescribed laudanum for you and, unless you're a bloody martyr, you'll take some of that as well . . . after we've talked.''

Her thoughts were tumbling in her aching head. She'd gambled and lost—like Richard. Only, it was much, *much* worse, for she had staked and forfeited Tony's future, *and* she had cheated the Earl of Worth! But, if she explained why she'd done it, perhaps she could salvage some of the wreckage she'd caused. The earl was holding a tight rein on his temper and was trying to speak calmly with her, but she was well aware of the underlying fury waiting to be unleashed on the slightest provocation. Should she throw herself on his mercy and beg for leniency on Tony's behalf?

Don't jump the gun! Wait until you've heard his questions, advised her common sense.

Olivia forced herself to relax—no small matter with a shoulder which would not permit relegation to the back of her mind. "Let me have the medicine,'' she said by way of conciliation.

"That's more like it,'' he said approvingly with a detestable smirk. With his free hand he propped up her head, then held the glass to her lips. When the last drop had disappeared, he replaced the glass on the nightstand and leaned back in his chair.

"Well now, let's talk. Since you look amazingly like Tony, I assume you are not some stranger who by chance stumbled onto a good scheme. You must be Miss Olivia Fenshawe. I've not had the felicity of meeting you previously, but Sir Richard had mentioned your name while I was at Fenshawe Court. You were in Bath at the time, I believe?"

A raised black brow and the eloquent silence demanded a response. She could detect no hidden threat or devious trap in his words and replied in the affirmative. "Yes, my lord, on both counts."

"Why then this masquerade?" he demanded.

This was her cue! She should have been exultant that he'd made it so easy for her to explain, yet she hesitated. To tell him now that Tony had *refused* to work for him, had run away instead, might indeed ring the death knell to all her hopes for Tony's future.

Olivia groped for words, trying to gauge his reaction before she committed herself to any particular course of prevarication. "Tony was . . . unavoidably detained, my lord, and so I . . ."

"So you determined to use the opportunity to catch yourself an earl! But—" his long, tanned finger stabbed at her, "you've bitten off more than you can chew, my girl. *I* am in a position to breeze through a bit of scandal, while *you*, the sister of Sir Richard Fenshawe, are not!"

_____CHAPTER 3_____

Olivia's eyes widened. He thought—He believed—It was too obnoxious to put into words! She was so furious that not even the excruciating pain in her shoulder could keep her prone.

"You go beyond the pale, my lord! How dare you say I came to entrap you! Were you the last man on earth, I'd want no part of you!"

Exhausted by her efforts, she sank back against the pillows. Drawing on her last resources of strength, she pressed a shaking hand to her temple and ordered, "Get out!"

Olivia heard the soft scrape of a chair and closed her eyes in relief. It was very quiet; he must have tiptoed from the room. The silence, however, was soon shattered when his voice boomed out again.

"You're even more of a bloody fool than I believed possible. Why would you risk your reputation if you didn't come to snare a matrimonial prize? What nefarious reasons can you have to impersonate your brother?" His eyes narrowed and raked over her face and slight form under the thin coverlet. "I'll have you taken back to Fenshawe Court."

She flinched, and he was quick to realize her vulnerability. "Unless . . . ! But before we go into the details of my possible plans for you, tell me why you were so certain that it was Lionel who shot you."

"I saw him. He was leaning out of the carriage, but as soon as he realized that I was looking at him, he withdrew and pulled the curtain."

"Lionel did carry a grudge against you, and he is hotheaded enough to consider a stain on his vest a killing offense—" The earl was pacing restlessly, one hand stuffed into the pocket of his coat, the other ruffling his black hair.

Fascinated, Olivia watched as his long, muscular legs, encased in buckskin riding breeches and glossy Hessians, measured the length of carpeting between the massive chest of drawers by the door and the fireplace behind her bed, reducing the vastness of the chamber to a mere cubbyhole.

"The gun just *might* have been aimed at you," he conceded. "But I'm convinced, had you not fallen against me at that precise moment, *I'd* have been hit. If the assailant was Lionel, the shot must have been meant for me—indubitably so, for the second shot was aimed directly at my head!''

He halted abruptly and swung around to fix his blazing eyes on Olivia. ''Dash it all, girl, but you saved my life!''

''That's certainly no reason to sound so embarrassingly grateful!''

His mood changed like quicksilver. ''Ah, but I *am* grateful, my dear.''

A smile, as charming as it was devastating to the unprepared Olivia, changed his saturnine features into a most attractive, beguiling countenance. He approached the four-poster and possessed himself of her right hand, raising it to his lips as he bowed with inimitable grace. Even his eyes glowed with warmth and animation, and she felt unaccountably shy when his lips brushed lightly against her knuckles.

''However''—although a smile still lingered, his expression had resumed the familiar, cynical look—''that still won't let you off the hook. While you lay cradled in Morpheus's arms, I've been busy scheming. All I required to set my plans in motion was confirmation that Lionel *indeed* was present in that coach. Now I am in need of your aid, Miss Fenshawe; in return, I promise absolute silence with regard to your stay in my house—unchaperoned.''

''No! I only want to get away from you.''

He held up an admonishing hand. ''Before you voice such unequivocal refusal, you should listen to and weigh my proposal. You have few alternatives; your choice should not be a difficult one to make. Number one, I can show you to the door, and within moments you'd be torn to shreds by the wolves of the night.''

The earl paused to let his dire prophesy sink in. Satisfied by Olivia's silence—her cheeks paler than before—and ignoring the mutinous spark in her hazel eyes, he continued, ''Or, as I said before, I can have you shipped back to Fenshawe Court. I feel certain Sir Richard and his most charming lady would bid you a *most cordial* welcome.''

Against her will, a weak chuckle escaped her cracked lips

but changed into a most uncomfortable cough. Immediately he was beside her, supporting her head with a strong arm and offering a drink of water.

"I know this is taxing your strength," he admitted wryly. "If only you were more cooperative, a mite less stubborn, you could be resting peacefully in no time at all."

"And if *you* would desist from badgering me, I could be asleep *right now*."

"But since I'm the one whistling the tune, I'll lay before you the third—and last—alternative."

"I'm all ears, my lord."

"I want you to pose as my fiancée."

Olivia blinked and swallowed hard. What manner of trick was he playing on her?

"Why?"

"It's rather a long story. I wouldn't wish to tire you unnecessarily." His voice dripped concern and solicitude.

"Cut line, my lord, and kindly explain."

"See here, Olivia! One of the first lessons as my 'fiancée' you will need to learn is how to speak in a ladylike manner. I can't have the *ton* accuse me of having picked you up in the stables."

"I won't be your fiancée—ever!"

With a disturbing gleam in his dark eyes, he countered, "I've only asked you to *pose* as such, my dear. Come now, we are wasting time. Will you cooperate or not?"

"Must you always have the last word?" she muttered crossly. "Give me a reason why you require a pretend fiancée, and I'll let you have my answer."

Lord Worth heaved an exaggerated sigh and explained in a bored voice, "I returned from the Peninsula last May, and since that time three attempts on my life have convinced me that someone feels I'd be of more use dead than alive."

Despite her determination not to become embroiled in the earl's affairs, Olivia's interest was piqued. "Lionel Worthing, your heir!" she exclaimed.

The heavy lids and thick lashes drooped and hooded his eyes, and although he nodded briefly, Olivia had a feeling that there was more on his mind than suspicion of Lionel alone.

When he looked at her again, his expression was bland. "I won't bore you with the details now," he drawled. "We'll have ample opportunity during our 'engagement' for long, cozy chats. For now you must accept my word that this is necessary. I'm out of patience with Lionel's cat-and-mouse games; I want to force his hand. What better way than to announce my betrothal and lead him to believe I'll wed and set up my nursery before the year is out?"

"Why do you not go to Bow Street and lay your evidence before a magistrate?"

"I have no evidence. You say you saw Lionel in the carriage. Do you believe your word, the word of a masquerader, would carry any weight in court?"

Olivia responded only with a rueful little smile.

"Precisely," he said. "And there is another reason why I cannot go to Bow Street. Tell me, Olivia," he demanded suddenly. "Tony ran away, did he not?"

"Yes," she replied, flustered by his sudden change of topic.

"Would you have told me that had you not been unmasked?"

"No, my lord."

"Will you request the aid of a Bow Street runner if your brother does not show up in the near future?"

"Of course not! Oh, I see. You hope to avoid a scandal by apprehending Lionel yourself."

"Not only that, but consider what my mother would feel were she to learn of my cousin's perfidy—or what my Aunt Lydia's sentiments must be if her only son were dragged before the courts. I will deal with Lionel myself—there's no other way."

"But what will you do once you've caught him at . . . at attempted murder? You cannot believe that he would not try again!"

"I imagine Lionel might be persuaded to accept a substantial draft on my bank and a one-way passage to India if I threatened to disclose his scheme to Aunt Lydia. In his own way, Lionel does love his mother and would not want to cause her pain."

"In that case he might accept your offer," she agreed. "But I don't see how I can help you. He'll certainly recognize me."

"I have a plan," said Lord Worth and darted a quick glance at her. "Would Tony be inclined to take up the post as secretary at a later date?" he asked.

Her breath caught sharply. Was this a new threat he planned to hold over her head? "He might," she replied cautiously.

"And I might just take him on then." His penetrating eyes seemed to see straight into her brain and recognize the hope that had flared up at his words. "It would suit me rather well, in fact. Tell me, what fib have you told Richard explaining your absence from Fenshawe Court? Surely you didn't come with his blessings?"

Olivia blushed. "I told him I'd been bidden to Bath to keep Grandmama company."

He grinned. "Ah, the redoubtable Lady Fenshawe. I've had the pleasure of meeting her at one of my mother's soirees."

"Then you will understand that Richard would not question her about me, or anything else for that matter."

"Good. You see, my dear, I shall give out that I'm escorting the injured 'Tony Fenshawe' home so that he may recuperate in the bosom of his loving family. Then I'll return to town some weeks later with Miss Olivia Fenshawe, my betrothed. Naturally, we'll duly announce our engagement in *The Times* and the *Gazette* a sennight before I introduce you to society. The real Tony may safely turn up at any time after your recovery without oversetting the apple cart." A frown puckered his forehead briefly, then he added, "There's little fear, I think, that he'll show up any sooner."

The ghost of a smile flitted across Olivia's face as she recalled the Herculean effort it had required in the past to coax Tony out of the sullens. "No fear at all," she said. But it mattered not, she told herself, for she would not agree to this fantastic scheme. It was one thing to pose as Lord Worth's secretary, but quite another to play the part of his fiancée.

Yet the powers of his persuasion were such that Olivia found herself dragging up desperate excuses to escape her inevitable fate. "I am not acquainted with anyone in London who could put me up, and you cannot very well deposit me in a hotel!"

"By the time you are well enough to play your role, my mother will have returned from Bath. Her chaperonage here at Worth House will satisfy even the highest stickler."

"And where shall I recuperate? Surely you were jesting when you said you'd take 'Tony' to Fenshawe Court!"

"How well you understand me. Do you recollect that we planned an excursion to Hendon? That's where you'll rusticate until you are fully recovered. My old nanny and I will prove excellent nurses, you'll see."

Her mind reeled, and she found it annoyingly difficult to focus on the earl's placid features or examine his arguments for a fault. "But . . . not now," she protested weakly as the hopelessness of her situation suddenly drained her of her last reserves of strength. "I'm in no shape to travel anywhere now."

"Better now than later, Olivia. It looks like you're headed for some rough times."

His hand felt cool and comforting on her forehead. Did he indeed look anxious? She tried to shake her head at this absurd thought, but, strangely, her neck and head were made of naught but pliant beeswax and would not move to her command.

"Temperature's rising," she heard him mutter in a distraught voice. "Nanny will know best how to deal with a complication like this."

"Oh, do be careful, Miss Olivia!" Nanny Brimstoke fluttered around the trunk of the old apple tree in her orchard and squinted against the brilliant rays of the late September sun.

Olivia laughed, feeling free as a bird after her long confinement.

"I'm safe," she called. "This branch is quite sturdy." To prove her point, she jiggled the limb on which she perched with her legs dangling at least five feet above the ground.

Nanny closed her eyes. She was getting on in years and was too old, she thought, to watch over a wild youngster—although by rights Miss Olivia should have outgrown her hoydenish ways long ago.

Olivia peered down at the slight old woman who'd looked after Lord Worth until he was old enough to be turned over to a tutor, and who'd nursed her—admittedly with the earl's capable assistance—through three extremely tiresome weeks of convalescence. A mischievous smile flitted across Olivia's face, briefly highlighting her dimple. She called, "Hold open your apron, Nanny! I'll toss you some apples for that pie you want to bake for his lordship."

"Now, Miss Olivia—"

But protest was futile. Nanny Brimstoke pursed her mouth in disapproval and watched as Olivia gathered her skirts, swung her legs up onto the branch, and raised herself to balance precariously on the swaying limb.

With one hand pressed firmly against the gnarled trunk, Olivia dared a step toward a cluster of red-cheeked apples dangling just out of her reach. *A pox on my shoulder and that exacerbating sling!* she fumed. To have come this far and then be unable to pick the apples was most annoying. In fact, she felt like a bloody fool.

Having inadvertently used the same epithet the earl had bestowed on her the day she'd been shot, she was even more determined to accomplish the feat.

Nanny was still watching and, being very familiar with the workings of a stubborn mind, hastily summoned her most persuasive arguments when she saw Olivia's predicament.

"Give it up, child, afore you tumble from the tree and find yourself laid up again. 'Twould, no doubt, go even worse with you this time because you're still weakened from the fever that ravaged your body. Pray consider if picking a few apples is worth the risk of another ten days in bed!''

''But you said you wanted some apples because his lordship is very partial to apple pie.''

Nanny snorted. ''You don't care two raps about what Master Fabian likes or dislikes!''

Olivia laughed and slipped her arm from the sling. ''But I care about *you*, and if you want to please that autocratic man, you'd best be quick about it. He should have been here hours ago. Watch out now, open your apron!'' The first apples plopped down into the serviceable, striped cloth.

''Careful! I don't want them bruised. You are very harsh in your judgment of his lordship, child. Why can't you see he has only your best interest at heart?''

''*My* interest, Nanny? Ha!'' In her indignation Olivia almost lost her balance and grabbed at one of the higher branches for support. Immediately she was punished by a stab of pain in her left shoulder. Breathing heavily, she retreated a step toward the safety of the trunk. ''He is an egotist! He only wants to *use* me in some nefarious plot. How many more, Nanny?''

''Two more will do nicely, thank you. But consider, you'll be his fiancée. As such you can demand the respect of all the *ton*.''

''*Pretend* fiancée, Nanny—not that I'd want it any other way. And I don't care tuppence about the *ton!* If you have enough apples now, I'll come down.''

''Do.'' Nanny gathered her apron around the apples and turned to leave. She hesitated, then looked up into the tree once more and said, ''If your engagement is announced in *The Times*, Master Fabian will never cry off.''

''And you think I'd leave it at that?'' Olivia lowered her posterior back onto the branch and looked round-eyed with surprise at the old woman.

''You could do worse, my girl,'' muttered Nanny Brimstoke. She marched off with her bounty, with not a backward glance to spare for the girl in the apple tree, and disappeared in the cottage.

"Well now!" said Olivia in exasperation. "How am I to get down?"

"How did you get up?" inquired a lazy voice.

Startled, she almost jumped off. Craning her head, Olivia peered down around the trunk of the tree at Lord Worth and scolded, "How can you be so ungentlemanly as to sneak up on a person from behind and eavesdrop?"

"If you wouldn't talk to yourself, I wouldn't have been put in a position to 'eavesdrop.' Moreover, I would not have caught you in a very unladylike position. Come now, we have important matters to discuss."

He held out his arms, and without protest she slid down into their secure hold. Olivia reeled dizzily as his fingers tightened around her waist. Surely her spinning head was due to her exertions and not to the disturbing warmth of his touch!

Hastily she twisted out of his clasp and retreated to a safe distance. "I still say you sneaked up on me," she accused. "I would have noticed had you approached openly from the cottage."

"I got off at the garden gate," he explained patiently. "But why is your arm not resting in the sling, and how came you to be stuck in the tree?"

"Some pesky boy slunk by and stole the ladder." Olivia slipped her arm through the cloth loop and glanced sheepishly at him, embarrassed to have to admit that a *child* had outwitted her and left her stranded. She hadn't even had the sense to ask Nanny Brimstoke to search for the ladder.

Lord Worth only nodded and said, "That would be Jonathan—a redheaded pest of a boy? I'll box his ears if you like. He played the same trick on me last autumn."

"He did?" Immensely cheered, she decreed magnanimously, "Never mind then. He must be the same Jonathan that Nanny is always talking about. He lends her a hand with some of her chores, and we wouldn't want to antagonize him."

"As you wish, my dear." A very understanding twinkle lit up his eyes as he steered her toward Nanny's ivy-covered home.

As soon as they stepped through the front door, Nanny came bustling from the kitchen, wiping her flour-dusted hands on her apron. "There you are, Master Fabian! I was getting a mite worried when you didn't arrive at noon, but I felt sure the smell of fresh-baked apple pie would bring you in time for supper."

She smiled complacently and offered her wrinkled cheek for his kiss. "There now!" she declared with satisfaction. "Miss Olivia, you take his lordship into the parlor and serve him a glass of my dandelion wine." Turning to her former nursling, she added, "That'll wash the dust out of your throat, Master Fabian. And you ought to take a few maca- roons or a slice of my fruit cake to tide you over until supper."

He grinned. "Still the same dear old 'Brimstone.' Will you ever stop worrying and telling me what to do, love?"

"How can I? I've had charge of you since you were born, and change my ways I cannot. Off with you now, and don't either of you dare come to the kitchen poking your noses in things that don't concern you."

Lord Worth blew her a kiss, then opened the first door to his right and gestured Olivia into the parlor. "Sit down," he invited. "I'll pour the wine. I know!" He held up his hand when Olivia opened her mouth. "The *good* crystal."

She couldn't quite suppress a smile. Of course, he'd know Nanny's little idiosyncrasies even better than she did. "How old is Nanny?" she asked.

"She must be approaching eighty—no one knows for certain. Nanny grew up in Northumberland; 'twas therefore never quite convenient to check the church register—and I've never dared ask her."

Olivia chuckled. "She'd box your ears, no doubt; but she should not be living by herself," she said, turning very serious. "Yesterday she dropped a can of hot water and scalded her foot."

"Is that an accusation I read on your face? Believe me, for years I've tried to install some young woman from Worthing Court here in the cottage, but Nanny sends every one of them back with a flea in her ear. Small wonder I called her 'Brimstone' in my youth, don't you think? Thank goodness, she cannot object to Jonathan's assistance. His mother is bedridden, and the family needs every penny he can earn."

Olivia frowned.

"What is the matter, Olivia? You looked at me just so when you observed me kiss Nanny the first time."

"Forgive me for staring, my lord. Do you mean to tell me that *you* hired Jonathan to help Nanny?"

"What would be so unusual about that?"

She blurted, "It is rather difficult for me to reconcile the thoughtful man who shows every consideration to his dependents with the Lord Worth who accepted my family home as the stake in a game of cards."

At once his face assumed a haughty, arrogant expression. "I realize your opinion of me is none too favorable. Perhaps some day I shall tell you about that game of faro, but it is of no import at the moment. We have more pressing matters to discuss."

"For instance, my lord?"

"For instance, my dear, as my 'fiancée' you must learn to address me as Fabian, or, if that is repugnant to you, you must call me Worth."

"Must I?"

A dangerous gleam appeared in his eyes. "Olivia," he warned softly, "I believe I made it quite clear that, in return for my silence about your stay at my house, I require your full cooperation."

"But since Lord Charles and Nanny Brimstoke absolutely swear on your honorable character, I cannot believe that you would tout my scandalous behavior before the world and ruin me!"

She heard the sharp intake of his breath and, for a moment, feared she'd overtaxed his patience. He took up the crystal goblet and drank deeply of the wine. As she'd noticed on previous occasions, his mouth puckered and an almost imperceptible shudder shook his broad shoulders. Of course! He *hated* dandelion wine but did not refuse it for fear of hurting Nanny's feelings.

When the glass was empty, he set it carefully on the polished tabletop. Clasping his hands behind his head, he leaned back against the soft cushions of his chair. "Call my bluff, Olivia," he murmured, fixing her with an inscrutable look.

Olivia blinked in astonishment, and her thoughts tumbled wildly. Should she follow her instinct? Her intuition told her he would never do anything dishonorable. During the weeks of her convalescence, he'd been with her almost daily, shouldering the greater part of nursing her to spare Nanny. He'd borne the brunt of her ill temper when she was feverish or, later on, bored, and most of the time he had been charming, even entertaining and fascinating with his wide range of knowledge and diverse interests. Then she'd felt that she could like and trust him. But when he was cold and remote—as now—he was like a different person, someone she didn't know at all, and an inner voice reminded her of the hardships he'd directly or indirectly caused her and Tony.

There was too much at stake—Tony's future, even her own—to put her trust in anyone but herself. No, much as she'd like to be rid of his disturbing presence, she dare not risk a refusal. Besides, she owed him something for his care, didn't she?

"I'll cooperate, Worth."

"Very well."

He sounded tired, even disappointed. She'd expected satisfaction at her capitulation or, at least, an I-knew-it-all-along grin, not this dispirited, two-word phrase. Unsure of her position, she squirmed in her chair and finally took refuge in the dandelion wine as he had done earlier.

"Have you sent the notice to the *Gazette*?" she demanded when the silence grew too thick.

Lord Worth looked up sharply. "I won't do that until you can function comfortably without the sling, which should be some time next week. I'll bring Sir Whitewater for a visit on Monday and let him judge whether your shoulder has healed sufficiently."

"Well . . . what then did you do in town if you didn't announce our 'engagement'?"

"I checked on my mother, who has returned from Bath. Then I called on Charles and talked about the enchanting Miss Fenshawe I met at her brother's home."

Olivia snorted skeptically. "You do not plan to take him into your confidence about the sham engagement?"

"No one but you and I will know."

"And Nanny," she corrected.

His brows snapped together in a frown. "You confided in Nanny? Dash it, Olivia! Why? I took great pains to explain to all my staff that you'd taken Tony's place to bail him out of some mischief, and that no harm was done since you'd be Lady Worth before long."

"But I won't be, will I? And Nanny would not utter a word about me since it also concerns you very closely."

"Granted, but pray do *not* confide in anyone else. I do not want even the whisper of a doubt to reach Lionel's ears." His fingers tapped rapidly against the glasslike top of Nanny's table. "Do you have any notion at all of Tony's whereabouts?"

Her mouth drooped. "No, and I'm beginning to feel anxious. I was certain he'd show up at Worth House after a few weeks of roaming, but now it's been five . . . no, more like six weeks, since he disappeared. I have nightmares that he may have enlisted and is somewhere in Spain or Portugal, perhaps wounded . . . or worse!"

"That's very unlikely. Even if Tony did enlist, he could hardly have seen much action during the short time he's been gone. Don't fret, an enlisted man's life is rough, but hardly intolerable—" He broke off. The Peninsular campaign was not a subject he cared to discuss.

"They why are you so concerned about the supply lines if

there are no hardships? As if fighting bloody battles with the wrong caliber ammunition weren't enough, our soldiers don't even get their rations on schedule!" Threatening tears made it impossible for Olivia to continue. She hung her head, turning her face away from him. Under no circumstances would she appear a watering pot before the hardhearted earl!

A chair creaked and his footsteps rang loud and forceful on the oaken floorboards, then stopped beside her. He placed two fingers under her chin and gently but firmly raised her face to his. "If your brother has not turned up when we're installed at Worth House," he told her, "I'll have some inquiries made. Do you think he may have sold his horse?"

"I cannot imagine that Tony would part from Thunder," she whispered.

"In that case, he would be with a cavalry regiment—if, indeed, he enlisted. Lieutenant Bramson, an officer in the Horse Guards, will have no trouble at all checking the rolls of the enlisted men."

Abruptly he let go of her chin and walked away. "Don't worry so much, Olivia," he said gruffly from the doorway. "Concentrate on being a convincing fiancée and let me handle the search for Tony."

Bemused and feeling rather bereft after the sudden withdrawal of his warm hand, she boosted her low spirits with a defiant, "Yes, *my lord*."

When Sir Whitewater arrived, he pronounced himself well satisfied and decreed that henceforth a sling would not be necessary to the healing process. He laid no restrictions on Olivia's return to a normal life, except to caution her to use common sense. Although she'd always carry a tiny scar high on her left shoulder, clever fashioning of her gowns would allow even the most daring décolletage, he told her with a twinkle, and left the chamber in Nanny's wake.

Lord Worth personally drove the physician back to town in his curricle, had a brief chat with his mama, and sent notices of his engagement to *The Times* and to the *Gazette*. He then departed for Hendon again to devote the next four days to his "fiancée," so that she might feel at ease with him in her new role and learn to display a respectful, even loving manner toward him for their first confrontation with the curious members of the *ton*.

The Earl of Worth and his "fiancée," Miss Olivia Fenshawe, entered London on the eve of the last day of September 1812, shielded from inquisitive eyes by the velvet curtains of the earl's crested traveling chaise. Upon Lord Worth's explicit order, the old coachman Bert drove the chaise first to the eastern section of town, down Houndsditch and the Minories. When Bert rapped the whip handle sharply against the carriage, Worth pulled aside the curtains and invited Olivia to take a peek.

"May I present for your edification one of our city's most memorable sites, my dear? The Tower of London, a convenient place to hide disobedient wives and fiancées."

She saw the quickly suppressed grin and the merriment in his charcoal eyes, heard the laughter in his deep voice, and countered promptly,

"And very handy to incarcerate overbearing lords!"

_____ C H A P T E R   4 _____

With sublime disregard for the pristine surface of his mahogany desk, Fabian propped his booted feet on the polished wood. He paid no heed when a stack of gilt-edged invitations was knocked to the floor in the process, but stared straight ahead, his brow creased, and his mouth drawn taut, with deep vertical lines at the corners.

Had he made a grave mistake in demanding Olivia's help?

Undoubtedly she was an unprincipled baggage. No young lady of breeding and sensibility would dare show herself in male attire. She also displayed a lamentable tendency to quibble and question his authority.

Like when she'd met his mother for the first time and realized that the dowager truly believed her to be his fiancée. . . . He'd had to drag the girl into his study to keep her from blurting out the truth.

"How could you deceive your own mother!" she'd stormed. "That sweet, gentle lady. It's . . . criminal!"

"Pray keep your voice down, Olivia! Do you want all of London to witness your fishwife manners?"

"My manners? If that don't beat the Dutch! My manners are not half as shocking as your behavior! Why must you lie to the dowager countess, and make me a part of your deception?"

"Because Mama is a trifle too fond of sherry. Mind you, she'd never get bosky, but the wine does loosen her tongue. Now, will you kindly concede the decision making to me?"

"Of course, my lord!" The defiant toss of her head indicated clearly that her thoughts still ran contrary to her tongue. "But I feel *very* uncomfortable. Do you realize, Worth, that your mama is planning to take me to Madame Bertin's to have me outfitted? And that she asked Signor Giuseppe to style my hair?"

"I have no objections, child."

His voice was bland, and the look he passed over her cropped hair and faded morning gown with the unfashionably full skirt gathered at the waistline proper was disdainful. Olivia scowled. After all, next to Tony's outfits she had no frocks with her but her traveling gown and this old rag which she'd worn day after day in Hendon.

"Do not patronize me, Worth! I hate being called 'child'—I may tolerate it from your mama or Nanny Brimstoke, but not from you! And if you must behave in such a disagreeable manner, I hope madame and signor will fleece you of your last penny! They're devilishly expensive.''

"Olivia," he warned softly, "pray curb your unruly tongue. And there's no chance I'll be bankrupted by the charges of one couturiere and a *friseur*."

"Oh!" She had stomped her foot and flounced from the study.

Then why on earth was he smiling at the memory of her provoking behavior? Well, for one thing, Olivia did not bore him, and she did not toady to him like so many of the simpering young ladies who tried so hard to catch his attention. In fact, on the only occasion Olivia had given in to him without a fight, saying simply, "I'll cooperate, Worth," he'd been hit by such a wave of disappointment that it had taken all of his willpower not to shake her by the shoulders or go storming off like a disillusioned youth.

Truth to tell, the brunt of his disappointment had lain in the fact that she did not trust him sufficiently to defy his orders. That knowledge hurt—unreasonably mayhap, but he wanted her to cooperate out of her own free will, not because she felt coerced.

But what utter nonsense! He'd put the ultimatum to her, and she must do his bidding—not that he would ever follow through on his threat to expose her masquerade! Why he would not was another question he could not answer to his own satisfaction. After all, she was naught but a shameless adventuress. Wasn't she?

A brief knock on the door and the tempestuous entrance of his cousin provided a welcome distraction from his jumbled thoughts. Lionel paused briefly on the threshold, then minced toward the desk.

"At last, Fabian!" A scented handkerchief in his long, pale fingers fluttered in agitation, while several fobs and other furbelows strung across his waistcoat jiggled in rhythm with his heaving chest.

"You've missed me, Lionel?" A raised brow denoted the earl's incredulity.

"Don't talk fustian! You must know why I'm here, why I've wanted to see you for several days, in fact!"

"Of course," agreed Fabian smoothly. In one fluid movement he took his feet off the desk and rose. "You wish to felicitate me upon my betrothal and drink my health. Pray take a chair, Lionel. All that dancing fal-lalery about your person quite cuts up my peace of mind."

Impatiently Lionel brushed his forearm over the swinging and jingling accessories to still their disruptive motion. The gesture broke the slender gold chain to which his quizzing glass was attached, and it dropped soundlessly onto the rug.

"How could you, Fabian!" Lionel sat down abruptly. "How *could* you engage yourself without a word to me!"

Fabian busied himself at the credenza and returned with two glasses of Madeira. "I wasn't aware I required your permission, Lionel."

"I am your heir, yet I had not an inkling of the matter! Consider my sentiments, my embarrassment, when I was quizzed by the fellows at Watier's and Brooks's."

"But surely you must have read the announcement. It appeared in both *The Times* and the *Gazette*."

"What good is a notice in the papers, pray tell, when one has to wait forever before one of the old dodgers at the club sets aside a copy? Besides, most of my friends had read the announcement at breakfast and pounced on me before I had time to pass my hat to the porter."

"I feel for you, Lionel, but I had no notion that you had to give up your subscription to the papers. Are you so badly dipped?" He watched his cousin through hooded eyes and pushed the Madeira closer to him.

Lionel disregarded Fabian's unspoken invitation to drink, merely sat up straighter and ran a finger behind his stiff collar as though it were choking him. "Never mind my subscriptions, Fabian! The point is, you should have informed me personally before you brought your engagement to public notice."

"The point is," replied Fabian softly, "it is none of your business what I do, or omit to do."

Unheeding, Lionel accused, "With this dastardly deed you brought every deuced shopkeeper running to my door, hounding me with their demmed bills! I have not a shred of credit left to my name!"

"Could it be that you'd led the merchants to believe I would not marry? How on earth did you convince them, Lionel?"

"I *am* your heir!"

"You may be my heir presumptive, but whatever made you believe I would not beget a direct heir? I am not in my dotage, Lionel! I enjoy the best of health, and I'm in prime condition with my fists, with the rapier, and with pistols. And so you may inform Frederick!"

Lionel paled. He compressed his thin lips while his feverish eyes darted hither and yonder to escape Fabian's penetrating look. "F-Frederick?" he asked finally, then dove for the glass of wine and emptied it in great gulps. Tiny beads of sweat pearled on his forehead. With trembling fingers he replaced the goblet on the desk, pulled out a lace-edged handkerchief, and dabbed it to his lips and moist brow. "What do you mean?"

"I mean your groom, my dear Lionel. Your half brother, named after your father because not only does he have the black eyes of the Worthings, but also the mole on the left temple like your sire and you."

"What does that have to do with the bill collectors pounding on my door?" blustered Lionel. "What can be done about *that*, pray tell!"

"I'm afraid you've none but yourself to blame if your scheme backfired," replied Fabian coldly. "And now—" He pushed back his chair and rose. "I think it best to terminate this discourse before you say something you may regret later on."

Lionel got up as well, but he was unable to let go. "No one believed that after your disappointment with Melissa Vernon you'd be caught again. And by a nobody, a chit from the country!" he spat. "I wager she's related to Richard Fenshawe and that popinjay who played at being your secretary for a few days. You've chosen your brood mare from a *truly excellent* stable!''

Fabian's fist crashed down on the mahogany desktop, capsizing one of the wineglasses. ''That's quite enough from you, cousin! You'll do well to remember that you're speaking of my future wife.'' He had not raised his voice, but the anger blazing from his dark eyes was sufficient to snuff Lionel's courage.

In the sudden silence, the slam of the front door and female chatter in the hall were clearly audible—the dowager Countess of Worth and Olivia had returned from their shopping expedition.

''Robinson,'' Lady Worth was heard to inquire. ''Is my son still closeted in the study?''

The butler murmured an affirmative reply, and Lady Worth suggested, ''Olivia, dear child, you go on ahead and surprise Fabian. I have a crow to pluck with Natty. Would you believe that after thirty years of dressing me, she still fastens my hats too tight? I have such a headache, I swear she must have driven one of the hatpins straight into my skull.''

Fabian groaned inwardly when the ''dear child's'' footsteps clicked across the marble floor toward the study. What execrable timing!

Lionel scowled and turned toward the door in the half crouch he assumed when riled. However, he jerked upright and took two involuntary steps backward when the door opened to reveal a striking young lady, the spitting image of Fabian's popinjay secretary.

A jonquil walking dress worn with a light brown spencer hugged the exquisite lines of her figure; dainty, heeled half-boots of the softest kid covered her slender feet; a tasseled reticule swung jauntily from her wrist; and she carried a parasol fashioned to match her outfit.

Lionel swallowed hard and let his gaze return to her face, which had occasioned him such a shock. He gaped at her short brown hair gleaming softly with a hint of chestnut and curling stylishly around a piquant face dominated by a pair of wide, hazel eyes. There was a dimple at the corner of her mouth, but it disappeared when she encountered his unblinking stare.

Olivia frowned haughtily and turned to Fabian. "I'm sorry, dear," she said softly. "Robinson did not warn me you had company. My mission can wait until you're free."

Olivia would have withdrawn promptly had not Fabian crossed the distance quickly with his long stride and pulled her inside.

"How charming you look, my love," he murmured, "and what excellent timing. I want you to meet my cousin, Lionel Worthing." With an arm around her shoulders he led Olivia toward the gaping young man by the desk.

"But . . . but that's . . . impossible!" stammered Lionel, groping in vain for his quizzing glass. "Now where could the dratted thing be?" he muttered.

"I beg your pardon, sir?"

Olivia regretted the words the moment they left her mouth, for Lionel's fumbling hands stilled in their search and his eyes bored into her. "It *is* you!" he hissed and passed a trembling hand over his eyes. "What's this foolish masquerade, Fabian?" he demanded, then shook his head as though to clear it when the elegant young lady before him had *not* changed back into Fabian's boorish secretary who'd worn the most atrocious checkered waistcoats.

"Lionel!" Fabian's voice was sharp. "What is the matter? Will you not greet my betrothed?"

Lionel set his chin mulishly. He inched closer to Olivia and subjected her, and especially her bosom, to such an intent scrutiny that she felt stripped of every stitch of her clothing. "Your betrothed?" he scoffed. "Ha! That's rich. I'll eat my fob watch if this ain't your secretary!"

"Bon appetit." Fabian's hold tightened around Olivia until a twinge of pain in her shoulder made her stir restlessly. Immediately Fabian released her and went to perch on the edge of his desk. "Had I realized that you'd already imbibed too much, I would not have offered you any

Madeira. You must be as drunk as a wheelbarrow, Lionel, if you believe my fiancée to be her own brother.''

"He . . . she . . . but such likeness is impossible!'' blurted Lionel.

"*You* should know better than anyone that it's quite possible,'' said Fabian.

Lionel ignored him. "Are you and Tony Fenshawe twins?'' He stepped closer to Olivia—so close that the scent of his hair pomade tickled her nostrils—and peered shortsightedly into her face.

Olivia's skin prickled uncomfortably, but before she could decide whether to make a cowardly retreat or laugh at his behavior, he took a step backwards, and the high heel of his pumps came in contact with glass, scrunching it into the rug.

Lionel yelped and jumped aside to reveal the sorry remains of his quizzing glass. His color rose and his dark eyes, so like Fabian's, narrowed to slits.

"Oh! Now see what you made me do!'' he shouted.

Déjà vu. The thought flitted through Olivia's mind quick as a phantom lizard, and a chuckle rose in her throat. *Oh, no! Not another challenge!*

Fabian slid off his perch and approached his cousin. Did he intend to fight her battle for her? she wondered. Her amusement dissipated into thin air, leaving a hollow feeling in the pit of her stomach. This, her first meeting with someone who'd seen her as Tony, was not going well at all. She must allay Lionel's suspicion and, at the same time, she must do something to ease the tension between him and Fabian. Suddenly she knew how to handle the situation.

"La, Mr. Worthing!'' she simpered. "I declare I'm at a loss. Whatever can you mean, I made you do it?'' She fluttered her lashes at him and smiled coquettishly like a girl who expected to hear the old excuse that he didn't know what he was saying because her beauty had completely clouded his brain.

But Lionel did not respond at all. He was either a dunce, she decided, or else he didn't know how to flirt. Undaunted by his silence, she tried again. "I know I shouldn't say so, not when you're the gentleman who tried to fight a parlous duel with Tony; but I'm so *thrilled* to make your acquaintance!" Olivia held out her hand, palm down, like a queen sure of her courtier's devotion.

Lionel goggled, then bowed over her hand with exaggerated elaboration. "Servant, ma'am," he choked out.

"Oh, sir!" Olivia retrieved her hand and pressed it to her heaving bosom. "What a rogue you are, sir!"

"Olivia!" Fabian's tight voice brought her up short, and when she darted a cautious peek at him, she encountered a most formidable scowl. Surely Fabian must realize what she was up to? Surely he was supporting her foolish role by enacting the jealous lover? "One moment, please," she told him repressively. "Can you not see I'm busy, my love?" and turned the full force of her sparkling eyes back on Lionel.

"And now poor Tony's laid up with a bullet wound in his shoulder. . . thanks to you, Mr. Worthing." Olivia sighed dramatically.

"Eh?"

"La, sir! Could Tony be spinning a yarn? He maintains 'twas *you* who shot him for spoiling his vest," she simpered. "He swears he saw you in the carriage."

Lionel's face turned a sickly hue of yellow. He cast an apprehensive glance at Fabian, then quickly looked back at Olivia, who appeared to be the less dangerous foe. "Miss Fenshawe—"

She interrupted breathlessly. "And now you wish to punish poor little me for making you step on your beautiful quizzing glass . . . . Now, I wonder what punishment you have in mind, sir?" Olivia cocked her head and pushed out a trembling lower lip, thus achieving a fair semblance of a sultry pout.

Lionel stared at her for a long, suspenseful moment, and gradually the hunted look disappeared from his eyes and was replaced by mirth and some excitement. "Miss Fenshawe," he tried again but choked with suppressed laughter. Hastily he bowed and then, his color alarmingly high after his earlier pasty appearance, he turned to Fabian, who had resumed his perch on the desk and watched with cynical detachment the antics of his fiancée.

"My felicitations, Fabian!" Lionel's nasal voice rose to a high pitch as malicious pleasure in the situation bubbled over in him. "You've got yourself a right 'un. Begad! What a joke the fellows at White's will think this bit of news. The great, infallible Worth caught in parson's mousetrap by a foolish, simpering chit!" Shaking with glee, Lionel made them an elaborate leg, then stalked off, shouting to Robinson for his coat and hat.

Olivia followed cautiously and peeked around the doorjamb into the entrance hall to watch his departure. When the slam of the front door "made assurance double sure,"* she whirled around and turned sparkling eyes on Fabian to share the wild elation she felt at having routed the enemy, but was soon brought to realize that the earl did not in the least share her sentiments.

"What an idiotish thing to do, Olivia," he said, holding on to his temper with difficulty. "Disabuse yourself of the notion that a simpering fool would do for my fiancée! I expect you to behave with decorum and circumspection. If word of this foolishness gets around . . . !" Distaste and censure flared in his smoldering eyes, and he shuddered. "It simply doesn't bear thinking of!"

"Well!" she exploded. "Here I do my utmost to divert your cousin's suspicions, and you accuse me of folly and worse! Be assured, my lord, I never intended to play *that* stupid role again after today."

"Then you are even more of a fool than I feared. Once Lionel gets over his glee, he'll still be none too pleased that we are betrothed; and when he finds out that you've hoaxed him, he'll be as mad as fire. He'll make your life miserable when I'm not near to protect you."

*Shakespeare, William. *Macbeth*, iv. i. 83.

"What could he possibly do?" she scoffed.

"But why the deuce did *you* do it at all?" Fabian came straight to the point. He slid off the desk and in two quick strides stood towering over her. "Even if Lionel was suspicious, he could have proven nothing unless you were careless enough to expose your shoulder to him. And once your brother returns and takes up his post, Lionel will be utterly convinced that he never met you before today."

"*If* Tony ever shows up again!" she retorted bitterly and turned on her heel.

Not trusting in his ability to keep a tight rein on his vexation much longer, Fabian watched her go in silence. *I already rue the day I asked you to act as my fiancée,* he seethed. *How shall I feel in a week or two?*

What an impetuous, exasperating girl! His long fingers flexed as he recalled her simpering performance. She'd made a laughingstock of him! He'd wring her neck for certain if she played such a trick on him again!

Feeling too agitated to sit down and work at his desk, Fabian sauntered over to the window and looked morosely over the square. What a brilliant day it was; a warm, golden autumn day—a stark contrast to his bitter mood. It was a day made to order for a drive in an open carriage . . . with a lovely companion beside him. Olivia? Bah! Fortunately her very waywardness would make it easy to keep his disdainful distance—she'd looked too enchanting with her hair styled by a master's hand and gowned in the latest, high-waisted fashion.

Scowling, Olivia ran upstairs. What a provoking man the earl was! She had entered the study with the best of intentions, merely wanting to show off her new finery— well, mayhap she'd also wished to hear a compliment or two on her miraculous transformation from dowd into a young lady of fashion. Surely it was only natural to expect some praise; much of the success of her new position as Worth's "fiancée" would depend on her appearance. In any case, 'twas monstrously unfair that once again she'd had to bear the brunt of his displeasure when it had really been Lionel's fault. Besides, Worth could have put a stop to her performance at any time, had he wished it.

Olivia halted briefly on the second-floor landing to gaze at a portrait of Fabian Worthing, Sixth Earl of Worth, painted when he was only eighteen years old. *Gracious, he must have come into the title at a very tender age!* He looked stunning in a rust-colored hunting jacket, his dark hair windblown after a day of hunting with the Quorn. . . .

Most arresting was the expression of his eyes and the smile the artist had captured in the portrait. No world-weary, drooping lids concealed the pleasure and exhilaration Fabian must have felt at the conclusion of a successful day riding to the hounds; and his mouth with its sensual lower lip was curved in a singularly attractive smile.

Transfixed, Olivia stared at that mouth. Only once during her five-week acquaintance with Lord Worth had she encountered that heart-stirring smile. Oh, he was pleasant and warm when he was addressing his mama or Nanny, and, on occasion, even when dealing with *her*. But generally his way of showing amusement consisted of a slight twist of his lips.

What could have happened to him to make him so detached and cynical? When Lionel Worthing had been caught in the web of his own dastardly plotting, would Fabian feel carefree and jaunty again—like the youth in the portrait?

Olivia tore herself away and slipped into her bedroom, shutting the door firmly behind her. Naturally, as the earl's "fiancée," she was no longer stashed away in a corner bedroom, but had been installed grandly in one of the airy guest suites close to the stairway. Her two gowns had looked rather forlorn in the huge French wardrobe, and she'd had nothing but her silver-backed brush and comb set to place upon the top of the elegant Hepplewhite dresser; but now a bottle of perfume, a jar of lip salve, and a small porcelain container of powder had been added. The drawers were bursting with lace-edged, silken undergarments, stockings, gloves, and shawls. And—to check if Lizzy had taken proper care when hanging up her new acquisitions, she flung open the wardrobe doors—she was the proud possessor of a sprigged muslin gown and a ball gown! More garments, cloaks, and a riding habit would be delivered just as fast as Madame Bertin's seamstresses could flash their needles. Olivia ran her fingertips along three hatboxes on the shelf above the dresses and admired a pair of white satin evening slippers she'd be wearing in a few hours to Lady Wanderley's ball.

She trailed into the sitting room and huddled in the window seat. According to the dowager countess, old Lady Wanderley was a very discriminating hostess. Only the crème de la crème of London society was privileged to receive a gilt-edged invitation to her annual ball. Lady Wanderley always gave the ball during the Little Season, always asked a group of musicians from the Hanover Square Rooms to provide the music, and always fell asleep halfway through the evening.

At least Lionel Worthing wouldn't be there; certainly he could not be considered crème de la crème. But how would one Olivia Fenshawe, insignificant miss from the country, fare? Olivia sighed and stared down into the narrow stretch of garden at the back of Worth House and the stone wall separating it from the neighboring gardens, from the carriage house and stables in the mews.

Richard and Harriet had not often permitted her to accompany them to social functions—although her name and Tony's had always been meticulously included in invitations from the few families who were on visiting terms with the Fenshawes. Grandmama, of course, had dragged her to balls at the subscription rooms and to her friends' entertainments, but she had been so obviously matchmaking that Olivia had visited her only when she had received a direct order to show her face in Bath.

Well, Merrie had done her best to school her in the social graces. She'd try to remember all the one thousand and one rules governing the deportment of a young lady, and take a first step toward earning Fabian's approval.

At eleven o'clock on the dot, Olivia floated gracefully to the ground floor. Her feet in the dainty dancing slippers barely touched the polished oak stairway, and the thin muslin of her ball gown clung deliciously to her person as she increased her speed of descent.

Alas, Fabian was before her, pacing the hall restlessly. His bold eyes raked her from head to toe, but no softening of his harsh features gave her the reassurance she craved. In fact, he looked so pointedly at her deep, square décolletage that she was convinced it was even more daring than she'd feared.

But he only said, "Splendid. Madame Bertin knows her business. Those puffy sleeves completely hide your scar."

"Oh." She released her breath in one relieved whoosh. So that was why he'd stared at her.

"But I suggest you run back upstairs and fetch a shawl, Olivia. This is October; you'll catch your death in that flimsy gown."

Olivia was about to enlighten him on this point when the dowager's voice drifted down to them from the stairs. "Not necessary, Fabian! Here, help the child with this." She joined them in the entrance hall and passed Fabian an evening cloak of brown velvet lined with silk in the same shade of ecru as Olivia's ball gown. "I told you, Olivia, that Natty would unearth it from the trunks in the attic. She knows where absolutely *everything* is kept. Let me look at you, child. Yes, now I'm doubly glad we chose the ecru muslin and not the white tulle. Besides, with your coloring you should not wear white at all; 'twould make you look positively insipid."

While Lady Worth was chattering away in her clear, high voice, Olivia had ample opportunity to flash a triumphant look at Fabian—which, of course, he did not deign to notice, concentrating only on draping the cape about her shoulders. But this should teach him not to jump to a premature conclusion! He seemed to think she didn't know better and would venture forth in short sleeves when only this morning the season's first layer of hoarfrost had covered the ground.

"We'd best be going," Fabian suggested when the dowager paused for a breath. "The chaise drove up ten minutes ago."

"Dear me, Fabian! Had I not heard you this afternoon bemoaning your acceptance of Lady Wanderley's invitation, I'd think you were *aux anges* to get there."

"I don't like to keep the horses standing in the cold, Mama."

The dowager cast a quizzical glance at her son and nodded to Robinson, who had appeared to throw open the door for them.

The carriage had barely started rolling when it began to pull up before an imposing house illuminated by countless flambeaux, and with scarlet-liveried footmen stationed along a strip of carpeting from the street to the great double doors of the mansion. Olivia's jaw dropped. Lady Wanderley was practically a neighbor, living just around the corner in Mount Street.

"Good." The countess nodded with satisfaction. "We are late enough to have missed the crush of coaches, but not too late to appear inconsiderate. If we'd left an hour earlier, Olivia, old Bert would not even have been able to pull out of the mews. Hundreds of carriages would have lined up along Mount Street and around Grosvenor Square."

"But why drive at all?" asked Olivia. "We could have walked the few steps."

"*Walked?*" repeated the countess in scandalized tones. "You would have us appear at a ball on foot, with our hair all windblown and cheeks aglow from the cold?"

"There is hardly a breeze tonight, and if pink cheeks are so gauche, why did you want me to purchase a pot of rouge?"

"Rouged cheeks are different," countered Lady Worth. "Thank goodness you didn't succumb to the lure of paint," murmured Fabian and offered an arm to each of his ladies. "You look glowing without the aid of cosmetics."

Was this a compliment or more of his sarcasm? Well, she'd give him the benefit of the doubt. "Thank you, my lord." She smiled at him and added, "You look quite dashing yourself." Her eyes roamed appreciatively over his dark coat and champagne-colored silk breeches, and lingered with some envy on his cravat tied in the *Trône d'Amour*.

"Call me Fabian, or Worth!" he hissed in reply, and then they were inside the ballroom, walking toward Lady Wanderley, who beckoned imperiously from her thronelike chair at the far end of the vast chamber.

All conversation in the ballroom ceased as the assembled company turned toward them and watched their progress toward their hostess; even the musicians had plotted against them and finished a contradanse just then, laying down their instruments for a respite.

Instinctively Olivia's head came up, and she straightened her shoulders as she concentrated on keeping a smile on her face.

"Good girl." Fabian's voice was as gentle as a breath, but she heard and drew courage from his presence. It wasn't so fearsome after all, having to face the exacting members of the *ton*.

"There you are at last, Worth!" shouted Lady Wanderley when they were still a good six paces from her. "I had just about given up hope of meeting your fiancée tonight. Thought you might prefer staying at home and sampling some of the gal's charms, eh, Worth?"

"My dear Lady Wanderley! You're quite your delightfully outspoken self, as ever," murmured Fabian as he bowed over her gnarled hand. "How I wish I had been born a few years sooner. I would have enjoyed paying court to you, ma'am. May I present Miss Olivia Fenshawe?"

The old lady nodded graciously and gestured for Olivia to take a seat beside her. Then she greeted the dowager countess with warmth and affection and pointed out, quite unnecessarily, the presence of some of Lady Worth's bosom bows. The countess was already surrounded by the beturbaned, excitedly chattering matrons.

"And you, Worth, you may take yourself off and find amusement elsewhere for a short while," directed Lady Wanderley.

Fabian bowed with exquisite grace and strolled off to solicit the hand of a delicate, fair-haired young lady for the next dance while Lady Wanderley turned her attention to Olivia.

"So, you're the chit who caught the elusive earl? Who'd have thought it, with your background and all. But you do have countenance—ye're no blushing, simpering miss. I like that. Most gals would have dropped in a dead faint had they heard my comments to Worth." She cackled gleefully.

"I've not had time yet to blush," confessed Olivia. "I've been too well occupied, first with overcoming my apprehension, then admiring your ballroom and the assembled company, ma'am. But what did you mean when you spoke of my 'background and all'?"

"Bless you, child! Don't you know about that faro game—what was it? Seven years ago? No matter. I always said Worth's pride and his sense of honor are too refined for his own good."

"Honor, ma'am? You speak in the same breath of Worth's honor and the card game that cost us our home?"

"Yes, I do! But apparently you don't share my opinion. Probably because you don't know the half of it. Didn't Worth tell you?"

"I've learned all I need to know from my brother, ma'am."

"Pshaw! Let me tell you, child! When your brother was found—" She broke off abruptly and looked about her, knitting her brows fiercely at two elderly ladies who were patently straining to overhear the interesting conversation. Then she whispered to Olivia in carrying tones, "A ball's not the place to enlighten you—too many curious ears about, and I know I holler when I think I speak quietly. It's on account of being partially deaf, you see. You come and visit me some morning soon, and I'll tell you all about it, but in return I wish to know what game you're playing at, gal. That you haven't tumbled head over heels for Worth I can see for myself—although I won't pretend to understand why you haven't. Now, if I were a few years younger . . ." She chuckled wickedly. "And why the hasty betrothal, gal?"

Olivia felt the blood drain from her face, then rush back to burn her cheeks with crimson, and hunted desperately for a few simple words of explanation, but her mind was blank. To make matters worse, Fabian came strolling toward them, to claim her for a dance, no doubt, as Lady Wanderley pointed out before Olivia had had time to compose herself.

It was with considerable confusion that she placed her hand on Fabian's arm. How could she have been so careless and given free rein to her feelings when the old lady spoke about that card game. Now she'd aroused Lady Wanderley's suspicions—and probably her "fiancée's" as well, to judge by the wary look he'd directed at her.

Thank goodness, the musicians were striking up a Scottish reel. There would be no opportunity for Fabian to question her about her conversation with their hostess—and hopefully the dowager countess had been too distracted by the other ladies' inquisition to have paid attention to Lady Wanderley's loud comments.

What on earth could Lady Wanderley tell her that she didn't know already?

CHAPTER 5

When the lively dance ended, Fabian steered Olivia purposefully toward a small settee at the far side of the ballroom. A sadly drooping palm spread its leaves over one end of the velvet seat, and gently billowing drapes nearby promised a welcome breath of cool air from an open window.

"Well?" Olivia seated herself primly and smoothed her long silk gloves over her elbows and along her upper arms. She could feel Worth's probing eyes on her face and turned away so he would not observe the telltale blush warming her cheeks.

"Now, why should I have the distinct impression that you've been up to no good, Olivia?" he asked and sat down beside her, much too close for her peace of mind.

With a longing glance at the refreshment table, which he observed but ignored, she replied haughtily, "I haven't the faintest idea, Worth. Oh, look! There's Lord Charles standing in that palm grove by the refreshments. Do let's ask him to join us."

She lifted her hand to beckon Lord Charles Baxter, but let it drop instantly with a startled look at Fabian even before he reacted and pressed his own large hand over hers.

"Precisely," he said and frowned at her. "There are pitfalls everywhere. Come." He pulled her off the settee and proffered his arm with a polite bow. "Let me *introduce* Charles to you."

"Please do," she said with feeling. "What a narrow escape! I'd be in a fine pickle now had I not caught my error. Gracious! Worth's fiancée waving to a man she could not possibly have met before!"

He caught the twinkle in her eyes and, despite his resolution to treat her with reserve, found himself responding to her mischievous smile.

"Imp!" he whispered into her ear and steered her around a group of giggling debutantes. "It may turn out rather interesting to watch Charles's face when he gets a good look at you."

"And *you* called *me* an imp!" she reproached him.

He laughed. "I can't deny that I'm curious about Charles's reaction. I wager it'll be more entertaining than this ball."

"Do you also feel it?" Olivia asked eagerly. "I mean, that this is rather an insipid affair? I feared 'twas my ignorance of town ways that made it impossible for me to appreciate the ball. It's *quite* different from what I imagined. For one thing, there are far too many people! One can't stand, or walk, or dance without having someone step on one's toes. Just look at the smudges on my slippers!" She halted and raised the scalloped hem of her gown to display the abused footwear.

"Charming, quite charming, indeed," he murmured with an appreciative glance at her neatly turned ankle.

She studied his face briefly, then dimpled. "Abominable, quite abominable, indeed!" Olivia said. "I wonder you dare show me this raffish side of your character when you're forever preaching propriety to me."

Laughter lurked in his charcoal eyes as he took a firm grip on her elbow and guided her through a particularly crowded area of the ballroom. The evening might not be a complete waste after all, he mused. Indeed, it might turn out *very pleasantly*. "I wish I might show you just how raffish I can be in such delightful company as yours," he told her, "but I fear we must concentrate on Charles now. He and his friends are standing just beyond this cluster of gossiping matrons. Pluck up, my dear!"

"Don't fret," she said, deliberately ignoring the first part of his speech and the excitement it had caused to leap up in her. "Confronting Lord Charles cannot possibly be as bad as walking gauntlet across the ballroom, with deathly silence cutting a path ahead and a wall of whispering voices growing thick behind us."

"I apologize. I should have stopped and introduced you to some of these eagle-eyed ladies and goggling gentlemen, but I was too pleasantly occupied to give them a thought, and, I fear, we'd never have made it all the way to Charles's side. Observe them just a little and you'll notice they are like hungry hyenas waiting to fall prey upon my lovely betrothed who keeps me enthralled at her side without the least difficulty.''

"Oh! That's why you're behaving so charmingly toward me.'' Olivia could not help but feel a tiny stab of disappointment, but nothing on earth would induce her to admit to this. "Well done, Worth! But you need not overdo it. By now they must be quite persuaded that I have you in my pocket.''

"'Tis no hardship on me. You are adorable tonight, my love. Now, pray don't blush. After such a 'whirlwind courtship' as we entered upon, surely you'd be quite accustomed to even my most outrageous compliments.''

"You must credit *me* with some thespian accomplishments as well. A blushing fiancée will be more convincing than a poised and cool one.''

"Quite. But hush now, love. Charles has seen us.''

Indeed, he couldn't help but see them. Several friends at Lord Charles's side were nudging him and nodding their heads in Worth's direction. Lord Charles's eyes opened so wide that Olivia feared they'd pop from their sockets. He, like Lionel Worthing, had sustained a severe shock at the sight of her.

"Charles, my boy! Delighted to find you here,'' boomed Fabian and pumped his friend's hand heartily. "Let me make you known to my fiancée. Olivia has wanted to meet you this age.''

Lord Charles's blue eyes had never left Olivia's face, but now they narrowed. "Honored, Miss Fenshawe,'' he said. "But—pray forgive my curiosity—*why* did you want to meet me?''

She chuckled. "You shouldn't feel surprised, my lord. Both Fabian and Tony have talked about you so much that I felt a strong desire to meet this admirable man whose virtues they extolled.''

Lord Charles regarded her dimpling face intently, then a broad grin spread over his boyish features. "I can only hope, ma'am, that they mentioned my sagacity as well.''

Tarnation, she fretted. This could only mean he'd recognized her. Had her disguise been that transparent?

"I perceive, my friend," Lord Charles addressed Fabian, "that the three of us must have a long, private talk in the morning. Miss Fenshawe..." he gave her a broad wink, "must fill me in on all the news about Tony."

"Indeed she will. But how comes it that you—and our worthy friends here—are to be found in a ballroom? I was certain *nothing* could sway the lot of you to do the pretty at an affair like this." He raised his expressive brows at the half dozen gentlemen surrounding Lord Charles, and introduced them all in turn to Olivia.

"There was talk in the clubs that you'd be bringing your fiancée here," said Lord Roxbury, a dandified young man with tousled, sandy hair, freckles, and shirt points as high and stiff as Lionel Worthing's. "Nothing but that bait *could* have dragged us to Lady W.T.'s. Boring affair, ain't it?"

"Olivia, too, was just saying what a terrible squeeze it is."

"I did nothing of the sort, Fabian!" she protested. "I'd never speak so rudely!"

He laughed. "My sweet little peagoose, a 'terrible squeeze' is the accolade of every hostess's dream—a festivity, boring and insipid no doubt, but with every one of the invited two or three hundred of the crème de la crème having accepted and shown up."

"Well—" She looked about her with some doubt still lingering in her mind. "I suppose by those standards this ball must be counted a great success. But I'd hoped there would be lobster patties and champagne," she said with a disappointed look at the punch bowl on the refreshment table, "and waltzing. I was told the waltz is all the crack in London!"

"Not at Lady W.T.'s," explained Lord Roxbury kindly. "She don't approve of the waltz, you know. Too, too scandalous having members of the opposite sex clasp each other around the waist!"

Olivia's eyes met Fabian's gleaming ones. She had to bite

her lip to keep from laughing out loud. Who'd have believed that their outspoken hostess had this streak of prudery in her?

"But you *will* have lobster patties and champagne at supper. *That* is considered de rigueur," Fabian told her and pinched her wrist under the guise of holding her arm possessively while Olivia suffered all the agonies of one swallowing the giggles bubbling up inside her.

To give her mind a different turn, she asked Lord Roxbury, "Why do you call her Lady W.T., my lord?"

The innocent question threw Lord Roxbury and the other gentlemen into confusion. Some chuckled, some looked embarrassed; only Fabian had a lazy smile on his lips and watched them all with amusement.

"My dear Miss Fenshawe," said Lord Charles finally. "You put us to the blush. I'm afraid you'll consider us discourteous and lacking in respect for our dear hostess, but believe me, no slight is intended."

"Oh! It must stand for Lady 'Wicked Tongue'!"

Lord Charles grinned and whispered to her alone, "I always maintained you're a sharp 'un, Tony." Aloud he said, "Yes, indeed, Miss Fenshawe. I fear you must consider us quite beyond the pale."

It appeared Lord Charles was bent on spoiling her evening, thought Olivia. He had called her Tony! With a rather forced smile, she shook her head. "Not at all, my lord. And I'm sure Lady Wanderley would be the first to appreciate the nickname."

"Indeed, she would!" interposed Lord Roxbury. "And I wager a pony she even knows of it. Charles . . . ?"

"If you offered me double, I wouldn't take the bet, Roxbury. Who'd want to ask Lady W.T. if she knows of the name?" asked Lord Charles. Then he bowed to Olivia. "May I have the honor of this dance, Miss Fenshawe?"

She glanced at Fabian, and since he nodded quite unconcernedly, allowed herself to be led onto the dance floor. Fully aware of her unease, Lord Charles directed one of his disarming smiles at her. "Don't worry, Miss Fenshawe,

I won't ask any awkward questions tonight. I can contain my curiosity until the morning.''

"You may call me Olivia," she answered brightly just before the movement of the country dance took them apart. It was bad enough to know that he'd discovered her secret, but why must he harp on it? And where had she gone wrong? Thank goodness she'd not succumbed to Fabian's entreaties and accompanied him to the clubs as Tony, to be introduced to a whole battery of young men. 'Twas enough to have to cope with one—and then there was Lionel who might recognize her yet.

"You don't look as if you're enjoying your first London ball," remarked Lord Charles during one of the brief moments when they were reunited in the dance pattern.

"I *am* enjoying myself," she assured him. "But I do wish they'd play a waltz! Tony and I have practiced the steps, but have never actually performed it. Like Lady Wanderley, the staid hostesses in Bath and in our countryside frown upon the impropriety of the waltz."

"We'll see! Lady W.T. ain't asleep . . . yet," he replied with seeming irrelevance before he was carried along in the opposite direction.

There was one more dance, which Olivia performed with a stammering Mr. Wilburton, who was so painfully shy that he uttered no more than four words for the entire duration of the boulanger: "B-beg your p-pardon, Miss F-Fenshawe!" when he trod on her already bruised toes.

When supper was announced, she ate the lobster patties Mr. Wilburton fetched from the buffet tables in an effort to atone for his clumsiness on the dance floor. In fact, she ate more than her fill of the delicacies so that she wouldn't hurt his feelings by a refusal, and drank several glasses of delicious champagne until Worth finally removed her glass and placed it out of reach.

A very few minutes after the last guest had abandoned the depleted buffet tables and drifted back into the ballroom, Lady Wanderley fell asleep.

"Let's slip away now to find some livelier entertainment,'' suggested Lord Roxbury to the others with a speaking glance at the nodding ostrich plumes on their hostess' slipping turban.

"What? Oh, not just yet. Pray excuse me a moment,'' begged Lord Charles and withdrew.

He returned presently and stationed himself close to Olivia. Mischief was writ all over his face, and he gave her a broad wink.

"What's up, Charles?'' demanded Fabian of his unusually animated friend.

"Nothing at all,'' replied Charles airily, but pounced on Olivia the very instant the musicians picked up their violins. "May I have this dance, Olivia?''

It was a waltz.

"Oh, no, you don't!'' Fabian stepped between them, his hand clamping around Olivia's wrist, pinning her to the spot although she'd given no sign of wishing to leave. "You'd best make good your escape before Lady Wanderley awakens,'' he warned his friend. "I wouldn't put it past her to rake you down with a fine-tooth comb if the music rouses her and she finds you on the premises.''

"But who will waltz with Olivia? We can't allow her to leave her first London ball without having waltzed.''

"Don't trouble your head, Charles.'' Fabian turned to Olivia with a wry smile. "You probably don't deserve it, my dear, but you have a perfectly capable fiancé to perform this service for you. May I have the honor?''

"P-pardon me,'' interrupted Mr. Wilburton, blushing furiously. "Does Miss Fenshawe have p-permission to waltz?''

Fabian frowned. "I suppose not. I am sorry, my dear, but we had better not offend any of Almack's patronesses.''

"I do not require their sanction, Fabian.'' Olivia chuckled. This time it was *her* turn to instruct the lofty Lord Worth in the proper procedures. "No betrothed or married lady does!''

"In that case, by all means let's waltz.''

Pink-cheeked, her hazel eyes alight with pleasure, Olivia laid her hand in his. She felt the firm pressure of his fingers under her shoulder blade as she was whisked onto the mirrorlike dance floor and hastily suppressed a gasp at his intimate touch. A warm glow spread through her body despite her best efforts to remain cool and detached.

Unaccustomed to champagne, she'd felt a trifle lightheaded after supper; now, with the lilting tune arousing her blood, and Fabian's delightful if disturbing proximity sending delicious tingles down her back, she was a sprite, an elfin creature who floated about to the entrancing sounds of Pan's pipes.

They did not speak, but their eyes were riveted on each other, aglow with the magic of the moment.

He is smiling at me! thought Olivia.

She is intoxicating, mused Fabian.

Instinctively they moved a fraction closer together, each savoring the other's touch and scent. Her eyes darkened, and she moistened her suddenly dry lips when Fabian slid his hand to the small of her back.

Then their dream world was shattered by Lady Wanderley's shrill voice and the discordant screech of a violin as the musicians stopped their fiddling, and the dancing couples around them drew hastily apart.

"Imbeciles! Depraved monsters!" screamed the outraged old lady. "How dare you provide the music to this improper, to this, this . . . scandalous dance in *my house*!"

"Well, my dear—" Fabian removed his arm from Olivia's back and released her hand. Now that the music had stopped, he was not at all loath to be brought back to earth. What foolishness was this! To let himself get carried away by a dance, by close contact with Olivia! He cleared his throat and told her, "This interlude provides a good excuse to search out my mother and order the carriage."

"Yes, indeed," said Olivia. A dull ache in the region of her stomach and a sudden throbbing in her head made her voice sound flat. Too much champagne, she thought gloomily. If only the dance hadn't ended so abruptly. . . .

Lady Worth was found in the card room, a glass of sherry and a small stack of gold coins at her elbow. She voiced no regrets when asked if she was ready to leave—on the contrary.

"Oh, what splendid timing, Fabian! Just imagine, I'd won three hundred guineas, but was beginning to lose it all to that sly fox, Winchelsea. You saved my day; I still have fifty guineas left!"

The footman in the hall sprang to attention and sent a second footman to call for Lord Worth's carriage. By the time Olivia and Lady Worth had donned their cloaks and Fabian had retrieved his hat and cane, the chaise was at the door.

With one foot already on the coach steps, Olivia suddenly pulled back and breathed in great gulps of the cool night air. It was the worst of punishments to have to be cooped up inside a stuffy carriage now.

Fabian, who had first helped his mother into the vehicle and had then taken Olivia's elbow to assist her up the steps, regarded her pale features and stated dryly, "The effects of a first grand ball crammed with champagne, lobster patties, and waltzing."

A shaky laugh escaped Olivia's dry throat. "You would know, Worth. But, indeed, I think I must learn to carry my wine better."

"I generally walk home after attending a stuffy party," he offered diffidently. "Would you care to accompany me?"

"I most certainly would." She felt instantaneous relief and stepped down to allow Fabian to bid his mama a good night.

When the coach had lumbered off, he gallantly offered his arm and steered her around the corner into South Audley Street. "Would your poor, bruised toes permit a stroll around the square before we return home?"

"I think they would revel in it! Do you realize, Fabian, I haven't been able to take a proper walk since our aborted walk to Tattersall's? I must confess, though, that walking on the city's cobbled streets is not the same as striding about in the country."

"Do you miss the countryside?" There was a note of

surprise in his voice. The young ladies he knew had moaned and groaned when they'd had to spend some time at their country homes.

Olivia mulled over his question for a bit, but finally she admitted, "Yes, I miss it greatly. When I lived at Fenshawe Court, I often pined for a visit to London, but if your mama's accounts of a lady's life in town paint a true picture, then I'd rather stay in the country forever. Nothing but shopping for gowns, paying morning calls, giving teas, attending balls—and wherever I go I must take a maid, a footman, and the carriage!"

He chuckled. "What would be *your* notion of having a good time in the city?"

"Going to Somerset House to study the paintings, visiting Bullock's museum, Hookham's library and the book shops, seeing the historical sights . . ."

". . . such as the Tower," he interjected.

A gurgle of laughter escaped her. "You are not convinced then that a view of the intimidating structure was sufficient to impress me? Must I walk inside where, no doubt, the very walls are permeated with the fear and anguish of those poor incarcerated souls who perished there?"

He appeared to consider the question seriously before he replied. "Nay," he said. "I can see 'twould be too much for a young lady of your exquisite sensibilities. I'll take you to enjoy a gallop in Richmond Park instead. What else would you like to do?"

"Get lost in the maze at Hampton Court, take a peek at Almack's famous assembly rooms, and attend a session in the House of Lords, to listen from the visitors' gallery to the speakers rip at each other," she rattled off breathlessly.

"I perceive that we must allow time for some of those amusements to make your enforced stay in town a pleasant one. Would you also enjoy the opera or a play?"

"Indeed, I would. Do you have a box at the Covent Garden Theatre?"

"And at Drury Lane," he confirmed. "And at the—"

"Listen!" interrupted Olivia in an urgent whisper. "Do

you hear something or someone stalking around in the enclosure?''

They had been strolling along the wrought-iron fence surrounding the garden in the center of Grosvenor Square and had entered a dark area with the next streetlamp still some distance off at the corner where Duke Street entered the square.

''No,'' he murmured, reluctant to have their tête-à-tête disrupted even by an imagined intruder. ''I heard nothing.'' Nevertheless, he tightened his grip on his solid ebony cane and led Olivia toward the other side of the cobbled street, where several lanterns in front of the mansions provided a safer environment.

But they did not reach the other side. Two muffled figures vaulted over the iron fence and brandished wicked-looking clubs.

''Outta the way, leddy!'' hissed one of them.

''Stand behind me, Olivia!'' commanded Fabian and wielded his cane like a sword.

Olivia watched helplessly as the two ruffians attacked Fabian, and were driven back again and again by his swift, powerful parries and lunges with the cane. But twice, while he was staving off one attacker, the other succeeded in landing a blow on his right shoulder. Her stomach knotted painfully. If he should lose his cane or sustain a hit on the head. . . .

What to do? If only she had a sword, or even a pistol! She must do something, anything; mayhap draw one of the assailants away from him!

''I'll get help, Fabian!'' she shouted. ''Hold them off!'' Olivia picked up her skirts and darted away.

Her maneuver was successful; one of the men started after her. Olivia was very swift, but since she had no intention of leaving Fabian to fend for himself, she flitted hither and yonder without gaining any distance from her pursuer. His labored breathing rasped loud and fearsomely close behind her. Soon he would capture her!

Capture . . . That triggered a memory.

Olivia put a hand to her mouth and produced a series of ear-piercing, staccato yells. She broke off abruptly when the ruffian was so close that she felt his breath hot against her neck. Her skin prickled and her fingers trembled as she undid the frogging of her cloak. She grabbed the smooth material firmly with both hands, raised her arms high above her head, and at the same time, spun around.

The cape billowed like a banner, and she swung it with all her strength at her pursuer, then let go. Finding himself suddenly blinded, he dropped his cudgel to tear the stifling cover off his head, but tripped over his own weapon and crashed heavily to the ground.

Since he was lying on the club and she couldn't get to it, Olivia used her beaded reticule to strike at his groping hands, but she knew she would not be able to hold him down long. Already he was on his knees, ripping at the shroud over his head with one hand and searching for his club with the other.

Hurry! Oh, please hurry, Fabian! she prayed silently.

After an eternity of apprehension, listening and swinging her little bag at the struggling footpad, she heard Fabian's fleet steps just as the thug lumbered to his feet.

"Stand aside, Olivia!" panted Fabian.

Deftly he connected his fist with the bearded jaw the man had carelessly exposed when he'd succeeded in partially removing Olivia's cape, and without having uttered a sound, the footpad hit the ground again.

Fabian swung around and took Olivia by the shoulders. Gently shaking her to and fro, he said gruffly, "Demmit, gal, I was certain you'd been hit by that . . . oaf when your cries ceased so abruptly. Why on earth did you yell like that? It curdled my blood, but fortunately, it also threw my assailant off balance and I succeeded in felling him. *Are* you unharmed, Olivia?"

"Of c-course I am. Only n-now I'm beg-ginning to feel chilled," she managed to assure him despite suddenly chattering teeth.

Fabian's eyes carefully traveled up and down her shaking

form to reassure himself that she was speaking the truth and was indeed unhurt. Finally satisfied, he let go of her, removed his own coat, and laid it around her shoulders before kneeling down to inspect the sprawling figure on the cobbles.

"He's still out cold."

"N-No wonder, after your d-deadly uppercut!"

Fabian grinned at her, but made no comment on her knowledge of boxing cant. "I had to use my cravat to tie up the other fellow. Do you have anything I could use on this one?"

"Sorry, m-my lord, I'm n-not wearing a s-stock tonight," she replied jokingly with a rather weak smile.

"Well, if you don't feel he merits the ripping of your petticoats, I'll have to tie him up in your cloak."

"Your m-mama won't like that."

"I'll buy her a new one, and we won't have to tell her. But let's get you home now to some cognac and a hot bath."

"Are you l-leaving them here strewn a-all over the square?" she asked, scandalized.

"I'll send some footmen to deliver them to the constable. Come now, let's bustle. You're shivering—and you sound just like Wilburton."

He took her hand in a firm grip, and together they hurried to Worth House, where he unlocked the front door and pulled Olivia into the dim entrance hall. The dowager having safely arrived and retired some little while ago, no lights save a single wall sconce in the hall had been left burning, and the footmen, knowing better than to wait up for his lordship, had sought their own beds. Fabian lit an eight-branch candelabrum and in its comforting, warm pool of light escorted Olivia into the study. He stoked up the still glowing embers in the fireplace, added kindling and some small logs, and had a roaring fire going in no time at all.

Leaving Olivia ensconced in a chair near the soothing warmth, a rug wrapped around her legs and a glass of cognac in her cold hands, he rushed off to rouse Alders and his stoutest footmen. He gave a brief explanation and sent them into the square to collect the hoodlums, then called for the young maid who'd been assigned to assist Olivia.

"Lizzy, get a hot bath ready for Miss Olivia immediately and bring some tea into the study."

When he rejoined Olivia, the glass in her hand was empty, and she greeted him with a rather bemused smile. "How is your shoulder, Fabian? I was afraid they'd improve their aim and split your skull if I didn't draw one of them off."

He shrugged carelessly. "I'm in good shape. After all, 'twas only a glancing blow. How are *you* feeling now?"

"Much better, thank you. Only a trifle dizzy," she admitted sheepishly.

"Cognac is said to have that effect at times. Don't fret, you'll drink some tea presently and will feel as right as a trivet."

"Tea . . ." she murmured, "the wondrous panacca." With some effort she roused herself from her dreamy state. "Worth, why would those two footpads be lurking in Grosvenor Square? I shouldn't think they'd find business very lucrative here. After all, it was pure chance that we happened by."

"I generally walk home and take a turn around the square," reminded Fabian dryly.

"Oh . . . ! Lionel?"

"Although I'm loath to believe such of my own cousin, I must certainly weigh the possibility."

"But so soon? Why, he learned of the engagement only this morning!"

"No, my dear. He learned of it when the notice appeared in the papers. And why should he wait? Lionel is an impatient man. He knows my habits well and he'll snatch at every opportunity. But the next opportunity must be arranged and masterminded by me. . . ." Lost in thought, he poured some cognac for himself and drank slowly.

"It may be for the best after all," he mused absently, "that Charles is coming later on this morning."

Before he could elaborate, or Olivia could question him, a knock heralded the arrival of Lizzy carrying a loaded tray. Carefully depositing it on the desk, Lizzy dropped a curtsy. "I'll be back presently to fetch ye for yer bath, miss." She was gone again before Olivia had time to thank her.

Frowning, she accepted the tea Worth had poured and exclaimed, "Here it is past three in the morning, and Lizzy looks as neat as a pin from that immaculate mobcap to her buttoned shoes—as though she'd never been to bed yet!"

"Unless you told her *not* to wait up for you, she couldn't very well retire, dear." Fabian picked up his cognac again, walked over to the window, and leaned his back against the sill.

Olivia blinked. "Are you telling me that Lizzy requires my permission to go to sleep?"

Amused, he nodded. "Indeed, my love. As a general rule, the staff retires after the tea tray has been taken up to my mother. But Natty takes her orders only from Mama, and Lizzy takes hers from you."

"Tarnation! I wish I'd been told. The poor girl! She must believe me a veritable dragon!"

"My poor Olivia! You made an excellent secretary, but your qualifications as a lady leave much to be desired—and you have much to amend!" he added sternly. "Where, for example, did you acquire the habit of yelling like an Indian on the warpath? I'm surprised you didn't bring the whole square down on us, armed to the teeth with guns and swords. And where on earth did you pick up 'tarnation'? That's a rare one."

Successfully diverted from her distress over Lizzy, Olivia chuckled. "Envious of my vocabulary, Fabian? Years and years ago one of our neighbors had a cousin from America staying with him, and he taught Tony and me all sorts of clever things. He'd have been proud—I believe I achieved a rather good imitation of a Cherokee war cry."

"Amazing that after all those years you should have remembered childhood games . . . and while you were being chased by a dangerous criminal."

"Well, actually it was only about four years ago, and he was forever chasing me, breathing down my neck—" She stopped and colored. "In any case, when the footpad came running after me, I suddenly remembered."

"I understand." Fabian grinned knowingly. "And I'm almost convinced that the ways of a hoyden are more alluring—and more useful to me—than the immaculate manners of a delicately reared young lady would be."

Olivia was puzzling over his words, undecided whether they denoted approval of her actions or not, and did not realize Fabian had left his position by the window until he stood before her chair, his eyes alight with laughter and his mouth curved in the breathtaking smile she'd hoped to see bestowed on her again.

"Thank you, my dear. For the second time you've had a hand in saving my life." He then picked up her hand, turned it over, and pressed a lingering kiss first on her wrist, then in her palm.

Little shivers of delight raced up and down her spine.

"Cold again, Olivia?" he asked and sternly suppressed the teasing smile that tugged at the corners of his mouth. "Come, I'll help you upstairs. Lizzy should have your bath ready by now."

"If that be all, miss, I'll blow out the candles, but I'll leave ye a small light on yer nightstand in case ye should waken from a bad dream."

"Thank you, Lizzy. But I believe I may be too tired even for nightmares," mumbled Olivia, relaxed and drowsy after a luxuriously hot, scented bath. "Only two more things, Lizzy."

"Yes, miss?"

"Promise you'll not wait up for me again, even if I forget to tell you to go to bed."

"Oh yes, miss. Thank you, miss! And t'other thing ye want me to do?"

"Tomorrow—nay, later on this morning I want you to ask

one of the footmen to hang Lord Worth's portrait here in my bedroom. You know, Lizzy, the portrait in the hall . . .''

"I know, miss. It's smashing, ain't it?"

_____CHAPTER 6_____

"But how did you tumble onto the truth so quickly, Charles? I believe my performance as Tony was excellent— he himself couldn't have done better, and I hoped, nay _expected_ to be accepted as his sister without a question.''

Despite Fabian's disapproving frown and Charles's grin, Olivia perched herself on the edge of the huge desk and swung her legs. The three of them were closeted in Fabian's study, with the door shut firmly against any prospective callers.

"Can't say that it was any one thing in particular that tipped me off, just the way you smiled at me with that tiny beauty spot right next to your dimple, and the way you held your head. You'd dimpled at me just so after the bit of swordplay with Lionel when I offered you some cognac. And then, of course, your reaction when I warned you about my knowledge, which had really been a shot in the dark then, but _that_ gave you away for certain.''

"Zounds! I could have bluffed it out.''

Fabian snorted and propped one arm onto the carved mantel, contemplating the tips of his gleaming Hessians as though their aspect was of greater interest than the ongoing conversation.

A tiny frown appeared on Olivia's forehead, and she watched him covertly. After his charming manner of the previous night, she could not help but be piqued by the earl's black mood and disdainful attitude this morning. Had he changed his mind? Did he now resent that she'd assisted him in routing the attackers? Or mayhap lack of sleep or worry about his cousin lay at the root of his harshness.

"I say, Olivia," demanded Charles. "Do you consider your position on the desk as being seated? If so, I suppose I might sit down as well, but I don't wish to offend."

Another snort was audible from the vicinity of the fireplace. Pointedly turning away from Fabian, Olivia smiled at Lord Charles. "Pray be seated, and tell me why you didn't make the mistake—as did Lionel—of believing me to be Tony dressed up as a girl."

"What a cork-brained notion! Lionel has more hair than wit if he jumped to that conclusion. Fabian would *never* foist a man on us dressed up as his fiancée. It ain't good *ton*!"

"Thank you, Charles." Fabian propelled himself away from the mantel and came to sit next to Olivia, draping his arm around her waist.

She stiffened and tried to squirm unobtrusively out of his clasp, but her movement caused a possessive tightening of his grip. How like him to pretend to be the smitten fiancé right after his derisive behavior moments earlier!

"Let's get to the point," said Fabian coolly. "You came to find out why my fiancée masqueraded as her baby brother. Well, that was to help him out of a scrape, and now she's *posing* as my betrothed to help *me* out."

"Posing? You mean you're not betrothed at all?"

"We are *not*," confirmed Olivia.

Lord Charles rubbed his temples and frowned. "I don't understand," he complained. "How does that help you, Fabian? Why would you need a 'fiancée' all of a sudden?"

"I wanted a device to back Lionel into a corner. Now he's feeling a desperate need for haste, and sooner or later he'll make a mistake. Then I can *finally* lay my hands on him and send him one-way to India."

For a long time Charles said nothing; he just stared hard at Olivia, then at Fabian. "Always told you to do something about that cousin of yours—ever since you sold out!'' he grumbled finally. ''He's a curst rum touch, if you ask me. What made you change your mind? You were not always convinced he's the instigator of—'' He broke off and looked questioningly at Fabian, who shook his head at him. ''But why this elaborate charade, Fabian?'' he demanded.

''Elaborate, my friend? It's the simplest trick of all, or did you have a better plan?''

''No,'' admitted Charles. ''But you can't have considered the consequences! When we've flushed Lionel out in the open, and I've no doubt we shall, is it your intention to cry off from the engagement?''

''Olivia will.''

''You'd have her branded a jilt? Can't ask it of her, Fabian!'' Charles shook his head decisively. ''She wouldn't have a shred of reputation left, not after Melissa, and not as long's her name's Fenshawe.''

Fabian's arm dropped from Olivia's waist. '' 'Twould be worse were I to cry off,'' he countered in a tight voice.

''Then why the deuce did you do it?''

''Stop!'' cried Olivia. ''Both of you! Will someone kindly explain what this is all about?'' She glared at Charles. ''Why the deuce *can't* Fabian and I dissolve the engagement whenever we wish?''

Lord Charles jumped visibly at being thus addressed. ''For goodness' sake, Olivia! Mustn't speak like that. If anyone were to hear you, they'd think you weren't a lady!''

''*You* obviously don't consider me a lady, else *you* wouldn't have sworn in my presence.''

''Olivia, I beg your pardon! It just slipped out.''

''Then tell me, please, what this is all about.''

''Can't. It's Fabian's prerogative—or else you'll have to go to your brother for an explanation.''

''Richard?''

Charles nodded and signaled frantically to Fabian to rescue him from Olivia's cross-examination.

''Let it be for now, Olivia.'' Fabian sounded distracted. He slid off the desk and started pacing. ''Someday I'll explain it all to you. Now, let's get back to the point. And there,'' he sighed, ''I must admit I hadn't considered the difficulties pertaining to a termination of my 'betrothal,' but I'll think of a solution presently.''

''Why can't you stay engaged to her?'' asked Charles reasonably. ''She's a taking little thing. Well, not *little* precisely, but she makes a man feel protective somehow.''

''Her fragile appearance is deceptive, my friend.''

Undeterred, Charles continued, ''Might have an odd kick to her gallop now and then, but you've never been overly fond of the well-behaved, insipid young misses, Fabian. Olivia might just be what you need to lift you out of the dismals.''

Fabian's head jerked around, and he regarded his friend with narrowed eyes, but before he could reply, Olivia spoke up in icy accents.

''If you two *gentlemen* have quite finished discussing me as though I were not present, then heed this! I *won't* stay betrothed to Worth for a single moment after this is over!''

Charles was unruffled by her outburst. ''Then you must each find someone else to become engaged to.''

Olivia and Fabian looked at each other—she questioning and rather confused, Fabian with that guarded, impossible-to-read look in his eyes that she knew so well. Charles had sounded so authoritative and final that Olivia could almost believe there was no easy way out of this sham engagement. But to get betrothed a second time merely to dissolve the first engagement? Surely that was carrying it a bit far.

''I'd be willing to honor my commitment,'' said Fabian slowly, hesitating as though every word were torn from him against his will. ''But it shall be just as you wish, Olivia. You need not feel obligated to me in the least, and you need not decide now. There'll be time aplenty later on.''

''Thank you, Fabian. You're most considerate, I'm sure,'' Olivia murmured, then dropped her eyes. He must not see how his reluctant proposal had hurt her. She studied the delicate pattern on her sprigged muslin gown . . . three tiny violets surrounded by a circle of moss roses . . . seven green leaves . . .

There was no reason to be upset. After all, she had no intention of agreeing to his proposition. No, thank you, my lord! She was much better off without him. He needn't have spoken of a possible marriage at all! Anger boiled up in her breast when she thought about the unruffled calm with which he'd spoken. Why must Worth always disrupt her barely soothed feelings! *You and your scheming!* she seethed. *See where it got us! And what, I wonder, would Charles say if I told him that you blackmailed me into this outrageous charade?*

The silence in the study grew thick and palpable. She looked up. Both men were watching her, Charles quizzingly, and Worth, Worth was . . . amused! The glint in his eyes sharpened when he met her stormy look.

Olivia tossed her short curls and slid off her perch. With a dignity and hauteur even Grandmama would have envied, she inclined her head toward the two gentlemen. "Pray excuse me now. If there's nothing further to discuss, I'll be on my way. I have an engagement with Madame Bertin."

"Of course, my love." Fabian took her hand and kissed her fingers one by one as they lay so obviously reluctant on his own. "Still trying to bankrupt me?" he whispered. "Remember, it's a wasted effort."

"By no means wasted, Worth!"

"Well—" said Charles when the door had closed with a crash behind Olivia's stiff back. "I fear you've made her very angry."

"Olivia has a volatile temperament," said Fabian diffidently.

"I didn't gain that impression at all," protested Charles. "She is certainly out of the ordinary with her frank manner and outspokenness, but not at all shrewish."

"Perhaps we just don't hit it off. I blackmailed her into this scheme, don't you know."

"You *what*?"

"I told her if she wanted to be assured of my silence

regarding her stay at my house as 'Tony,' she'd have to do my bidding for a while.''

"Why, you scoundrel, you'd *never* have exposed her!"

"But Olivia doesn't know that."

"No. And you're disappointed," said Charles with a knowing look at Fabian's harsh features. "You've always wanted everyone to trust in you, but you're not prepared to explain yourself or let a person get close enough to gain an understanding of your sterling qualities. And besides, your expectations of women were always too high."

Fabian sighed. "Perhaps it is asking too much that she should trust me. She does *not* know me well, and . . . I do try to get a rise out of her at every opportunity," he admitted. "But it was *not* unreasonable to expect Melissa to be still betrothed to me when I came home on furlough after Coruña—if that's what you refer to as expectations 'always too high.'"

"Your name appeared on the casualty list," reminded Charles.

"But surely Melissa could have waited a trifle longer than three months before accepting Graintree's proposal. Why, she didn't even put on black gloves for me!"

"You're not wearing the willow for her still, are you?" asked Charles, incredulous. "Besides, you should've known Melissa wouldn't want to miss out on a season simply because she believed her fiancé lost to Napoleon's war."

"She was perfectly willing to come back to me," mused Fabian. "Almost fainted dead away when she saw me at Almack's and realized she could have had an earl after all, instead of a mere baronet. But by then I'd realized that I didn't care two hoots about her, and I gave her and Graintree my blessing."

"Then why won't you consider marrying Olivia?"

Fabian raised his brow. "You were present when I offered, dear fellow. Have you already forgotten that she refused me?"

"That wasn't an offer, Fabian—it was an insult! Sometimes I wonder if I know you at all anymore. One minute you're charming and urbane, next you've turned stiff, arrogant, and unapproachable. It makes my fist itch to plant you a facer and crack some of that armor you put up around yourself.''

"Charles, I am sorry if you feel I've given you the Turkish treatment.''

"Well, it's not that exactly, Fabian. Mind you, I've seen you freeze some unlucky fellow with just a glance, or annihilate him with a cutting word or two. Personally, I regret that you, that you . . . shut me out when I touch on a personal matter. You didn't use to do that, Fabian. Remember when we were at Oxford? Our walking tour of the Lake District? Or Scotland? But I noticed the change in you immediately after the fiasco with Melissa. I blamed it on that at the time, but surely not now?"

"Certainly Melissa added her mite to change my attitude toward women," admitted Fabian, twisting his lips cynically. "But Melissa had nothing to do with my frame of mind at the time. Nothing at all.'' Fabian cast his mind back to that January of 1809, remembering the 250-mile march over rugged terrain; and then the French had caught up with them three days after they'd reached Coruña. "No one who'd been with Moore and watched him die just as our ships came to take us off would have been in a jocular mood— around anyone," he said quietly.

"I grant you that. I can also understand why you were as touchy as a bear with a sore tooth when you returned after Fuentes de Oñoro with a ball in your arm; but why are you still aloof and harsh a year after you sold out?"

"Really, Charles! I cannot perceive how this rehashing of my past has the least bearing on the subject."

"Oh, no? Did you not feel what I am talking about? The barrier crashing between us, your shutting me out the instant I touched on your selling out? And did you not try to give me a set-down with your 'Really, Charles!'? And when Weybourne—your very dear friend Dickie Weybourne who'd arranged your passage from Fuentes de Oñoro—was home on leave at Eastertide, you would have cut him at White's had he not simply grabbed your hand and clapped you on the shoulder!''

"Had my very good friend not shipped me home whilst I was in no position to gainsay him, I'd not have had to listen to my mother's pleas to sell out!''

"Dammit, Fabian! You should thank God that your friends got you onto a transport home for medical care! Had you remained there, you'd have lost your arm, perhaps your life, despite Alders's efforts, and he'd be the first to attest to that.''

"My duty lay with my division, Charles. But I let tears and remonstrations about filial duty, duty to the family name, and duty to the tenants sway me. I sold out.''

"Your mother was right, and you know it. Since there's no younger son to carry on, you do have a duty here at home. Isn't that why you're finally fighting back to prevent everything from falling into Lionel's greedy hands, to be squandered at the gaming tables? How long do you think your tenants would have had a roof over their heads had you perished on the Peninsula?''

"I should have been with my division at Badajoz, Charles! I deserted them!'' Fabian was very pale, with great beads of sweat pearling on his forehead and temples. His voice sank to a mere whisper. "They were butchered, Charles! I read the dispatches as they came in. All hell had broken loose— and I had sold out! For months afterwards I had nightmares— still do occasionally—always seeing myself in the enemy camp, fighting *against* my friends.''

"My God, Fabian! I knew you were affected when the first news trickled in, but I didn't realize how much you blamed yourself for selling out.''

Fabian sat down heavily in his chair behind the desk and propped his head wearily into his hands. Charles did not immediately intrude on his friend's grief, but when Fabian finally drew himself up, he poured some cognac and handed him a glass.

"So,'' said Charles. "You sold out for your mother's sake and found yourself embroiled in a far more vicious fight than you would have seen in the Peninsular campaign. Lady Worth does not know about Lionel, I take it?"

Fabian tossed down the cognac as though it were water and motioned for more. "No. And she'll *never* know if I can help it."

"I only wish I could be of more assistance."

"You *are* helping me," said Fabian firmly and, already regretting the weakness he'd displayed before Charles, changed the subject back to Olivia. "Were you serious," he demanded, "when you advised I marry the chit? Quite frankly, I was surprised to hear you suggest it."

"Well, you shouldn't be! You can't think I'd hold it against her that she's a Fenshawe? I know *you* don't. For years you've been at pains to cover up Sir Richard Fenshawe's infamy, and protected his younger siblings. You can't tell me you'll withdraw your protection now that you've met his sister, who's one of the most adorable little minxes it's been my privilege to encounter. I wouldn't believe you, not after watching you with her last night."

Fabian's lips curled briefly. "Last night, my friend, Olivia and I engaged in a little game of polite flirtation. After all, we have to be convincing as a newly betrothed couple. Besides, you heard her, Charles. She'll have none of me."

"Then you must change her mind. Now, let's get down to the first order of business. What are we to do about the attacks on your life?"

After her grand exit from the study, Olivia made a cowardly retreat to Lady Worth's apartments, only to be intercepted by Natty. "Sorry, miss, but ye can't go in now. Her ladyship's still resting."

"Oh." Olivia studied the tips of her green slippers. Was nothing going right for her this morning? "Please send me word when Lady Worth is ready to see me," she said. "We were to look in at Madame Bertin's for a final fitting of my riding habit."

"Madame will have to wait, miss," answered Natty repressively.

Olivia trailed to her own sitting room and was just about to curl up in the window seat when she heard her maid and a footman talking in her bedroom. Curious, she walked over to the connecting door and opened it.

"Oh, Miss Olivia!" called Lizzy. "Will ye come and see? How d'ye like it, miss?" she asked proudly.

They had removed three small sketches of the Lake District by the very promising artist John Constable from the wall facing her canopied four-poster, and hung the young earl's portrait instead. Now Fabian's beguiling smile would greet her each morning upon awakening—but somehow the prospect did not appeal as it had the night before.

"Thank you, Lizzy and . . . Jenkins, is it?" She nodded dismissal, ignoring Lizzy's moue of disappointment at her cool reaction to her "fiancé's" likeness. *Fiddle-de-dee*, thought Olivia, Lizzy should be glad she'd refrained from ordering the painting out of her room again.

Olivia glared at the portrait, then turned her back on it. It did not help; she could feel the laughing eyes bore into her back.

On sudden impulse she kicked off her slippers and exchanged them for half-boots. She snatched up a muff and pelisse delivered only a few hours ago by the mantua maker, and rushed downstairs.

"Must get away from here for a bit!" she muttered under her breath. She'd never touch champagne or cognac again—the stuff put daft notions in her head. Why on earth had she ever believed she'd want Worth's portrait in her bedroom? How the deuce could she think with him laughing down at her!

"May I call the carriage for you, Miss Olivia?"

Her hand tightened on the polished brass handle of the front door as she half turned and smiled at the butler. "No, thank you, Robinson. I am going for a walk."

"Very good, miss. I'll just see what's keeping Lizzy."

"I have not asked Lizzy to accompany me since I intend to take my walk in the enclosure, right here in the square."

"In that case, miss, you'd best take the key."

"The key?"

"Yes, miss. If no one has entered the garden as yet, the gates might still be locked." Robinson opened a small door under the stairway and fumbled inside, rattling several keys before he found the right one. "Here you are, Miss Olivia."

"Must I lock up again when I leave?"

"No, miss. At night one of the footmen is sent out to make sure all four gates are locked. Most of the other houses in the square generally send a servant as well."

All these elaborate precautions had not prevented two determined footpads from lying in wait for their victim in the secured garden, she reflected wryly as she crossed the cobbled street.

She need not have bothered bringing the key after all. The ornate iron gate across from Worth House was ajar, and vociferous young voices alerted her to the presence of others. Two little girls, about six and seven years of age, strolled chattering along the path, each clasping a doll in her arms. A nursery maid sat on a bench nearby, clicking her knitting needles busily, yet never taking her eyes off her charges.

The girls curtsied shyly, and Olivia smiled although her heart was wrung with pity for them. It was impossible for the poor little things to run or learn to climb a tree, clad as they were in frilly dresses over several starched petticoats and long, lace-edged pantalets. Mentally shaking her head at the unknown, unfeeling city parents, Olivia approached the gate opposite the one through which she'd entered. It, too, stood open.

Goose bumps formed on her back as she stepped out into the square. Just a little to her right was the spot where Fabian had been attacked the night before. Furtively she glanced about, but no hidden danger lurked anywhere—save for the danger that she might be observed from Worth House as she was leaving the garden. She turned and peered behind her, but no Lizzy or panting footman had been sent after her. The shrubbery in the enclosure was fairly high and, although almost bare of foliage, would obscure her next movements. . . .

She was just about to cross to Duke Street when she saw a hackney entering the square from North Audley Street. If only it were empty! Timidly she raised her hand and, wonder of wonders, the jarvey pulled up beside her.

"Where to, missy?" he asked gruffly and opened the door of his dilapidated coach.

"Number eleven Hans Crescent."

Merrie's small flat was dark and gloomy, and it smelled musty. Olivia flung aside the drapes in the sitting room and opened the tiny window wide to let in fresh air and dispel the faint aura of desolation and abandonment hanging over the place.

With her feet propped on a hassock, Olivia sat in her old governess's chintz-covered wing chair and stared with blind eyes at the dust motes dancing on the narrow beam of sunshine penetrating through the window opening. She was seeing a different house, where the windows were larger and plentiful, where servants would dust even during the owner's absence.

Fabian had hurt her this morning; first with the drastic change of his manner toward her, then by grudgingly "proposing" to her.

Foolishly she'd believed after the ball that they'd become friends and could brush through this masquerade counting on each other's support. *Friends!* Olivia snorted. As though she could ever feel so lukewarm about Worth. She either hated and despised him or, worse, felt hopelessly attracted to him. The sooner she could extricate herself from this tangle the better! Apparently her reputation was still endangered; in fact, just as much as it had been when she'd masqueraded as Tony. Worth, as the honorable gentleman everyone supposed him to be, could not cry off from the "engagement," and according to Charles, neither could she because of something Richard had done, and because of someone called Melissa.

Who was this Melissa? Olivia couldn't do anything about Richard and wisely vented her frustration on the unknown woman. Why the deuce had she not thought to ask about Melissa instead of ripping up at Charles! Olivia's fist crashed down on the arm of her chair, freeing a small cloud of dust to tickle her nose. With streaming eyes—dust was as good an excuse as any to let the tears flow—she dug in her muff to find a handkerchief, but not before she'd been attacked by a violent bout of sneezing.

No matter what might happen during the next days, she could not possibly remain engaged to Fabian after Lionel had left for India. Real engagements inevitably led to marriage, and marriage to Fabian was unthinkable.

She resolutely ignored a timid inner voice questioning why that marriage would be so distasteful and determined to get away from Fabian as soon as possible. She should have stood her ground in the study and remained to help with the plotting against Lionel. Fabian's famous schemes did not appear to work out quite the way they were supposed to. Undoubtedly *she* could have contributed some valuable suggestions. Her head was bursting with ideas. . . . Yes, indeed, she would return to Worth House and prod Fabian and Charles into action.

Having come to a decision, she jumped up, slammed the window shut, and drew the curtains. She raced down the three flights of stairs and burst out of the building. Unfortunately, she'd not had the foresight to ask the hackney driver to wait for her. Too impatient to stand still and await the arrival of another hackney, Olivia started walking toward Sloane Street, where she'd earlier observed several sedan chairs and coaches waiting for a fare.

"Miss Fenshawe!"

Olivia stopped and blinked in consternation at the dandy who'd pulled his canary-yellow and black carriage to a halt beside her. *Lionel Worthing!* Drat the man! She was in no mood now to speak with him, but he'd expect her to be the vapid, simpering fool she'd portrayed in Fabian's study.

"I thought I recognized that curly head of yours from as

far away as Sloane Street,'' he sneered. "May I offer you a seat in my phaeton?''

"La, Mr. Worthing! Fancy meeting you here,'' she replied faintly.

"Come,'' he ordered. "Get in. You shouldn't be walking alone in this part of town—or anywhere else for that matter.''

"My, how you do run on, Mr. Worthing,'' simpered Olivia and extended her hand toward him.

With surprising strength he pulled her onto the seat beside him. "Don't bother continuing the farce!'' he said scathingly. "I've had speech with Roxbury, who couldn't praise you enough for your beauty, charm, and your *enchantingly* frank manner. Don't ever try to hoodwink me again, Olivia! I do not care to be ridiculed.''

"I do not recall giving you leave to address me by my first name, Mr. Worthing! And if Lord Roxbury laughed at you, then obviously you had taken great delight in trying to embarrass Fabian with tales of our encounter yesterday. You didn't think *you* would end up the fool, did you?''

"Your tongue, *Miss Fenshawe*, will most assuredly lead you into trouble someday!'' Viciously Lionel tugged at the reins and turned his phaeton around. "Your brother Tony already had a taste of my temper, as you will recall. He might have been seriously hurt had not Fabian entered before I could skewer him!''

Her stomach tightened when she realized how deeply Lionel regretted the disruption of the duel, but she also recognized instantly that by not mentioning the gunshot as a punishment for Tony, Lionel had as much as admitted that the shot had been aimed at Fabian. He'd given her the ideal opening to fluster him!

"My brother *was* seriously hurt,'' she corrected. "You shot him. Don't forget, he *saw* you in that coach!''

"What?'' he asked and looked at her blankly for a moment.

Olivia's eyes widened. Had she made a mistake? Had it *not* been Lionel after all in the traveling chaise?

"Oh . . . yes, of course," he mumbled finally. "And it should teach all you Fenshawes a lesson." Then he asked with a nasty sneer in his nasal voice, "What were you doing in this neighborhood? Seeing a lover?"

"And what were *you* doing in Sloane Street?" she countered. "Seeing a cent-per-center?"

"None of your demmed business!" His whip cracked, and the horses, mismatched in every way but their coloring, increased their erratic pace.

His sawing at the reins did nothing to commend his driving skills, and she closed her eyes when he feathered the corner from Sloane Street into Knightsbridge without so much as a check for oncoming traffic. They teetered dangerously on two wheels and she was flung against Lionel. Shouts and curses rent the air and, very much against her will, her eyes flew open. A huge dray pulled by a team of six plodding Clydesdales was coming toward them! With all her might she dragged herself into the very corner of the box seat. The weight shift was sufficient to bring the two spinning wheels of the phaeton back in contact with the solid ground, and Lionel finally decided to move his carriage over to the left to make room for the dray.

"Well!" Scorn and fury blazed from her hazel eyes. "You may claim to be a good shot, even an expert fencer, but a whip you are *not*! You may let me down at Hyde Park Corner, sir. I'd rather walk the rest of the way."

"Are you chickenhearted as well as deceitful, Miss Fenshawe?" he asked with a smirk. "But I'll do no such thing. A fine to-do we'd have were I to allow Fabian's precious fiancée to walk unescorted!"

"And much you care! At least slow down if you wish to retain my companionship, because I'll not think twice before jumping off if you plan to take the corner into Park Lane at this speed."

"Damn your impudence!" he shouted, but checked the horses and continued at a more sedate pace.

An uncomfortable silence settled between them, Lionel seething with anger, and Olivia searching for an excuse to be set down before they reached Worth House. They turned into Upper Grosvenor Street, and still no convincing argument had occurred to her, and then they were in the square.

"I'll yet find out why you were in Hans Crescent, my fine lady!" muttered Lionel, pulling up before Worth House.

Olivia wasted no time on a reply, but scrambled off the box with more haste than grace, intent only on getting into the house before anyone could see her. Alas, she was too late to escape the icy wrath of Fabian's eyes as he chose that particular moment to exit Worth House with Lord Charles in his wake.

"Don't bother to thank me for returning your errant betrothed, Fabian!" called Lionel. "Believe me, 'twas no pleasure I'd care to repeat."

Fabian had neither a glance nor a word to spare for his cousin, but kept his blazing eyes trained on Olivia. With a muttered imprecation, Lionel took himself off.

Olivia had known she'd land herself in the suds if her exploit was discovered, but naturally she could not have foreseen that she would run smack into Fabian. She vowed not to cower and cringe before him, no matter how fearsome he looked.

"Fabian," she said with forced brightness as she started up the stairs, "Lionel *admitted* the shot had not been aimed at 'Tony' at all!"

"He did? How?" His black brows threatened to touch across the bridge of his nose as he scowled at her.

"Well . . . he said . . . he said that . . ."

"Never mind," interrupted Fabian icily. "We had already established that as fact in any case."

Lord Charles, who had prudently kept in the background, now cleared his throat to gain their attention. "Well, I'd best be off now," he said and doffed his hat at Olivia.

"Changed your mind, Charles?" asked Fabian. "You're not coming to Whitehall with me?"

Charles laughed and shook his head. "I can see that you're wanting a word with Olivia. I'll see you both tomorrow."

"Coward," drawled Fabian and bestowed a cynical look on his friend.

"Oh, I freely admit I'm too lily-livered to stick around when a lovers' quarrel is brewing; but keep in mind our little talk, Fabian! And you might take Olivia to Whitehall in my stead," he recommended.

Fabian looked none too pleased with the suggestion, and Charles turned to Olivia with a grin. "I feel for you, my dear. I, too, quake in my boots when Fabian fires that I'll-brook-no-nonsense look at me. But remember, his bark's worse than his bite!" He flung this last statement over his shoulder as he ran down the wide marble steps.

Olivia watched his departure with envy. "Pray excuse me, Worth," she murmured and tried to slip past him. "Lady Worth might be waiting for me."

His hand shot out and gripped her arm with unnecessary force. "My mother left to pay a call on one of her friends. Pray spare me a few moments of your precious time. Let's step into the study where we can be private."

Just then Fabian's prized chestnuts, hitched to a gleaming black curricle, swept around the corner. The diminutive tiger on the box pulled them up with a flourish and called out proudly, "They's in fine fettle today, milor'!"

Fabian watched for a moment as Clem struggled to keep the restive pair under control, then made up his mind. "Clem can't hold the horses much longer; you'd best come with me in the curricle, Olivia." He scowled at her, making it quite clear that she was not to take this as a freely extended invitation, and started down the stairs. Since he did not release his grip on her arm, she had to follow willy-nilly and climb up beside him. Only then did he let go of her.

"I won't need you, Clem," said Fabian when the tiger had jumped off the box and prepared to scramble onto the small perch at the rear of the curricle. Fabian flicked the reins, and they were off before Olivia had time to arrange her skirts decorously about her feet.

CHAPTER 7

"Where were you?" demanded Fabian.

"Out. Will you let me handle the ribbons?"

"No. Where did you go?"

Olivia had not really expected that he would permit her to drive the chestnuts, nor had she expected he would forget about her escapade if she avoided his question. "Hans Crescent," she said quietly.

"Who did you see? And pray make your reply a comprehensive one. I dislike having to extract answers one by one—like rotten teeth!"

"I saw nobody; I simply sat in my old governess's empty flat for a span, then left because I wanted to offer you my assistance in plotting the trap for Lionel."

"Ah! I had wondered why you carry a key on that chain around your neck!" he exclaimed.

"How did *you* know about the key?" asked Olivia with asperity.

"Have you forgotten, my dear, that Alders and I had to remove your shirt when you were shot?"

Noting the mocking gleam in his eyes, Olivia blushed profusely. "Lecher!" she hissed and averted her face hastily.

Fabian chuckled. His ire had cooled when Olivia had disclosed her hiding place, and her ill-concealed embarrassment amused him. "Little peagoose! How on earth could we have removed the bullet unless we bared your shoulder? But let me assure you, the proprieties were observed at all times. Indeed, you expose more of your charms in Madame Bertin's gowns than I glimpsed the day Alders performed the surgery."

She vouchsafed no reply, merely fanning her heated face with her muff. After watching her for a moment, Fabian said casually, "If you should feel the need to escape again, pray take Lizzy along. It really is not safe for a young lady to be out on her own."

"Then I needn't 'escape' at all if I must drag a maid or a footman along."

"Lizzy need not go inside with you," Fabian explained. "She could wait in the coach, unless you intend to behave as stubbornly as today and refuse when Robinson offers to have the carriage brought around."

Now that Olivia's secret hideout had been discovered, his suggestion sounded very reasonable; however, she had no intention of conceding to him on all points and remained silent until they pulled up before an imposing structure in Whitehall.

"Where are we going?" Olivia asked, studying the many government buildings with interest.

"Headquarters of the Horse Guards." Fabian jumped down, tossed the reins to one of the urchins loitering about in hopes of earning a penny, and extended his hand to help Olivia from the curricle.

"Oh! Are we to see your friend the lieutenant?"

"Lieutenant Bramson. If Tony enlisted, we should learn today where he is. I'd sent word to Bramson as soon as we arrived in town."

"Thank you, Fabian!"

"Don't get your hopes up," he warned. "If Tony's as interested in horse breeding as you make out, he may very well be in Ireland."

Fabian nodded to the guard who stood rigidly at attention; the guard sprang to life, clicking his heels, and then rushed to open the heavy door for them.

"I didn't realize we could simply walk in without any questions asked," marveled Olivia.

"You can't. But I come here often . . . on business."

Their footsteps echoed eerily in the long, empty corridor. Halfway down the hall they turned left and ascended a long flight of shallow, wooden steps, then turned left again and, after a cursory knock on a narrow door, entered a large office.

The young man behind the littered desk jumped up and hastily buttoned his scarlet tunic. "Worth! Good to see you. The old man hasn't sent you to pester me in weeks. Don't tell me you fellows at the ministry are slacking off?"

"Just enough to lull you, Bramson; then we'll pounce again." Fabian grinned and shook hands with his friend, then took Olivia's arm and pulled her forward. "Let me introduce Lieutenant Peter Bramson to you, my dear. Peter, meet my fiancée, Miss Olivia Fenshawe."

"Delighted, Miss Fenshawe." The lieutenant bowed over her hand, an admiring gleam in his light brown eyes. "Worth, as usual, has carried off the prize! But mayhap now that he's out of circulation, I'll have a free field with the fair maidens."

"With *some* fair maidens perhaps, but not with Olivia," warned Fabian, and to Olivia he said, "You must excuse him, my dear. He's a sad rake, I'm afraid."

Olivia blushed. Would this playacting never end? To cover her embarrassment, she asked, "I understand you may have news of my brother, Lieutenant. What have you found out?"

Now it was the young officer's turn to look harassed. "Pray be seated, Miss Fenshawe." He snatched a bundle of maps off a chair and offered the seat to Olivia, then performed the same service for Fabian by pushing a tall black hat and a pair of white gloves off the second chair.

"This is a . . . delicate, extraordinary affair," Bramson muttered as he sat down behind his desk again. "I wish you'd come alone, Worth."

"Is Tony injured? Dead?" cried Olivia, half rising from her chair.

"No, no! Not at all, Miss Fenshawe!"

"What is it, Bramson?" Fabian pressed Olivia down and kept his hand reassuringly over her own. "Did you find his name on your rolls of newly enlisted?"

"Yes. Right here in the Horse Guards."

"Can I see him, Lieutenant? Is he still in town?" As the

heavy burden of worry about Tony lifted, Olivia beamed at the young officer.

"Well, it's not as simple as that. Here, Worth! You'd best read this report and see for yourself."

"A report?" Fabian's brows knitted together as he reached for the papers Lieutenant Bramson held out to him. "What's the young varmint been up to now?" Fabian read silently. He gave a start once, but said nothing until he'd come to the end of the last sheet.

"Devil a bit!" He turned to Olivia. "Your brother has deserted."

Olivia blinked. "Impossible!" she exclaimed and shook her head vigorously. "Tony may be a here-and-therian, but he knows his duty to his country. He's wanted to fight Napoleon ever since he came down from Cambridge. He'd *never* desert!"

Without a word, Fabian passed her the three sheets of paper covered tightly in bold black writing. Olivia scanned them quickly. "Oh! How unfair!" She read over a part of the report again to make quite certain she had not misunderstood, then said indignantly, "That officer intended to *steal* Thunder from him!"

She paled. "Will Tony be shot if he is caught?"

"No, of course not," assured Fabian hastily with a frown at Lieutenant Bramson. "Olivia, why would Tony react so violently when he learned that he must exchange his horse for another?"

"Tony would not have signed up had he been told beforehand that an officer could take his pick of the horses. You see, Thunder is more than just a horse—he's Tony's friend. Tony raised him from a colt, broke him to bridle, and trained him. He's always ridden Thunder himself, save for the year he spent at Cambridge, because Richard would not pay for stabling. Then only I was allowed to exercise him."

"If the horse is so precious to your brother, why would he want to take him abroad at all . . . as cannon fodder?" asked the lieutenant.

Olivia blanched again, but replied with asperity. "As little as Tony would consider himself cannon fodder, he would not believe Thunder was in danger as long as they were together. In any case, he'd never leave him at Fenshawe Court again, because Richard *will* try to ride him . . . with spurs! Thunder is a valuable Arabian; Richard would have ruined him,'' she added contemptuously. "If only Richard had bought Tony a commission, none of this need have happened!''

Fabian had listened to her outburst in thoughtful silence. At her last words, his face cleared and he turned to his friend. "Bramson, with me to vouch for Anthony Fenshawe, could you place him with the Light Bobs as an ensign?''

"Your own division? Hmmm. Striking an officer . . . and desertion. These are no light charges. It's asking a lot, Worth, but with your name to back up my request, we might be able to pull it off. Mind you, he'd have to show up within two weeks! Replacements are due to ship out on the twentieth.''

"I'll have him here. Come, Olivia. We must look for your elusive little brother.''

"But what about the charge of desertion against him?'' she asked.

"If he gets his colors in the next week or two and is shipped out to the Peninsula, who'd stand up to say he had deserted?'' Lieutenant Bramson directed an encouraging grin at her. "With Worth backing your brother, I've no doubt that *all* charges will be dropped once I present the matter to Major Tomlinson.''

"Thank you, Lieutenant. I'm happy to have made your acquaintance!'' she called as she was whisked out the door by Fabian. "What now?'' she inquired breathlessly. "How can you be so certain you'll find Tony in time?''

"I can't be certain. Think, Olivia! Where, in or near London, would he most likely hole up. He has no money, no clothes but what he's wearing on his back, and he has a valuable horse to look after.''

"A livery stable,'' she replied promptly as Fabian handed her into the curricle.

Fabian pressed a coin into the urchin's grubby hand, and

off they went at a spanking pace. "I'll send Clem and some of the grooms to scour the better stables and also the posting houses."

Olivia cast a worried look at him. "Won't it be awkward?" she asked. "Would you have to tell them about the trouble he's in?"

"They already know he's in a scrape. Remember, that's the excuse I gave for your taking his place. We need give no other reason for wanting to find him," he reassured her. "But if the search of posting inns fails, where else might he be hiding? Think, Olivia! Your brother's life may depend on it."

She was no longer listening. "Tony will be as pleased as Punch," she mused. "But how will we reimburse you? An ensign's pay cannot be much. It may take years for him to repay you—unless I can find another position. *After* we've caught Lionel," she added hastily.

Fabian threw her his unreadable look. "Don't worry about it. For the moment we are engaged, and as your betrothed it is clearly expected of me to do something handsome for your brother. Later on, when Lionel has been taken care of, we can discuss the matter again. By then you'll have earned a generous fee for your 'performance.'"

"A fee? But you said I would be aiding you in return for your silence!"

Fabian's jaw tightened. He'd had enough of being the blackguard in Olivia's eyes. Now was the time to redeem himself. Now that he was in a position to be of real help to the younger Fenshawes, he'd make it clear that she was under no obligation to him whatsoever! Having come to this conclusion, Fabian relaxed and leaned back against the squabs.

"You have earned a fee already," he told Olivia. "And in my opinion, Tony's commission as well. Let's call it quits and start anew. Olivia, would you consider acting as my fiancée as a gesture of goodwill?"

Her eyes grew wide as she stared at him in stunned

silence with her mind awhirl. He was sincere! Her intuition about his character had been correct. She *could* trust him.

Taking her silence for a refusal, Fabian swallowed his disappointment and said quietly, "In that case, I shall provide your transporation to Fenshawe Court or wherever you may wish to go. It was extremely generous of you to have helped me as much as you did. And don't worry about Tony—I'll find him." Almost as an afterthought he added softly, "I never would have breathed a word about your masquerade to anyone."

"Oh, you misunderstand, Fabian!" Finally roused from her state of numbness, Olivia was horrified that Fabian should believe her capable of turning her back on him now. "I just couldn't find my voice, Fabian! But of course I'll see this through—even if it were not within your power to help Tony."

"Thank you, Olivia."

His smile, as captivating as the one in the portrait, melted any reservations she might still have held. Carried away by the impact of his devastating charm, she called out, "Beware, Tony! You're about to be turned inside out!"

"Will you still be in such high spirits when Tony stands before you in his new uniform, taking his leave of you?" Fabian asked.

Instantly she sobered. "No, of course not, but I hope that for Tony's sake I can show a cheerful face. He's been hankering after a pair of colors for ever so long, and he says it's his duty as the younger son to fight Napoleon."

"Ah, yes! The prescribed duties of the younger sons—the first younger son destined for the army, the second for the church, the next for the law, etc., etc. And an *only* son, Olivia? Might he not feel the call of duty from various directions?"

She looked at him with troubled eyes, uncertain if he even expected a reply, so abstracted and remote did he sound. When he raised his brows quizzingly, she felt cornered.

"I don't know the answer, Fabian," she said. "But I fear

that a man called upon to make that decision is in a most unenviable position."

"Indeed."

Again she shot him a worried look. She could not tell from his toneless voice or the expression on his face if he was being sarcastic or if he merely agreed with her. A short while ago, when she'd believed herself blackmailed by him, she would not have hesitated to question him, but now, having promised rashly to continue as his betrothed, she felt as shy as a young girl at her first Queen's Drawing Room.

Fabian himself broke the long silence and changed the subject. "Did you not order a riding habit from Madame Bertin?"

"Yes, I did. And what's more, I was supposed to see her for a final fitting today, but I fear it may be too late now," she said, disappointed that she must wait an extra day for the coveted garment and postpone a ride in Hyde Park yet again.

As though he'd read her thoughts, Fabian promised, "I'll take you to Madame Bertin's after I've spoken to Clem. Charles and I have planned an excursion to Richmond Park for tomorrow afternoon, and I imagine you'd as lief go on horseback as in the carriage."

"Oh, yes," she agreed fervently.

Presently Fabian pulled up in the mews behind Worth House. He wasted no time in rounding up Clem and three of the stable lads and gave them their instructions. "I have reason to believe that Miss Olivia's brother is working at one of the livery stables or posting inns," he told them. "I want you to find him with all possible speed. You won't have any problem recognizing him as he looks much like Miss Olivia."

"Leastways like she did as 'Master Tony,'" interrupted Clem with a wide grin splitting his face.

Fabian frowned at him, but Olivia chuckled. "Quite so, Clem. Also keep your eyes open for a gray Arabian with a bit of black markings on his left foreleg. That's Tony's Thunder."

"When you find him," admonished Fabian, "get back here immediately and report to me. Look lively now!"

The four men bowed, donned their caps, and left the mews at a brisk clip.

"Wait!" Olivia called, picking up her skirts to dash after them. Obedient to her imperative summons, they halted, but were undecided whether they dared turn back after the earl had ordered them off. She caught up with them while they were still arguing the point.

"Tell my brother that I'm at Worth House," she panted, "and that I require his aid *immediately*. He's bound to come with you then. . . ."

When the grooms had disappeared from view, she added softly, ". . . and he won't have an opportunity to slip away again."

"Little schemer!" Fabian sauntered up to her and chuckled approvingly. "But now to your riding habit. Do we go directly, or do you wish to take some refreshment before we leave?"

"Let's go immediately. No doubt Madame Bertin will offer us a dish of tea."

They climbed back into the curricle and set off for Bond Street. In the fashionable shopping street, they encountered several ladies and gentlemen of Fabian's acquaintance and many a bow had to be exchanged, but he stopped for no one so that very shortly they entered the elegant rooms of Madame Bertin, couturiere, who once had the honor of dressing the late Queen Marie Antoinette.

Madame was gratified that the Earl of Worth had troubled himself to accompany his fiancée to her establishment. Not only did she offer tea and delicate petit fours, but she insisted that Olivia model the riding habit and other gowns her seamstresses had completed.

Fabian took all the attention he was attracting in his stride. He nodded his approval of a mauve morning gown and a mint-green merino walking dress with a rust-brown bodice, flounces, and matching spencer; with an appreciative gleam in his eye, he commended Olivia and Madame

Bertin on their selection of a severely cut scarlet riding habit with black velvet trim and frogging, and a plain white lawn shirt and stock; but he stared dumbfounded when Olivia paraded before him in a ball gown of gold satin shot with emerald, draped cunningly across the small scar on her left shoulder, but leaving her right shoulder bare.

Golden flecks of mischief danced in Olivia's eyes as she smiled at her "fiancé." "Do you find it to your liking, my lord?" she asked demurely.

Fabian rose and slowly walked all around her. If he had a quizzing glass, she thought, he'd put it to use now. He stopped behind her, and she felt his eyes burning the exposed skin on her back. Then his finger softly trailed along her shoulder blade, setting her skin afire. Quickly she pirouetted to confront him face to face.

"You have another beauty spot right there." Fabian turned her around and again his finger caressed her skin. "I fear, my love, I shan't be able to stave off the onslaught of lecherous admirers when you show yourself in this gown. How about a shawl or a tunic to wear over the dress?"

Olivia's face fell. Was he serious? He still stood behind her, and she couldn't see his eyes, which would have given him away, but Madame Bertin allowed herself a prim smile. "Milord pleases to jest, *n'est-ce-pas*? Do not worry, mademoiselle. Your fiancé is too great a connoisseur of the ladies' fashions to insist on spoiling the lines of this *robe très ravissante*!"

"You honor me, madame. But with her short curls Miss Fenshawe does not even have a hairpin at her disposal to defend her virtue."

Madame noted the martial glint in Miss Fenshawe's eyes and responded with a chuckle. "Your beautiful fiancée *indubitablement* will find the *stratagème* to escape unwanted attentions."

"Indubitably so, madame. Can you have the gowns delivered in the morning?"

"*Certainement*, milord. There is required only one or two stitches to make them perfection."

"Please, Fabian—" Olivia reached out and laid her hand pleadingly on his arm. "The riding habit is already completed. May we not carry it with us?"

"Certainly, if you won't mind being seen with a cumbersome bandbox on your lap! Go ahead, madame, have it wrapped."

"At once, milord." Madame Bertin bustled Olivia off to change out of the gold evening gown, and with her own capable hands folded the riding habit in tissue paper and placed it tenderly in a large box.

When Olivia returned from the dressing room, she found Fabian on the verge of leaving with the box under his arm. "You are in luck today, my dear, and need not share your seat with this parcel," he quizzed. "It's not as large as I'd feared and will fit into the boot of my curricle after all."

"How fortunate." She beamed at him while her mind was already busy scheming how to talk him into taking her for a ride that afternoon.

When Fabian had stowed away the bandbox and helped Olivia into the curricle, he watched her face—such a perfect mirror of her tumbling thoughts!—from the corner of his eyes as he guided his chestnuts through the now thronging afternoon traffic in Bond Street. Several times he thought she'd speak her mind, but each time her lips clamped together again and the small worry line on her brow deepened. It was not at all difficult for him to guess her dilemma. Amused to see the usually forthright Olivia try her hand, or rather her mind, at sophistry, he decided to let her dangle a bit, and thus the trip to Worth House was accomplished in complete silence.

Fabian pulled up before the front door and nudged her gently with his elbow to arouse her from her ruminations. "I shall let you off here, Olivia. Since I don't have Clem with me, I must perforce take the curricle to the mews myself. I don't dare trust my chestnuts to a footman."

"Of course." She rose, wondering fleetingly why he did not get down to help her from the box—after all, the horses were no longer so fresh that they'd bolt if he let go of the reins for a moment.

"I say, Fabian—" She sat back down again. "Might it not be a good idea if I went with you to get acquainted with the horse I'll be riding tomorrow to Richmond Park?"

"As you wish, my dear." Hiding a grin, he flicked the reins and moved on, turning into South Audley Street, and then made a sharp left into the mews which ran between Grosvenor Square and Mount Street.

The head groom came running and took charge of the chestnuts, informing the earl that none of the lads had returned as yet from their errand.

"I suppose it'll take them all of today and possibly tomorrow, Sam," said Fabian, looking sternly at his head groom. "You and Ted ought to be able to carry on by yourselves for a bit."

"Natcherly, milor'," replied Sam, affronted. "Excepting when her ladyship requires me to drive her in the landaulet, seeing as old Bert's laid up again with that rheumaticky leg of his. I dunno as Ted would be able to harness yer chestnuts, milor'."

"Don't worry, Sam. It wouldn't be the first or the last time that I hitched them up myself." Fabian took Olivia's elbow and steered her toward the stalls. "Oh, Sam!" he called over his shoulder. "There's a bandbox in the boot. Have Ted carry it up to the house right away."

Olivia stood transfixed, staring at the fourteen sleek horses that regarded her with solemn eyes over the stall doors. "I hadn't realized how many horses you keep in town!" she exclaimed.

"It's a nuisance in some ways," Fabian admitted, "since I also have to bring a number of grooms to exercise them. But I like to be able to mount my friends for excursions, like the one to Richmond tomorrow."

"*Are* we friends now?" she asked curiously.

"As much as we can ever be," he said.

They regarded each other soberly, even warily, for a few moments; then Olivia shook off the sober mood and bantered,

"Just listen to us sound off as though we're enacting a Cheltenham tragedy! Come, introduce me to your cattle, my lord."

They stepped closer and Fabian pointed to the four stalls at the far right. "You know my grays, of course. The two empty stalls next to them are for the chestnuts, and the two bays are kept at my mother's disposal to take her about town in her landaulet. Only these eight beauties here are bred for the saddle." Then he nodded toward the last empty stall at their left. "I'd meant to fill that spot last month at Tattersall's, but my secretary managed to spoil my plans." Grinning widely, he took her arm again and led her toward a little mare who tossed her head and whinnied in delight at their approach.

"Which one shall I ride tomorrow?" asked Olivia with a longing glance at the large roan in the stall next to the empty one.

Fabian followed her look. "Oh, no, my lady! That is Chichester, and only I ride that gelding! I thought I'd try you out on Maisy here until I know how you handle yourself in the saddle." He fondled the little mare's ears and watched the mulish expression on his "fiancée's" face with barely suppressed amusement. "Maisy's past her prime now and safe for even the most timid of riders," he needled.

"I can handle *any* horse, and I would prefer something a bit more spirited, if you please!"

"I certainly wouldn't want to give the impression that I doubt your word, my love, but try to understand the dilemma I find myself in. After all, it has not been my privilege to observe you on horseback, and I could be placing your limbs—and your life—in jeopardy were I to mount you on a horse that is too strong for you," he said very reasonably, all the while intent on studying the tops of his Hessians so she wouldn't recognize the wicked, teasing smile playing on his mouth.

Olivia's eyes flashed. "That can be remedied! Give me five minutes to change into my riding habit, and I'll show you that the horse I *can't* handle hasn't been born yet!"

Fabian gave such a shout of laughter that Sam, who was just leading the chestnuts into their stalls, turned curiously and stared at him in amazement. It was a sound he hadn't heard from his lordship in years.

Fabian laughed again at Olivia's outrage and said, "Don't fire up at me, love. It's just that I'd almost come to believe you'd lost your heart and would *never* ask for a ride this afternoon. There must have been something very forbidding about me today that you didn't dare."

"You devil! I have a good mind not to—"

"Yes?" he prompted when she fell silent.

Suddenly she chuckled. "You *are* a devil. Of course I wouldn't refuse to ride, and you know that very well! But it is most impertinent of you to lead me on."

"You must forgive me, but I find I cannot resist coaxing that certain flash of anger to your eyes—and it does not require very much coaxing at that!"

Startled, she looked at him. His dark eyes shone with warmth and laughter; they radiated tenderness yet held hers with compelling force. Her knees felt oddly weak, and it required all of her willpower to break the bond. Slowly she lowered her lashes.

"I won't flash anymore . . . for now. So we might as well get ready. Which horse may I ride, Fabian?"

He pointed to a nervous black stallion. "How about Firebrand? He's very aptly named, I warn you, but he'll set off your new riding habit to perfection. Come now, I'll show you a shortcut through this back door and the garden behind my house. And while you change, I'll try to wheedle cook into preparing a sandwich made with the fresh bread I smelled this morning and some slices of ham cured at Worthing Court. Would you care for a sandwich?" he asked politely.

"Yes, please. I'm ravenous."

"Small wonder. We both missed luncheon. I had planned to eat with Charles at Brooks's after our business at Whitehall, but since Charles so cowardly deserted me—"

"And *you* practically kidnapped me and kept me a prisoner at your side," she quipped. "We must now both of us make do with scraps."

_____CHAPTER 8_____

A chill wind rustled the last autumn leaves clinging tenaciously to the majestic oaks, the slender birches, the elms and beech trees as the small cavalcade of six riders galloped across Richmond Park. With dusk almost upon them, the sun had lost its brilliance, the last rays of rosy glow having no fire to warm the shivering party.

Olivia nudged Firebrand's flank and slowly gained ground on Fabian, who was ahead of them all on his powerful Chichester. *What the deuce was ailing the man?* she asked herself for the umpteenth time. At the Star and Garter, where they'd stopped to refresh themselves with tea and cakes for the ladies and a glass of arrack punch for the gentlemen, he'd sat as though nailed to the settle, and ignored every one of her reminders that the shadows were lengthening.

Fabian had been in an expansive mood, entertaining their companions, Lord Charles and Emily Carrington, Lord Roxbury and his sister Lady Ruth, with anecdotes from his Oxford days and humorous tales of army life in Portugal—like when he'd had to give up his tent to some two dozen scrawny chickens during a rainstorm, because he'd had the foresight to erect his shelter on an elevated spot where the gushing waters did no more than leak through the roof and soak everything inside. The chickens, destined for the pots of the officers' mess, had been voted more valuable by his fellow officers than the comfort of their brigade major. . . .

It was difficult to imagine the fastidious Earl of Worth feeling at home anywhere but in London—and mayhap at his country estate—yet she felt instinctively that even as he was getting doused by the torrents of rain, he'd laughed with his friends and helped shoo the squawking chickens into the tent. Of course, he'd had Alders with him. Undoubtedly his batman had proven himself capable of keeping the brigade major's gear in exemplary order.

Olivia bent lower over her horse's neck. How hard it was to catch up with Fabian. He was riding hell for leather, as though Old Boney himself were somewhere ahead, just waiting to be taken, and not driving his army through the ice and snow of the early Russian winter.

Charles, too, was acting strange. For the past ten minutes or so he'd completely ignored Miss Emily Carrington, whose escort he was—and if ever there was a girl in need of a patient, tenderhearted escort, it was Emily, who clung for dear life to the pommel and reins of her staid mare. Naturally, she had fallen behind and was now clucked over by Lord Roxbury and his sister. Charles was too busy playing some kind of game, driving his large, rawboned chestnut on, then holding him in, and all the while searching among the trees and shrubs to either side of the bridle path for some elusive thing. . . . By George, he was trying to catch up with her now!

"Come on, Firebrand!" she urged. "Let's show him a clean pair of heels." Finally she had come within shouting distance of Fabian. "Worth!" she hollered. "Are we having a race?"

Without slackening his pace, he looked over his shoulder at her, displeasure clearly visible on his face even at this distance. "Get back! Stay behind Charles!" he ordered and turned his attention again to the path before him, just in time to duck under a low-hanging branch.

But Olivia was not one to remain in the rear, and she gave both gentlemen a good run for their money. She clung like a burr to Fabian, never more than a few paces behind him—consequently swallowing a great deal of dust—and neither did she allow Charles to pass her. The three of them charged out of the park at a full gallop and then, as though on command, bridled their horses when they'd reached the road.

Immediately Fabian rounded on her. "Why the devil did you not do as you were bid!" he stormed. "Now the whole demmed excursion was for naught!"

"For naught?" Her voice rose indignantly. "Do you mean the only purpose for this outing was to teach me a lesson in obedience?"

Too angry for words, Fabian tightened his grip on the reins and threw her a furious look. Had they been dismounted, she felt certain he'd have shaken her until every bone rattled in her body.

Olivia looked to Charles for enlightenment. "Well, what have you and Worth been up to? Did I spoil a race, or why were you trying so desperately to get past me?"

"You see, Olivia," he blustered, "we'd meant to trap Lionel today. When I invited Roxbury to this expedition yesterday, I made damn sure—oh, pardon me, my dear—I took great care to let Lionel overhear the particulars."

She snorted and turned to Fabian. "And you believed he'd actually come out here, hide behind a tree, and shoot at you again?" A delicately arched brow raised quizzingly told Fabian clearly what she thought of his plot.

"If you hadn't stayed so close to me, he'd have had a very good opportunity, and Charles was right there to give chase," he pointed out scathingly.

"It didn't stop him the last time I was so close to you."

"But then you were dressed like a man!"

"Ah! I understand. It makes no odds to shoot another man accidentally, but a woman makes all the difference in the world. For certain, Lionel would show all due respect and reverence to a lady!"

"Stop bickering, you two," admonished Charles. "I hear the others approaching, and I must think of an excuse for deserting Emily to the tender mercies of Roxbury and his sister."

But Olivia had yet another argument to present. "Even if Lionel had come out to Richmond Park to waylay you, he would have had no opportunity to take a shot at you when we first arrived, because we all stayed together in a cluster. Surely while *you* kept us at the Star and Garter for two whole hours, he must have given up and returned home to a snug fire and a bottle of wine instead of kicking his heels in this cold wind."

"We stopped for two hours at the Star and Garter because I wanted to cross the park as near dusk as possible."

"Then we should have started from town at a later hour!"

"That, my little know-it-all, would have been too conspicuous. Who ever heard of a party leaving London in the *late* afternoon for an excursion to Richmond?"

They glared at each other, forced into silence by the approach of the three stragglers. Apparently Lord Roxbury had done his best to soothe the two ladies in his company, for they gave every appearance of enjoying themselves.

Emily Carrington raised her blue eyes shyly to Lord Charles and smiled at him. "I hope you had a good race, Charles. It looked like fun, and I wish I'd had the courage to participate, but as you know I am too timid to gallop for long."

"I was a brute to desert you without warning, Emily." Charles eagerly grasped at the excuse she had unwittingly offered him. "I only pray you will not refuse me next time I ask you to ride out with me—although I would more than deserve it if you did!"

In one accord Emily and Charles turned their mounts toward London and cantered off, exchanging tender smiles along the way.

"*I* only wish next time you'd fill me in on your plans, Worth," grumbled Lord Roxbury, "so that I might either join you in the race or else beg off from the excursion altogether, instead of being stuck with a prattling schoolroom miss." He cast a darkling glance at his sister, which caused that young lady to giggle—but then, Lady Ruth was only sixteen, not far removed from the schoolroom after all.

The four riders caught up with Emily and Charles before long, and they all reached London in good spirits although it was getting colder by the minute and darkness had enveloped them for the last few miles. Lord Roxbury and his sister resided in Curzon Street and were the first to take their leave. The others continued along South Audley Street until they'd reached Grosvenor Square, where Emily and Charles took their departure.

"I live just a few doors down in Upper Grosvenor Street," Emily told Olivia. "Please come and see me if you find yourself at loose ends. I'm at home most days to keep Mama company. She's an invalid, you see. And if my timidity hasn't given you a disgust of my companionship, perhaps we could ride in Hyde Park together one afternoon. I envy you your good seat, Olivia," she added with a disarming smile.

Remorse over her earlier, uncharitable thoughts about Emily's lack in riding skills brought a flush to Olivia's cheeks. "I should like that very much, Emily. I understand it's impossible in any case to gallop in Hyde Park during the fashionable hours of the afternoon." Then, thinking that poor Emily had looked rather wistful and pleading, Olivia also promised to call on her. She waved a cheerful farewell and turned her horse into the square. She and Fabian had only ridden a few yards when Olivia pulled up Firebrand sharply.

"Lud!" she exclaimed and stared in consternation at a large, cumbersome chaise before Worth House. In the pool of light from a tall gas lantern she could make out four outriders sitting to attention on their horses while several footmen ran to and fro, carrying trunks, valises, and even a huge chest from the carriage into Worth House.

Fabian frowned at the commotion before his home. "Do you know which royal personage is descending on my humble abode?" he demanded, a terrible foreboding filling his heart.

"Grandmama," breathed Olivia.

"That's who I feared it might be. It appears that even the

old ladies of Bath read the London papers. Oh, well! It makes no odds now—''

He set Chichester in motion again. When Olivia gave no sign of wanting to follow his example, he reached back and grabbed Firebrand's bridle. Pulling Olivia along, he led the horses around the chaise and dismounted. ''Jenkins!'' he shouted while helping Olivia down.

The footman, recognizing his master's voice despite the scolding of two parakeets in a gilded cage right next to his ear, promptly dropped the valise he was carrying and hoisted the bird cage off his shoulder. Jenkins received the bridles with a wide, happy grin and marched off toward the mews.

''We shan't see him again for a while,'' said Olivia enviously.

Fabian chuckled. ''Shall I call him back? Perhaps you'd prefer to take the horses to the stables, and mayhap even spend an hour currying them?''

She tossed her head and preceded him up the front steps where a tall, gaunt-faced woman in black bombazine stood supervising the unloading.

''Good evening, Fletcher.'' Olivia smiled at her grand-mother's dresser. ''Did you have a good journey?''

''As good as could be expected,'' the woman replied dourly.

''Well, I suppose I'd best change before I greet Grandmama —I must look a fright. Where is she now, Fletcher? Resting?''

''Yer grandmother is in the salon with Lady Worth, taking a dish of tea. She won't be none too pleased if ye dally too long, Miss Olivia.''

''Hanged if I do, and hanged if I don't,'' muttered Olivia crossly. ''Grandmother would give me a piece of her mind were I to appear in all my dirt before her.'' She picked up the skirt of her riding habit and rushed upstairs, two steps at a time.

Lizzy was in her bedchamber, laying out a change of clothing. ''Oh, miss! Ye do be late. Milady's all aflutter on account of Lady Fenshawe's unexpected visit, and cook's fretting over the braised goose; you'd think the Prince of Wales hisself had come to visit. I brung some warm water up with me, miss . . . lessen it got too cold now. What with ye—''

"Thank you, Lizzy." Ruthlessly Olivia cut off the flow of words. She stepped out of her rumpled riding habit and washed quickly before donning fresh garments. The long-sleeved gown of amber kerseymere sported a multitude of tiny buttons down the back and on the tight cuffs, and after some struggle she submitted meekly to her maid's assistance. The soft woolen material clung snugly to her figure and felt warm and comfortable to her chilled limbs.

Barely fifteen minutes had passed since Olivia's return to Worth House, and she felt justifiably confident that even her cantankerous grandmother would be unable to find fault with her appearance. She'd brushed her tangled curls until they shone, and her cheeks glowed rosy after her long outing. Olivia cast a last critical look in the tall cheval glass, then hastened from the room to join the dowager countess and her grandmother downstairs in the salon.

A liveried footman stationed in the hall rushed ahead and flung open the door for her. She saw at a glance that her grandmother was in excellent spirits—meaning that her thin lips were less pursed than on other occasions, and that her dark, finely stenciled brows showed perfectly rounded arcs instead of reproving, triangular peaks. Olivia blinked when the old lady, on seeing her in the doorway, actually permitted herself a smile. It was no more than a slight uplift of the corners of her mouth, but it looked decidedly like a smile.

"Come in, come in, gal!" ordered Lady Fenshawe. "Don't stand there gaping. Haven't you a kiss for your grandmother?"

She and Lady Worth were ensconced in deep chairs by a roaring fire, and as Olivia crossed the colorful Aubusson carpet in the center of the salon where such elegant pieces of furniture as three Sheraton chaise longues, dainty chairs of the Queen Anne period, and several elegant side tables promised comfort and convenience, she could feel the heat from the enormous fireplace increase with every step she took.

Gracious, this was unbearable! What she wouldn't give to be able to run upstairs again and change into a muslin frock, or to tear open the four tall windows in the salon. The heavy brocaded drapes, though stunning in their red, jade, and gold pattern, made the hothouse atmosphere in the room appear even more oppressive.

But it would not do to excuse herself now. The dinner hour was upon them, and she must at least try to get along with Grandmama, a high stickler for punctuality. She couldn't afford to set up her grandmother's back, else she'd not learn until several days had passed why the old lady had ventured out on the hated journey from Bath to London. Surely it was not to congratulate her granddaughter on her betrothal, although, admittedly, Grandmama was looking as pleased as Punch.

Then Olivia saw that the two ladies by the fire had exchanged their teacups for glasses of sherry. No wonder Grandmama was feeling rather mellow! But it would not last long. There, she had found her lorgnette and was holding it to her eyes. . . .

"What on earth—! Are you wearing a wig, gal?"

"No, Grandmama. What a surprise to see you in London. I trust you suffered no ill from the journey? Grandmama, you look splendid." Olivia bent down and kissed the wrinkled cheek, then turned to greet the dowager countess.

"I hope you didn't worry on our account, ma'am. I apologize for returning home so much later than I'd anticipated."

"I shan't fret as long as I know you're with Fabian, dear. I know he'll keep you safe," replied Lady Worth complacently. "Pull up a chair, dear, and take a glass of sherry with us."

Lady Worth poured another sherry which Olivia accepted gratefully, but pull up a chair she would not. There was no fire screen in sight, and mayhap she could escape the worst of the heat by walking around.

This arrangement did not suit Lady Fenshawe however.

Her beaklike nose came up, and she dropped the lorgnette on its heavy gold chain back onto her majestic bosom. "Stand still, gal!" she commanded. "If that ain't a wig, what the deuce is it?"

"It's my latest hairstyle, Grandmama. Fashioned by Signor Giuseppe himself."

"Hmm." Slightly mollified, the old lady continued in less aggressive accents, "Trying to set a style, are you? But *short* hair? I never saw the like of it! None who knew you this summer in Bath would credit it."

Olivia sighed, wondering if she'd have to listen to another homily on her ungrateful behavior in Bath, but her grandmother's thoughts had taken a different turn.

"Got yourself engaged, too," grumbled Lady Fenshawe looking rather pleased nonetheless. "Worth is not a bad catch—not bad at all, considering you got him to the sticking point all by yourself. Mind you, I could have done better for you had you asked for my advice."

"A duke, perhaps?" Fabian had entered quietly and stood smiling in the doorway. "Let's see now, whom do we have available? There's Clarence, of course. He is free of Mrs. Jordan now, and Miss Tylney-Long would have none of him. And then there's . . ."

"Rubbish!" declared Lady Fenshawe and waved the earl closer.

Relieved, Olivia sought refuge on a chair far removed from the leaping flames. She dabbed her moist forehead inelegantly with the cuff of her sleeve—in her haste to greet Grandmama she'd forgotten to bring a handkerchief—then concentrated on her sherry. Let Worth do the pretty and suffer all the tortures of hell. He deserved it, too! After all, her grandmother's arrival was just one of the many consequences he hadn't taken into account in his nefarious schemes.

But he, if he had to roast in hell, would not roast alone. After Fabian had greeted his mother and charmed Lady Fenshawe by kissing her hand and murmuring outrageous compliments on her purple and black striped gown, he smiled at Olivia and extended his hand toward her.

"My love," he said, caressing her with his deep voice. "You'd not be so cruel as to deprive us of your presence. It's been thirty-eight minutes since I feasted my eyes on you last!"

Olivia shot him a look that should have mortally wounded him, but her grandmother applauded his blandishments.

"Spoken like a true courtier, Worth. I feared that the young men of today knew not how to charm a girl, but I perceive I've been wrong. Move closer, Olivia. I haven't seen you for over four months—and that's the truth, even if your young man here gives you honeyed phrases."

"Fabian would not offer Olivia false coin!" Lady Worth defended her son loyally, only to spoil the effect with her next words. "He may have the reputation of a rake, but he's always sincere."

Sincere? thought Olivia. *No, accomplished would have been the better term.* If Lady Worth could have observed her son during Lady Wanderley's ball, her eyes would have been opened to Fabian's extraordinary ability to dissemble. Resigned to her fate, Olivia rose and dragged herself toward the scorching flames and her grandmother's searing tongue. How could the two old ladies stand it? She might even faint before she got there. Olivia was spared this ignominious fate by the timely arrival of the butler announcing dinner.

"Good," declared Lady Fenshawe. "I'm devilish sharp-set. The food at the posting inns is deplorable, and indigestible to boot. Your arm, Worth!" she commanded.

Fabian bowed. "My pleasure, ma'am."

"And I shall have Robinson as my escort," said Lady Worth, "so that you may take in both the Fenshawe ladies, Fabian."

Dinner, although it consisted of only two courses—no company having been expected—nevertheless appeared interminable to Olivia. Her grandmother and Lady Worth were agreeing happily on the discomforts of travel, dwelling in gruesome detail on being bounced in poorly sprung carriages over roads consisting of nothing but ruts and bumps despite the new covering of macadam over stretches of the Bath Road, the unaired bedding at the inns, and the inconsiderate ways of young bucks who forced their racing curricles past slower vehicles and generally cut up the peace of mind of unprotected female travelers. Fabian, too, added his mite, but Olivia remained silent, using the time to speculate on the reason for her grandmother's visit.

If Grandmama merely wished to express her opinion of the betrothal, she would have done so by letter. So what did she want? Had she learned something of Tony's disappearance? Olivia's heart gave a lurch. Then Tony would really be in the basket. Grandmama would never forgive him for running away. "Backbone and a stiff upper lip" was what she'd always preached, and she would have expected Tony to serve Fabian for at least a year, no matter how hard it would have been on Tony. Or perhaps Grandmama had discovered that she'd stayed at Worth House before Lady Worth was in residence, or—

Finally the covers were removed and the servants withdrew, but instead of leading the ladies from the dining room, Lady Worth suggested they join Fabian in a glass of port. Lady Fenshawe voiced no objection and therefore Olivia, impatient to get to the point and emboldened by several glasses of wine served at dinner, took a great swig of port, then blurted out, "Why have you come to London, Grandmama?"

"To buy your trousseau, gal! Did you fear I'd come to drag you back to Bath?"

Olivia choked on a mouthful of the port she'd unwisely continued to sip, and Fabian jumped up to pound her on the back. When Olivia had recovered, he removed the goblet from her tight clasp and said with a grin, "Vile stuff, ain't it, my love? Perhaps a glass of lemonade would be more to your liking?"

"Fiddlesticks!" declared Lady Fenshawe. "This is a perfectly unexceptionable port. Reminds me of the bottles of '98 my late husband had laid down. He never did get to sample more than a bottle or two, and it's all wasted on Richard now."

"This is an '04 vintage, but, I believe, quite as palatable as the '98. I recall—"

"You're too young to recall anything of great import, young cawker!" interrupted Lady Fenshawe. "And in any case, I haven't risked my neck on those execrable roads to discuss the merits of port. Olivia, I've planned a two-week stay in town. I meant to put up at the Poultenay, but Alicia has graciously offered me a room here. I appreciate it, Alicia," she said to the dowager countess with one of her rare smiles.

"Naturally you must stay here," confirmed Fabian and earned himself a reproachful look from Olivia. "And as to the trousseau, you will do just as you wish, of course, but Olivia does not appear to lack in anything."

"Truly, Grandmama. I do not need any more clothes, and surely you do not wish to purchase linens for me to embroider? You know I cannot set a straight stitch!"

"What treachery!" Fabian raised his brows and regarded Olivia severely. "You did not tell me, my love. Who, I ask, will hem my handkerchiefs and embroider my slippers?"

"Do it yourself," replied Olivia crossly.

The two older ladies exchanged glances. Lady Worth rolled her eyes resignedly, but Lady Fenshawe rapped her knuckles sharply on the tabletop.

"Olivia, behave yourself!" she commanded. "Now, back to your trousseau. Do you take me for a dolt, gal? I saw at a glance that your gown was not one I purchased for you in Bath. Where *did* you get it, and how, if you have more than one, did you pay for them?"

"I did not steal them, Grandmama! Fabian—"

Aghast, Olivia bit her lip as she suddenly realized the significance of what she'd been about to say—she'd accepted gowns and other, more intimate garments from Fabian . . . like a kept woman! She felt the betraying color rush to her face and wished she could sink into the floor.

"The heat . . . so stuffy," she mumbled and lunged for the napkin beside the decanter of port. Fanning her flushed cheeks vigorously, she said, "Perhaps I *have* overspent myself, Grandmama, and if you would consider settling my accounts, I would be ever so grateful to you. Come, let me show you my new gowns.''

Olivia jumped up, eager to quit the dining room and Fabian's smoldering eyes, but her grandmother waved her back into her chair. "Tomorrow, child. You know I don't stay up late and I'm about to seek my couch. But before I retire, you'd best tell me about that young rapscallion!''

There was no doubt in Olivia's mind to whom her grandmother was referring. Richard had always been the "scapegrace,'' and Tony the "young rapscallion,'' but she pretended ignorance. "Who, Grandmama?''

"You know very well I'm talking about Anthony. What's this I hear about his catching a ball in his shoulder? Mrs. Kettering also mentioned he'd worked as Worth's *secretary*!'' Lady Fenshawe's long nose twitched in disbelief, and she subjected both Fabian and Olivia to a fierce glance through her lorgnette.

Olivia swallowed hard. Mrs. Kettering was one of Grandmama's cronies, an inveterate gossip. If Mrs. Kettering had been in town when the engagement notices appeared in the papers and London was abuzz with talk of her "romantic'' meeting with Fabian while he supposedly returned the wounded Tony to Fenshawe Court . . . Well, there was no help for it now. She must tell her grandmother the truth, before she learned it from the staff or Lady Worth.

"That was I, Grandmama.'' Olivia took a deep breath to steady her miserably quavering voice. "You see, Tony was too furious to take up the position because Richard had committed him to Worth without consulting him. And then Tony—I'm afraid Tony . . . ran away!''

Hiding her apprehension behind compressed lips and an unblinking stare, Olivia faced her grandmother, prepared to defend Tony's action after the old lady had vented her spleen. But her grandmother sat stock-still, incapable of uttering a single word. Fabian pressed the wineglass into her stiff fingers, and only after she'd taken a great swig of the restorative did she return Olivia's look.

"So," she said quietly, "Tony ran off somewhere and you, as usual, tried to cover up for his blatant stupidity by trying to hold down the post until he'd finally come to his senses." Lady Fenshawe seemed to shrink into herself. She looked suddenly very old and very tired. "That's why you've chopped off your hair, I take it?"

Olivia nodded mutely, and Lady Fenshawe murmured, "That boy has no bottom. But you're almost as daft as he is," she added softly. And if it had been someone other than her grandmother, Olivia would have believed she'd heard a hint of admiration in the low voice.

"This is a great shock to you, Lady Fenshawe." The dowager countess laid her hand comfortingly over the old lady's trembling one. "Perhaps you should learn the rest of the tale tomorrow when you're feeling stronger," she suggested gently. "I remember how shaken I was when Fabian told me Olivia's story—not that I thought ill of her for her daring, mind you. But I was thoroughly upset over the poor child's suffering."

"Mama," said Fabian quietly, "if Lady Fenshawe is to hear about it tomorrow, then *tomorrow* we'll talk about it."

Lady Fenshawe drew herself up and fixed Olivia with a piercing look. "Does your shoulder still pain you, gal?"

"Not at all—and there's hardly a scar to show, either. Come, Grandmama, let me take you upstairs." Olivia rose and walked over to her grandmother's chair.

Fabian forestalled her and assisted the old lady to her feet himself. To Olivia he said, "I should like a word with you. Pray join me in the library when you've seen to your grandmother's comfort."

"You two go right ahead then," said Lady Fenshawe testily. "Alicia will show me to my room."

"Of course." Lady Worth embraced Olivia in a flutter of silver-gray chiffon gown and shawls. "We can take a hint and shall allow you and Fabian a few moments of privacy. Good night, my dears."

When the two ladies had departed, Fabian cocked a brow

at Olivia, who was still standing in the center of the dining room. "After you, dear." He bowed.

She tossed her head and marched past him. "There had better not be a fire in the library," she flung over her shoulder.

"If there isn't, I'll light one . . . under your *derrière*!" he promised. "What the deuce are you trying to do by asking your grandmother to pay for your gowns?"

Olivia kept her temper firmly in check until they were in the large book-lined room, where the air was redolent with the scent of leather and tobacco smoke. When the door was firmly shut behind them, she rounded on Fabian, hands on hips. "You need to ask?" she stormed. "Well, let me tell you, Worth! I'd rather be beholden to my grandmother than to you!"

"You did not consider anything wrong until she mentioned your new clothes. Or aren't you the same young woman who's trying to bankrupt me?"

She colored again and became even angrier because of it. With a stomp of her foot to give emphasis to her words, she admitted furiously, "I know *now* that I've behaved like a nitwit in accepting the garments. But, dash it, Worth! Accepting clothes had become such a matter of fact for me that I didn't think of the impropriety of it until Grandmother asked how I'd paid for them."

A bit calmer, but still with bitterness in her voice, Olivia continued. "After my parents died, Grandmama sent me two gowns every year, one for summer and one for winter, unless she had me stay with her. Then I generally received an additional frock or a cloak. And Miss Merriweather would occasionally accept some serviceable castoffs on my behalf from charitable-minded neighbors. So, you see, although you offered me no castoffs, I simply accepted the gowns without thinking . . . especially since you'd poked such fun at my old blue cambric."

Fabian saw the hurt on her face, and pride struggling to overcome her shame. He turned away abruptly. Damn! He should have made that scoundrel Richard Fenshawe sign a second note—promising to care for his sister as befits a gentlewoman! Fabian's hand clenched. If only he could put them to use against Sir Richard, as they were itching to do.

When he had his anger under control, he faced Olivia again and said quietly, "I am sorry, my dear. I behaved abominably toward you."

She blushed again and indicated with a nod that his apology was accepted, but she did not meet his eyes. Olivia rather felt she ought to beg his forgiveness for her outburst, but feared to open her mouth lest she start bawling like a babe.

To divert her, Fabian suggested, "Let's talk about a new plan to outwit Lionel, unless you are too tired?"

"Oh, I'm not the least bit fatigued." Olivia perked up instantly, relieved to have the subject changed. She selected one of the leather chairs that stood grouped around a small table littered with agricultural tomes, political pamphlets, and one or two gentlemen's magazines, and sat down on the wide arm.

"This afternoon's undertaking was not at all well planned," she said with a deep furrow on her wide forehead. "You should have consulted with me, Fabian. For instance, you should have arranged for Lionel·to accompany us. Then he could have cut the girth of your mount while we were at the Star and Garter. . . ."

". . . and planted a burr under my saddle," interposed Fabian with a grin.

"Do be serious, or we need not be holding this conversation at all!"

He propped an arm against the mantel of the cavernous fireplace and obediently assumed a grave mien, but his eyes were still dancing when he assured her, "I am serious, my dear. But I have no wish to take a tumble—too easy to break one's neck—and I feared you were becoming a mite melodramatic."

"Perhaps," she conceded. "I take it then, you can come up with a better plan?"

"Yes. We shall set the wedding date . . . say three weeks from today. That will set the cat among the pigeons!"

"No!" said Olivia sharply. "Only consider, Fabian! If Lionel does *not* act, we might actually find ourselves walking down the aisle."

"There are worse fates."

"Yes, like getting killed!"

Fabian threw up his hands. "All right, let's devise a different scheme." With four long strides he was at her side and seated himself in the very chair where she was perching on the leather arm. "We must find a way to make Lionel believe he has lured me to some lonely spot. Then, when he attacks me, Charles will pounce on him . . ."

". . . and I will hold Lionel in check with one of your dueling pistols!"

"Do you know how to shoot?" he asked, diverted.

"No, but Lionel won't know that. So that's no reason to keep me out of your plans."

Carefully she wriggled a little farther away from his warm shoulder, but the slippery surface of the chair's arm proved treacherous, and she slid off completely. She might have ended up in an ignominious heap on the floor had not Fabian snatched her around the waist and hoisted her up again.

"Would you be more comfortable on my lap?" he asked with a great show of concern.

"I thank you for the offer, but I believe I shall be most comfortable seated across from you." Suiting the action to her words, she settled herself opposite Fabian, pulled up her legs, and modestly spread the folds of her gown over her slippered feet.

He frowned. When that brought about no change in her posture, he pointed out, "Surely that's not the way a young lady of quality should sit, my dear."

"Thunder and turf! Who are you to preach propriety to me, Worth? One moment you offer me your lap to sit on, and the next you are scandalized because I've tucked my feet under! Now, do you want to devise a plan to trap your

Bedlamite cousin, or do you wish to give me a lesson in deportment?''

"More than once have I been tempted to blister your backside," he said musingly. "I wonder what results I should . . ."

"The only result you'll be able to boast of is a drawn cork if you so much as lay a finger on me!"

His eyes glinted dangerously. "If that is how you were allowed to converse at Fenshawe Court, Sir Richard has a lot to answer for."

"Well, you are wrong! Richard had nothing to do with it. In fact, he and I have scarcely exchanged three words during the past two years. 'Twas Tony who instructed me. He had considerably broadened his vocabulary during his short stay at Cambridge and was eager to impart his knowledge to me. And as you may have noticed, Grandmama is not exactly a mealymouthed, retiring old lady!"

"Indeed. But I'm certain she'd be the first to point out that it won't do for you to copy her style. And I'm coming to believe that the sooner that young brother of yours is sent to the Peninsula, the better."

"Have you had news, Fabian?" she asked eagerly.

"Well, I've had word from Lieutenant Bramson that Tony's commission has come through; his orders are ready and waiting, but, unfortunately, Clem and the boys have been unable to find a trace of him yet. I've told Clem to widen the search. They'll start looking as far north as Barnet and Chingford, then they'll spread out to Ilford and Woolwich, to Streatham and Hampton, and scour the west as far as Hanwell."

"Please, Fabian, I should like to go out myself and search for Tony."

"I know the endless waiting has been hard on you, but I'm not certain—" Fabian broke off and thought for a moment, then snapped his fingers. "Why didn't I think of it before? You've been wanting to get lost in the maze at Hampton Court, you told me once. If the weather is promising, we'll set out early in the morning and we can stop and ask about Tony at every posting house on the way.''

Olivia's face lit up. ''Shall we take your curricle? Will you let me handle the ribbons?''

''Woman!'' he protested with a laugh. ''Will you never learn where to draw the line?''

Her face fell, and she heaved a disappointed sigh. ''When I was still 'Tony' in your eyes, you said I might drive your team to Hendon. At that moment I was gloriously happy that you believed me a man, because I realized you'd never have made the offer to a woman—and I was correct!''

''Then I must prove you wrong!'' He rose and extended his hands to help her off her chair. ''Get some rest, imp. I'll see you bright and early in the morning.''

Olivia's dimple appeared. ''Good night, Fabian. Sweet dreams!'' she called as she ran from the room up the stairs.

Fabian stood in the open door of the library, a bemused expression on his face. ''More likely nightmares about landing in a ditch with you at the reins,'' he muttered and strolled toward his study.

Well, at least she was going to bed in a happy frame of mind. What a mercurial girl she was—one moment ripping up at him, and the next, all anger forgotten, she was wheedling him into letting her handle his grays. And his own displeasure at her lack of decorum had completely flown his mind. . . .

Fabian poured himself a cognac, his mind trying to grapple with Olivia's accusation that he was a hypocrite. But was not all of society built on the assumption that men had more license than women? Olivia apparently did not feel compelled to abide by those rules. Well, he couldn't blame her. After all, it did seem rather unfair.

He swirled the amber liquid absently. What would it be like, he wondered, to be married to a girl like Olivia? Certainly never boring! But would she be able to keep his nightmares about the Peninsular campaign at bay when he would hold her in his arms at night?

He stared at the cognac in his glass—her eyes showed

little flecks of just that color when she was laughing. . . . Curious that she always addressed him as Fabian when she was pleased, and as Worth when she was out of charity with him!

_____ C H A P T E R   9 _____

Olivia disrobed slowly, her mind awhirl with sleep-robbing thoughts: finally she'd be able to take an active part in the search for Tony; she'd been promised the treat of handling Fabian's grays; and she would see Hampton Court. Strange that Fabian should have remembered her wish—

Tying the satin ribbon at the neck of her ivory lace nightgown, Olivia stared up at Fabian's portrait. Her face softened and a responding smile curved her lips as she studied the handsome youth. Several times this evening she'd caught glimpses of this other Fabian, the one who was teasing, gay, carefree—like when he'd twitted her about her outrageous plot, and when he'd called her an imp.

He'd also lost his temper more than once, she reminded herself sharply and turned away from the portrait. She snuffed the candles on her dresser, leaving only the small lamp on her nightstand burning, flung back the coverlet of heavy Nottingham lace, and climbed into the four-poster bed. While her eyes traced the brocade pattern of the turquoise and silver canopy, her mind lingered on Fabian's threat to beat her. He had most likely spoken in jest, yet his words had evoked immediate, ugly memories of Richard and his whip, causing in turn her furious response to Fabian. Somehow, though, they had concluded the evening amicably.

Olivia peered again at the portrait. It was too dark now to

distinguish the features, but she required no light to see, superimposed over the shadowy image on the wall, the expression on Fabian's face as he had watched her from the library door. She'd wanted to run back to him, to—

She did not want to think anymore, she determined, her cheeks flaming. Olivia tossed restlessly, then pounded her pillows to find a comfortable spot for her reeling head. She wanted to sleep, yet the bit of secret longing, well hidden at the very back of her mind, pushed and prodded until it finally burst forth and had to be acknowledged.

I wanted to throw my arms around him and hold him tight!

Rolling over onto her stomach, Olivia buried her face in the feathery softness of her pillows. *Daft!* That's what Grandmama had called her, and she was right! It was daft, even irresponsible, to fall in love with the man who'd enticed Richard into the faro game that had cost them their home.

She must not let it happen. Perhaps it was a good thing after all that she'd finally admitted her feelings to herself, for now she could guard against Fabian's charm and watch that her infatuation with him did not grow. Very soon now she'd be able to remove from Worth House, and she must make certain not to leave her heart behind.

Olivia finally fell asleep, only to be wakened moments later, it seemed, by the dour Fletcher. "My lady's been up for an hour, awaiting yer pleasure, Miss Olivia!"

"What time is it?" she asked sleepily.

"Past seven o'clock. Ye'd best come right away, and ye can have a cup o' tea afore it gets too cold."

Fletcher handed Olivia a robe of soft amber wool and hovered over her while she performed a very cursory toilette, then marched her down the hall to her grandmother's room.

Grandmama's impatient voice could be heard before the door was fully open. "There you are, Fletcher! For heaven's sake, cover up the bird cage again. Those pesky parakeets are noisier than a flock of geese. Then you may go."

Lady Fenshawe was seated at a small table by the window, a plate of buttered toast and a dainty tea service before her. She took one look at her granddaughter's pale, drawn features and waved her into the chair across from her own. "Have some tea," she said.

Obediently Olivia swallowed the hot brew her grandmother had poured and felt the soothing warmth settle in her stomach and clear her eyes. "Good morning, Grandmama. Did you sleep well?"

"I only rest easy in my own bed, and the sooner I get back to Bath, the better. Now, tell me all that's happened!"

Olivia complied, but made no reference to Lionel Worthing, to the attacks on Fabian's life, or the falseness of her engagement.

"And so I assume," said Lady Fenshawe when Olivia had come to a faltering halt, "Worth offered for you because he felt honor-bound to save your reputation. It's not the love match I supposed it to be after all. Hmm."

She looked at her granddaughter thoughtfully. "Is that why you want me to lay out my blunt on the clothes he's already bought you?"

"Yes," whispered Olivia. *But it's much worse than you can possibly imagine,* she thought despairingly.

Lady Fenshawe spoke up again, her voice a bit croaky, as though she suffered from a putrid throat, or as though she'd swallowed her tears to hide her misery from Olivia. "And Anthony has besmirched our name by deserting from the Horse Guards—"

"It will be all right, Grandmama. Fabian has purchased a commission for Tony in the Light Division; the papers are drawn up, and all charges against Tony have been dropped. We'll find him in time to ship out, and no one need ever know."

"I shall know," muttered the old lady. "Where on earth could the tiresome boy be? Have you checked with Miss Merriweather?"

Olivia shook her head. "Merrie is in Suffolk. Her niece is increasing."

Her grandmother was silent for a long time, lost in reflections. And none of them too pleasant, thought Olivia, to judge by her haggard face. Olivia poured more tea and sipped the strong beverage. She was startled when her grandmother suddenly sat up straighter, saying,

"*I* must bear the blame for all this! I should have taken charge of Tony and you seven years ago. But I'm a selfish old woman; I was worried that you'd bring upheaval and disruption into my ordered life. I left you at Fenshawe Court even when I knew how unhappy you both were with Richard and Harriet. And I did know—Miss Merriweather wrote to me once, but I ignored her."

Lady Fenshawe sighed and stared at her folded hands in her lap. They were trembling despite her efforts to still them. Quietly she continued. "When finally I deigned to notice you and asked you to visit me in Bath, it was too late. You resented me and cut your visits as short as your sense of civility permitted." After a moment she added in a whisper, "And I could easily have purchased a cornetcy for Tony."

Olivia looked at her grandmother with troubled eyes. Everything Grandmama had said was painfully true. A part of her wanted to cry out, *Yes! Why didn't you take us into your home when we were young and in need of guidance and protection? Why didn't you get Tony his commission?* But the deep lines of suffering etched suddenly on her grandmother's face kept her silent.

The old lady studied Olivia closely, searchingly, but when she realized that neither condemnation nor consolation would be offered by her granddaughter, she nodded as though accepting the inevitable.

"Only remember this, gal!" she said in her usual authoritative voice. "Should you decide you don't care for Worth enough to go through with this, you come to me. I still have sufficient spunk in me to help you through any scandal that might arise if you jilt him."

"Thank you." On impulse, Olivia rose and bestowed a quick, almost furtive hug on her grandmother. Neither one of them was accustomed to a display of emotions before the other. "I may just take you up on this generous offer, but let's give it some time, shall we?" Olivia wished she might avail herself of her grandmother's aid right now, but she could not leave Fabian until he'd put Lionel on a ship bound for foreign shores.

"If you will excuse me, Grandmama, I should dress. Fabian's taking me to Hampton Court, and we wish to leave early to make inquiries about Tony along the way."

Lady Fenshawe snorted. "Hampton Court? Have you looked out the window, gal? It's sleeting, and I'd wager a monkey the temperature will drop and turn everything to ice. I doubt Worth will risk his horses in this weather."

Her prediction proved only too true. When Olivia joined Fabian in the breakfast parlor, he rose and said, "I am so sorry, my dear, but it doesn't look at all propitious for an outing. I would not want to endanger the grays—or, for that matter, us—on a trip we might just as soon make tomorrow or the next day."

"Of course," said Olivia, feeling very relieved of a sudden that she need not be in close proximity to him for the better part of the day. "We shall go tomorrow. It's too early in the season for the sleet to last, and we still have two weeks to find Tony."

Fabian looked at her with concern. "You are not fretting yourself unnecessarily, are you, dear? We *will* find him."

"I must believe that, mustn't I?" She smiled, grateful for his confidence and encouragement, then went over to the sideboard to choose from the array of tempting dishes.

"What shall we do instead?" he asked when she'd poured coffee and started to nibble on a hot buttered scone.

Olivia blinked. Did he still wish to spend his time with her? That was not at all what *she* wanted. She'd rather make good use of this respite to get her emotions under control. She found it hard enough to meet his eyes when he spoke to her, always afraid he'd be able to see into her heart. To have him recognize her foolish love would be more than she could bear.

"Well?" he demanded. "Can I challenge you to a game of chess? I must warn you, though, that I'm generally held to be unbeatable!"

"Perhaps some other day," she replied, only half registering the taunt she'd have been unable to withstand at any other time. "I thought I might slip out and visit Emily Carrington. It's but a few steps to her door, and I don't believe there's ice on the ground yet to make it too hazardous to venture outside."

He regarded her for a moment, then said gravely, "As you wish, my dear. In that case I shall look in on Lord Bathurst. I've rather neglected my duties of late."

"What are your duties?" she asked, hoping to avoid a painful silence between them while they were finishing their meal.

"When I sold out, Bathurst appointed me his advisor. Whenever he receives dispatches, even private letters, from Wellington, I sift through the content, for Old Hookey has been known at times to exaggerate some of his problems shamelessly. Bathurst believes my personal experiences in the Peninsula to be helpful in the evaluation of the reports. Well—" Fabian tossed down his napkin. "I'll be off. Have a nice coze with Emily, and do take Lizzy with you."

Before Olivia had recovered from her astonishment at the precipitate conclusion of his breakfast, he had left the room. She sipped her coffee and frowned at his plate, filled with beefsteak and eggs. Had he felt rebuffed when she'd declined to play chess? He had not *looked* disappointed; but then, neither had he shrugged it off in his usual disdainful manner.

After pondering on his strange behavior for a few moments, she gave up the futile exercise. She had enough worrying to do about her own concerns. She could use a bit of distraction, and Emily might be just the person to provide it. Charles liked Emily, and that was a good enough recommendation for her. But she would not drag Lizzy along just to walk one block. No, not even after *my lord* had ordered her to do so. And if he learned of her defiance, so much the better. He'd be furious with her, and she could flare back at him.

Barely fifteen minutes later Olivia slipped out of Worth House. She had wrapped herself in a warm, hooded cloak and protected her feet with sturdy walking boots. Despite the driving sleet and a strong wind tearing around the corners of the mansions she passed, Olivia made good progress and arrived with glowing cheeks and sleet-coated eyelashes at Carrington House. Here she was met with the lowering news that Miss Carrington had been sent to the lending library by her ailing mama to find some amusing volumes for the invalid.

"Would you care to leave your card, miss?" asked the butler haughtily.

Olivia laughed. "I don't have a card, but kindly inform Miss Carrington when she returns that Miss Olivia Fenshawe inquired after her."

"Certainly, miss." The butler unbent sufficiently to bestow a thin smile on the unattended visitor. Apparently even he had heard that Miss Fenshawe was betrothed to the Earl of Worth, thought Olivia.

"Mrs. Carrington is still in her bedchamber," he continued. "But if you'd care to step inside, you could wait in the blue salon until Miss Carrington returns."

"No, thank you. Just see to it, please, that she receives my message."

Carefully Olivia descended the slick marble steps. When she heard the door close, she stood for a moment on the sidewalk, undecided what to do next. She looked over her shoulder toward Worth House but could not even see as far as the corner of Grosvenor Square through the thick veil of sleet and snow. Finally she proceeded in the opposite direction from Worth House.

She had tried to see Emily—that was all anyone could ask—and if she didn't feel like returning home now, she need not do so. *Gracious!* Matters had gone far indeed if she thought of Worth House as "home" already.

Olivia trudged on, a little angry with herself because she

could not control her wayward feelings, and a little apprehensive because the slush on the cobbles was turning to ice, making it difficult to walk. But somewhere ahead, near Park Lane, she would find a hackney. Grandmama had planted a notion in her head, and she wished to pursue it.

When she finally discovered a hackney, the driver at first refused to take her to Hans Crescent. "Nay, missy. I'll take ye 'ome if I must, but me an' me Warrior 'ere is bound fer 'ome as well. It's turning mighty nasty to be out an' about."

"Warrior?" Olivia smiled at the grizzled old man. "With a brave name like that, surely your horse would not want to miss out on a fare. I'll pay you double, plus extra for the waiting, if you take me to Hans Crescent and then home to Grosvenor Square. I shan't be above a minute at Hans Crescent," she promised.

The old man hesitated. Double fare and extra for waiting would just about make up for the loss he'd be taking on account of the weather. "In ye go," he finally grumbled. "But mind ye, we'll drive slow. Won't risk me Warrior's old legs fer no crazy notions ye nobs take into yer 'eads!"

And slow he was. Olivia felt certain she could have walked faster than this snail's pace Warrior was setting. At least she was dry and fairly warm inside the musty, rank-smelling cab. When they arrived at number eleven Hans Crescent at last, Olivia slipped from the hackney without a backward glance.

This time she did not climb the three flights of stairs to Merrie's tiny flat, but descended instead to the basement. An elaborate brass plate on the door informed her that the concierge's name was Mrs. Yates.

Mrs. Yates, as round as she was tall, came puffing to the door and opened it a crack. "What do you want? There's no vacancies right now. Come back in a month or so if you're still interested."

"Please, Mrs. Yates!" Quickly Olivia slid her booted foot in the crack to prevent the door from being slammed in her face. "I am Miss Olivia Fenshawe, former pupil of Miss Merriweather. I only wish to inquire if my brother has been here or sent a note for Miss Merriweather, because, you see, he's not aware that she was planning to go to her niece's in Suffolk.''

Mrs. Yates extracted a quizzing glass from the pocket of her voluminous black gown and subjected the young lady who was so exceedingly well informed about Miss Merriweather's whereabouts to a careful scrutiny. Apparently she liked what she saw, for she opened the door wide and invited Olivia into her parlor.

"Would you like a cuppa tea, dearie?" she asked. "I've just put the kettle on. You must be proper frozen from having been out in this weather."

"Thank you, Mrs. Yates. I appreciate your kind offer, but I must not dawdle. I've left the hackney waiting, and I know the driver is worried about his horse. Please tell me if a young man has inquired about Miss Merriweather."

"Well, a young flash did come by, oh, about two, three days ago. But he asked questions about all the tenants. Not that I gossip about the tenants, mind you, but he did let on like he might want to rent one of the larger apartments."

Olivia chewed her lip. The concierge's first words of affirmation had fanned the flame of hope in her breast, but it had soon dwindled and died. This did not sound at all like Tony. He would have asked outright after Merrie. But she pursued her questioning doggedly.

"This young man, did he look at all like me, Mrs. Yates? My brother and I are very much alike, you see. If I dressed up in his clothes, we'd look like twins."

"Dear me! You don't want to do that, love. I mean, a young lady to dress in breeches and all!" Mrs. Yates shuddered delicately, but returned to the point when she noticed Olivia's anxious eyes. "But no, he did not look at all like you. He was dark, with black, brooding eyes, and he was dressed real smart like. His vest was the most dazzling thing I ever clapped my eyes on, and his shirt points were so high and stiff that he couldn't turn his head for all that he wanted to." She giggled girlishly as she remembered the dandy who'd kissed her hand so gracefully.

"Come to think of it," she continued with a frown, "he inquired most partickerly after all my resident gentlemen. Wanted to know if a certain young lady visited them here."

"Thank you, Mrs. Yates. That was clearly not my brother," explained Olivia. The description of the young man fit Lionel Worthing to a tee, and she could hear his sneering voice asking her, "What were you doing in this neighborhood? Seeing a lover?"

Mrs. Yates had put her quizzing glass to her eye again, and the huge, distorted orb stared at Olivia disconcertingly. "But the young lady he described looked very much like *you*," she muttered.

"Well, the only person I visit in this building is Miss Merriweather," said Olivia dampeningly. "And you said no one has left a note for Miss Merriweather either?"

"No, dearie."

"Thank you very much, Mrs. Yates. I shan't keep you any longer from your tea. I will come back some other time to check if a note has arrived. And, please, Mrs. Yates, if it is not too much trouble, would you inform my brother Anthony Fenshawe, should he call, to come and see me at Worth House in Grosvenor Square?"

Impressed by the exclusive address, the concierge nodded vigorously. "No trouble at all, dearie. I'll see he gets your message."

Back in the hackney, Olivia shivered in a corner, her hopes dashed. It suddenly seemed like a harebrained notion that Tony should have come to Merrie's flat. He'd probably laugh and scoff at the idea that he should have sought assistance from his sister's old governess.

Then Olivia remembered Mrs. Yates's vivid description of the young man who had apparently inquired after her. Did Lionel Worthing indeed believe she was meeting a lover in Hans Crescent? What did he think he could do with the information? Carry tales to Fabian? She chuckled at the notion and felt somewhat better.

Olivia paid off the hackney driver, even gave him an extra shilling for Warrior's ration of oats, and slowly ascended the slick steps to the great front door of Worth House. The door was flung open by Robinson before she had time to grasp the knocker.

"Oh, miss! There you are!" He could say no more, but swallowed convulsively and pulled her inside.

"Why, whatever is the matter, Robinson? Surely you were not worried about me?"

"Yes, miss! That we were. There's my lord laid up above with a gashing head wound, fretting himself to distraction with worry about your safety, and . . ."

But Olivia paid him no more heed. As soon as she'd taken in that Fabian was wounded, she rushed upstairs and burst without ceremony into his sitting room.

"Fabian—"

She broke off in confusion when about a dozen people turned in unison and stared at her. There was the dowager countess with Natty and Grandmama supporting her; Alders and Sir Whitewater flanked an easy chair in which Fabian was sitting with blood spatters on his white shirt and a thick bandage around his head. She had barely any time to notice Lord Charles and Emily Carrington off in a corner of the room, and several footmen, grooms, and Clem all goggling at her, before Fabian hoisted himself up and took a step toward her.

"And where, may I ask, have you been?" he demanded through clenched teeth.

Olivia couldn't tell whether it was pain or anger that made him speak in such a strained voice. "Shouldn't you be sitting down?" she asked with a worried look at his bandage.

"I daresay, but I want an answer first!"

But more hands than he could ward off reached for him and led him back to his chair. Then Alders shouldered everyone aside and gently dabbed his master's moist brow.

Sir Whitewater cleared his throat. "I have done all I can for now, my lord. I suggest you rid yourself of all these well-meaning people and have a short talk with your fiancée to set your mind at ease. Then rest, rest, rest, my lord. I cannot stress enough that after a blow on the head such as you sustained, rest is of the utmost importance. We do not know yet whether there is a concussion of the brain to contend with, but if you should suffer from persistent headaches for more than a day or two, pray alert me immediately. Good day, my lord.''

The physician then turned to the dowager countess and bowed. "My dear Lady Worth. There is nothing you can do for your son at the moment. Why don't you lie down for a while? I'll leave a soothing draught with Natty, and should you be too overset to relax, you may take three tablespoons of the elixir in a small glass of water.'' He nodded to Lady Fenshawe to accompany the dowager countess while he conferred with Natty and Alders in the hall.

The other servants, after a questioning glance at Lord Worth, shuffled slowly from the room and clattered down the stairs.

Only Olivia, Emily, and Lord Charles remained with Fabian. He raised his brows and shot a less than welcoming look at them. "Pull up some chairs,'' he grumbled, "and stop hovering around me.''

Lord Charles grinned. "No, no, my friend. I'll leave the hovering to Olivia and Alders. Emily and I must be off.''

"I am so sorry, Lord Worth, to have caused so much unnecessary commotion.'' With a timid glance at his forbidding countenance, Emily Carrington tugged nervously at the velvet frogging of her dashing blue redingote.

Fabian waved aside her apology and awarded her a reassuring smile. "No harm done, Miss Carrington.''

"I hope you'll remember that line after we've left,'' said Charles, "and begin raking Olivia over the coals.''

"Oh, dear!'' Emily looked conscience-stricken. "I hadn't thought of that. Please, Olivia, you must believe that I did not mean to bring trouble on your head! When I returned from the lending library and learned that I'd missed your visit, I was very upset. And then Charles dropped by and offered to drive me here—you see, Mama did not want me to leave again, but she can never withstand Charles's pleas.''

Emily gulped in some air and then continued, the words

tumbling from her mouth like so many pebbles rolling down a hillside. "We arrived here just moments after Lord Worth had been carried into the house, and he was still downstairs in the hall. Naturally, Charles wanted to be with Lord Worth, and I asked the butler to let you know that I was here, but Robinson said you'd left the house and not returned yet. Lord Worth immediately became upset because he thought you were at my home. . . ." Her voice trailed off uncertainly.

"Never mind, Emily," Olivia replied soothingly. "I've weathered worse storms, and we shall have our visit some other day. If Worth places me under house arrest, you'll simply have to ask Charles to bring you here again."

"Be easy on Fabian today, Olivia," begged Lord Charles as he opened the door for Emily. "He does have a frightful gash on his head."

The door closed behind them, and Olivia and Fabian were left to eye each other warily.

"Where were you?" he demanded harshly.

Well, thought Olivia, *I suppose I ought to be grateful that his wound is not serious enough to rob him of the strength to shout at me.* "Do you realize, Fabian," she said musingly, "that you have spent quite a bit of your energy asking me just that particular question lately? But all in good time. First I wish to know what happened to *you.*"

Olivia threw off her cloak and pulled one of the heavy chairs closer so that she might sit facing him. He looked so pale and wan that she wished she had the courage to prop his feet on a hassock or ask him to lie down. Why wasn't Alders here to make Fabian behave sensibly?

As though he'd read her thoughts, Fabian said testily, "All right, I'll tell you, for I don't want to waste time arguing about who talks first. I've no doubt Alders will be here in a few moments and fuss around me like a mother hen."

He winced and touched his head gingerly. "Please go to the smaller of the two carved cabinets in the corner, the one with the jade and ivory dragons on the doors. You'll find a decanter and glasses inside.''

Without a word she did his bidding, glancing curiously about the room as soon as she was out of his range of vision. The strange mixture of solid English armchairs and ornately carved Oriental furniture—the side tables, chests, and cabinets all decorated with inlaid ivory, mother-of-pearl, and jade—was very pleasing to her eye, and the luxurious Persian carpet in dark, somber shades of blue, red, and gold blended the two worlds gracefully together. She bent to examine the strange lock on the doors of the cabinet, and found to her chagrin that she could not open it.

"Dash it, Olivia! Use the key!" instructed Fabian without looking around.

The key turned out to be a little brass lever on top of the cabinet. It resembled a folded-up letter opener and had to be inserted sideways in the lock. When she'd passed him a cognac and was settled across from him, he told his story briefly and baldly.

"I was set upon again, near Whitehall. This time my cane did no good—there were three ruffians. I doubt not that they'd have finished their task to the brutal end had not Lieutenant Bramson and some of his friends happened by and driven them off. Bramson took me home, and just as my mother and Alders were insisting that Sir Whitewater must come and that I must not be allowed to walk upstairs but must be carried, Emily and Charles dropped in.''

He looked at Olivia expectantly. "Your turn," he prodded.

But she was too distraught to think of anything but this latest attack on his life. "Lionel again—and you were unprotected!"

"Well, yes," he admitted. "I assume Lionel was behind the attack. Although I did not see him anywhere nearby, I did recognize his groom as one of the three Mohocks."

"You mustn't walk out unarmed anymore!"

"I shan't," he replied grimly. "I'm having a cane fashioned for me, with a sword concealed inside.''

Even that did not seem adequate protection to Olivia, but

as she was wondering how to convince him to take a footman or a groom on his perambulations without bringing to his attention that she had *not* taken her maid, he winced again and leaned his head wearily against the back of his chair.

"Now, will you tell me where you have been?" he asked in a tired voice.

"Only to Hans Crescent," she replied soothingly. "It occurred to me that Tony might have tried to get in touch with Merrie, but, as it turned out, 'twas just a foolish notion after all."

"And where was Lizzy while you were out?"

Tarnation! Even after a whack on the head he didn't miss a thing. "She was at home. You see, I did not think to go to Hans Crescent until *after* I'd learned that Emily was not at home. And surely you didn't expect me to drag Lizzy along just to walk the few steps to Carrington House?"

"Yes!" he rasped. "I do expect that you leave Worth House accompanied by a maid, even if you plan only to step next door. My God, Olivia! Don't you realize I was almost out of my mind with worry when I returned and learned you were not at Emily's? I thought Lionel had tried to strike at both of us at the same time."

"I am sorry, Fabian. But surely there is no point in his attacking me as well?"

"There is no rhyme or reason behind these attacks! Lionel is striking out blindly because he can see his objective disappear further and further from his grasp."

"You may be right. The concierge in Hans Crescent told me that a young man—and she described Lionel exactly, including his horrible vest—had questioned her about me and the gentlemen living in the building. You see, when he met me there last time, he'd assumed I was meeting a lover!" Olivia smiled impishly, her twinkling eyes inviting him to share her amusement.

A lopsided grin lit up his face briefly, but he pointed out instantly, "This proves my point. You *must* take Lizzy with you. Or better still, take Jenkins as well."

She had no time to protest because Alders erupted into the sitting room after the most cursory of knocks. "Pardon me, Miss Olivia. But Sir Whitewater would wish fer 'is lordship to take 'is rest now."

"Of course, Alders. I was just leaving."

Both Olivia and Alders ignored Fabian's objections that he had not concluded his talk with her. As she closed the door, she could hear the valet's bracing voice, "Come now, milor'! Let's 'ave no more nonsense from ye. I've put a nice 'ot brick in yer bed, and ye can sleep off most of the 'eadache."

Alders, the clucking mother hen, she thought. Chuckling softly to herself, she went downstairs to see if any luncheon had been prepared in all the confusion of the morning. As she crossed the hall, Robinson emerged through the green baize curtain at the far end asked, "How is his lordship, Miss Olivia?"

"He should be resting comfortably now, Robinson. Alders was with Lord Worth when I left, ordering him to bed."

"Thank you, miss. And what should I do about Clem, miss? He insists he must see his lordship—or you."

"Send him into the study then. I shall talk with him."

"Very well, Miss Olivia."

——CHAPTER 10——

Clem edged hesitantly into the study and halted a good five paces away from the mahogany desk where Olivia sat in Fabian's deep chair.

"Sit down, Clem," she invited with an encouraging smile.

Belatedly Clem snatched his cap off his head, then twisted it nervously in his thin, callused fingers. With his narrow, wiry frame, barely five feet tall, he looked more like a scared schoolboy than the earl's intrepid tiger who rode at the back of Lord Worth's racing curricle and didn't turn a hair when his master overtook a lumbering mail coach on the narrowest stretch of road. He did not avail himself of the proffered chair, but inched a trifle closer and peered doubtfully at Olivia.

"Well, I dunno if I'm doin' right by tellin' ye what me an' Ferdie found out, Miss Olivia. Mayhap I should wait until the guvnor feels spritely agin. Wouldn't want ter get yer 'opes up fer nothin'."

"Is it about my brother? Did you discover where he is?" Olivia shot up and ran over to Clem, shaking his arm in her excitement and impatience to learn more.

"Nay, miss." He blushed as dark as his freckles and retreated a step backward. "But mayhap we got a lead finally. Ye see, Ferdie an' me was goin' ter check the postin' inns up around Barnet's way, an' we'd just had a word with the ostler at the Angel—that's in Islington, miss—when we figgered we'd best turn back on account of the weather, ye see. But after a mile or so, me 'orse went lame. So we pulls up at the Scarecrow."

"At the Scarecrow? Is that an inn?" Olivia sat down again, convinced that this would turn out to be a lengthy interview. Poor Clem had a hard time getting to the point, and she feared if she were to hurry him she'd only make him feel more uncomfortable.

"Yes, miss. 'Tis a snug enough little place with quite a bit of traffic, but ordinary like we'd not 'ave stopped there 'cause they keeps only 'alf a dozen or so 'orses and only one groom. At the Angel they stable six dozen or more of prime cattle," he explained proudly.

Olivia fidgeted with one of the pencils on Fabian's desk. She had known that! She could even have pointed out to

Clem that the Bull and Mouth in St. Martin's-le-Grand had underground stables to accommodate *four hundred* horses, but she merely nodded, encouraging him to continue.

"So I sends Ferdie off to the public room to get us a tankard of barley broth while I takes the 'orses to the stables. An' sure enough, I finds a pebble lodged in one of Sultan's 'ooves. I pried it out with me pocket knife, and then I cast me ogles over t'other 'orses, just 'abit like ye might say, and there's this Arabian, gray with a black sock."

The pencil snapped in half, but Olivia did not notice. "Which leg?" she asked, leaning forward tensely.

"Left foreleg."

She had to take several breaths before she could speak again. "It could be Tony's horse. But you did not see my brother? Did you speak to the ostler or the landlord about him?"

Clem shook his head. "Nay, I didn't see Master Tony. And I didn't want ter scare 'im off if he was 'oled up there by askin' a lot of questions. I thought you and the guvnor would want ter drive out and see the 'orse for yerselves. But now, with 'im laid up an' all, I just dunno what to do."

"You did exactly as you ought," she told him, then rushed over to the window. One look at the glasslike sheen on the cobbles showed her that a drive to Islington would not be possible this day.

"You can take me to the Scarecrow tomorrow as soon as the sun is up to melt the ice," she declared.

Clem opened his mouth to speak, but thought better of it and only bowed his head to hide the worry in his eyes.

"Thank you for telling me about the horse, Clem." Olivia smiled at him, and when he still looked rather unhappy, she added, "You did right in telling me. Lord Worth would have wanted you to. And he'd want you to drive me to Islington. It's imperative that my brother be found soon, don't you see?"

Clem nodded doubtfully, and Olivia sent him off to the servants' hall for his dinner. She remained in the study long enough to steady her foolish heart, which was beating like a hammer in her heaving bosom, and to control her wide smile. It would not do to face Grandmama across the luncheon table all aglow and twittery, not when Fabian lay injured upstairs. She could not tell her grandmother about Tony—not yet. It would be too cruel should it turn out to be a false lead. But deep down inside she *knew* she'd find her brother on the morrow!

Fabian slowly pried his eyes open and squinted at the burning lamp on his bedside table. Dash it! Was he getting careless that he'd not turned down the lamp when he'd gone to bed, or had he been in his cups? More likely the latter; his head felt as though it were stuffed with cotton. Slowly he raised a hand to the most tender part of his head and encountered a thick bandage.

He sat up with a groan as memory returned. A pox on Lionel and on Frederick's strong arm! If only he could think of a way to stop them. Charles had been of no help so far, and Olivia was dreaming up plots even worse than his own.

Olivia! He groaned again, remembering his agony when he'd thought she, too, might have come to harm at Lionel's hands. Why would the dratted girl not behave like a lady and use his coach and take her maid along? Thank goodness he'd had sense enough not to let her know that the footmen and grooms she'd found in his chamber had been awaiting his directions as to where to start the search for her. The ungrateful chit would probably have laughed in his face.

But should he warn her about Lionel's groom? Frederick, he mused, was not exactly the obedient servant to dance to his master's tune. . . .

Deep in thought, Fabian stared at the chink in the curtains which showed a pale sliver of light, the first sign of dawn. He must have slept all of the previous afternoon and the whole night through. No doubt Sir Whitewater, the sly old fox, had conspired with Alders to mix laudanum in the glass of water he'd drunk before retiring. At least he felt better for the long sleep—not even a headache remained, just a tender spot where the club had connected with his skull and the awful padded feeling in his head that was the aftereffect of laudanum.

He tugged the bell cord sharply. Serve Alders right to have his sleep cut short. How dare he quack him! But when the valet came rushing into the bedchamber, his craggy countenance screwed up with anxiety, Fabian only said, "Do you think you could fix me a hearty breakfast? I don't believe I can get up without some sustenance in me. Feel as weak as a kitten, dash it!"

Alders's face lit up at this speech. "Of course, milor'. How about a few slices of sirloin? And would ye be wantin' tea or ale?"

"Tea. But mind you, *no* laudanum it it, Alders."

This earned him a reproachful look. "Ye know I wouldn't 'ave done it, exceptin' Sir Whitewater insisted on it. Said you'd be in a terrible shape if ye didn't sleep at least twelve hours."

He stalked off, and when he returned a scant half hour later with a huge breakfast tray, Alders watched with satisfaction as his lordship made short shrift of the slices of juicy sirloin and drank several cups of tea, a we-know-what's-good-for-you expression on his face.

Finally Fabian leaned back and motioned to the valet to remove the tray. "And now you may shave me," he said with a grin.

Alders almost dropped the tray. Ever since their return from the Peninsula he had tried, in vain, to convince his lordship that shaving him was part of a valet's duties. But it took a knock on the noddle . . .

Shaved, dressed, and with only a small gauze pad covering the cut on his head—after all, the wound had not been very deep but had bled copiously—Fabian made his way downstairs to the library. He was feeling very well considering the circumstances; all he required was a bit of quiet and the opportunity to blow a cloud, a habit he'd picked up in Spain.

Just as he was opening the library door, a slight figure

came sliding around the baize curtain that separated the kitchens and servants' quarters from the main part of the house. Fabian saw the shadowy movement from the corner of his eye and pivoted around, his fists raised in readiness for a fight.

"Eh, guvnor! No 'arm intended!" squealed Clem in dismay.

"What the devil! I'm beginning to see attackers at every corner. What are you doing here, my lad? Nothing amiss in the stables, I hope?"

"The 'orses is in fine fettle, guvnor. Nothing to worrit about. I'd come to see Alders, but seein' as ye are in fine fettle yerself agin, I might as well tell you the lay of the land."

"Well, come into the library then. I've no wish to have the whole household descend upon me, as they very likely will if we stand gabbing in the hall."

"Aye, guvnor." With a broad grin on his urchin's face, Clem followed Fabian into the room. His eyes widened with awe as he took in the book-lined walls, the slim stairway leading to the balconylike upper level from where even the highest placed book could be reached with the help of a short ladder. "Ye never read all of 'em!" he exclaimed.

"No." Fabian laughed. "I'm afraid many of the tomes must wait until I'm too old to do more than sit in a rocking chair and waggle my head. Now, what's amiss, Clem?"

Fabian lit a cigar and made himself comfortable in one of the leather chairs. He waved Clem into another, and, never having felt shy around his lordship, Clem plopped himself down and stretched out his short legs in imitation of the earl's negligent pose.

"It's Miss Olivia, guvnor."

Keen, dark eyes bored into Clem's. "Yes?"

"When Ferdie an' me were in Islington yesterday, we found what we thought was Master Tony's 'orse at the Scarecrow, an' I told Miss Olivia about it on account of yer feelin' queer as Dick's 'atband."

Fabian blew a smoke ring. "And I suppose," he said

slowly, "Miss Olivia wants to drive out to Islington and see the horse for herself, and she told you that I'd want you to drive her."

"Aye, guvnor."

Fabian gazed pensively out the tall windows overlooking the garden at the rear of Worth House. Timid rays of sunshine danced across the last golden blooms of a hardy chrysanthemum and glistened on the cascading waters in the tiny fountain. It promised to be a perfect autumn day, a day made for an outing. *She never did have her drive to Hampton Court,* he mused. A smile spread slowly across Fabian's face until even his eyes lit up with secret thoughts of pleasure.

"When Miss Olivia orders the carriage, harness the grays to my curricle. Just be sure to send me word, Clem. I'll be driving Miss Olivia myself."

Olivia stepped out into the corridor and softly closed the door to her sitting room behind her. After a quick, guilty look in the direction of Fabian's chambers, she tiptoed to the stairway, then picked up her skirts and ran downstairs. Only slightly out of breath, she greeted the hovering Robinson. "Is the carriage ready?"

"Yes, miss," replied the butler, who hurried to open the door for her.

She had taken but two steps down when she was brought up short by the sight of the prancing grays harnessed to Fabian's curricle, and Fabian himself holding the reins.

"What's delaying you?" he called. "Don't you know better than to keep a fresh team waiting?"

Olivia whirled down the last four steps and ran into the street. She accepted his proffered hand and swung herself onto the box. Before she could properly settle herself on the upholstered seat, Fabian flicked the reins and they were off at such a clip that she was flung against him.

"Whoa," she murmured and steadied herself carefully. "What are you doing out of bed? And where is your bandage?" she demanded.

"Under my hat." He grinned, then pointed with the whip handle at her bonnet. "You'd best tie those ribbons again, or your hat will fly off."

Indeed, the rakish bow she'd tied under her left ear was not strong enough to hold the frippery confection on her head, but neither did she want to choke by tightening it. With a pang of regret she removed the wide-brimmed black hat with the dashing white plume and Burgundy silk ribands and placed it on the seat between them. "It is meant to be worn in a *closed* carriage," she pointed out.

"Shall we turn back and take the chaise?"

"No." She presented a laughing face to him. "I doubt you'd let me sit on the box of the chaise to try out your grays."

"You may suffer a disappointment in the curricle as well," he warned. "After all, you planned to go to Islington without me, and I don't appreciate being left out of your schemes."

"Oh," she said in a small voice. "It was only because I thought you'd be too knocked up to go, and . . . and I was worried Tony might slip away again, and . . ." Olivia faltered, searching for words, but when she darted a cautious peek at his face, she saw the devilish lights dancing in his eyes.

"You're bamming me!" she accused.

"I couldn't resist. Forgive me, my love."

Fabian's smile made her heart swell in her breast, and when he passed the reins into her hands and sat back with his arms folded across his chest, she had to blink rapidly to clear her suddenly misty eyes.

He accepted my word that I can handle a four-in-hand! He trusts me with his priceless grays!

For a while they drove in silence, Olivia giving her whole concentration to the horses, feeling the tender mouths of the leaders, while Fabian enjoyed her rapt expression. Then, confident that she had their measure, she sighed blissfully and looked at him with gratitude and admiration mirrored on her face.

"What sweet goers, Fabian! And so beautifully matched! I'll never forget this drive. Thank you!"

"Best keep your eyes on the road, whipster," he replied gruffly. "There's a coach approaching."

The two vehicles passed each other on the narrow lane with an inch and a half to spare. "Well done," he said. "Who taught you?"

"Tony did. He taught me to ride, to fence, and to drive to an inch."

"But not how to shoot," he teased.

A tidal wave of color burned her cheeks, and Fabian had to strain to understand her words. "I didn't do too badly as long as Tony had me aim at wafers, but when he took me out after rabbits . . . simply couldn't stomach it. Don't join a fox hunt either," she added defiantly.

Fabian nodded. "That's all right, love. Oftentimes I, too, contrive to get lost before the kill."

So, he thought, *the intrepid young lady has some very tender spots.* He watched her idly while his mind tried to comprehend her complex personality. She was strong-willed and determined to a fault; too often had she pitted her stubborn mind against him. He knew her to be intelligent and courageous, thoughtful and polite toward the servants, and now he'd learned that she was tenderhearted toward animals. But was she capable of feeling any deeper emotions, or was she shallow and cold like so many of her peers? She obviously loved that rapscallion brother of hers, but that was not quite what he had in mind.

Could she, would she, allow herself to fall in love?

Well, why should she? Love was a futile emotion, a waste of energy. He knew firsthand. Olivia was too forceful to let herself fall in love.

Pity, he thought. *She's a romantic at heart, even if she doesn't know it. Just look at the things she does: masquerading as a man, charging off to rescue her brother. . . .*

The poor child had assumed too many responsibilities at a very tender age, and now she believed herself to be the knight in shining armor who must rush off to assist young men in distress. *He*, apparently, ranked at the top of the list, right next to her brother. How gallantly she'd drawn off the thug that night in the square. But she was playing the *wrong* role in her romantic dreams! What if he could make her realize . . . ?

The curricle rolled to a smooth halt in the courtyard of the Scarecrow. Quickly hiding his momentary confusion, Fabian jumped down and assisted Olivia to the ground after she'd handed the reins to a stable lad.

"Would you care for a cup of tea or a glass of wine?"

"No, thank you, Fabian. I'd rather look at the horse first."

"Of course." He asked the boy to rub down the grays and bait them, then turned back to Olivia with a smile. "For, whatever may occur, they've earned a bit of rest, and we shall certainly require some refreshment after we've talked with the ostler and the landlord."

She was willing to agree to almost anything if only he'd hurry and take her into the stables.

Fabian took her arm and led her across the yard to the low brick building. It was dark inside because all doors but the one through which they'd entered were closed, and before their eyes could adjust to the dim light, a giant of a man barred their way.

"Is there summat ye need?" he growled.

"We'd like to see the Arabian you've stabled here," replied Fabian. But not even his most commanding lift of a black eyebrow impressed the ostler.

"Effen ye need a change of horses, I'll get ye the best I have, but we've none to show nor to sell." He pushed closer and tried to edge the unwelcome visitors back into the yard.

"Bring a lantern!" commanded Olivia, planting herself firmly in his path. Fabian's strong arm around her shoulders was all the reassurance she needed to feel unafraid.

The huge man grumbled but finally retreated to the tack room, and when he emerged again, he was carrrying a smoking oil lamp.

The ostler's astonishment was plain to see as he held the

lamp high, and Olivia, quite accustomed to Tony's ability to charm his way into the most hardened hearts of ostlers and grooms, stepped forward and took the light from his slackened grip.

"I'm Tony Fenshawe's sister," she informed the gaping man. "I know he's in a tight spot, and I've come to help him."

But the ostler was not won over easily. He studied her for agonizing minutes before he finally nodded. "Ye're Miss 'Livia all right. Master Tony told me to let ye take his Lucifer."

"Thunder," she corrected quietly.

A grin spread across the man's face, revealing a wide gap where two upper teeth were missing. "And who might this gent be?" he inquired politely and fixed Fabian with a hard stare. Upon learning the name, his grin widened even more. Not because of Fabian's impressive title—by no means!

"Ye're the nob as Gentlemen Jackson keeps braggin' about! Pleased ter meet ye, my lord. I was used to spar with Mendoza."

The two men shook hands and were soon engrossed in reminiscences of great prize fights and amateur pugilism. Before long, Olivia was heartily bored and walked off with the spluttering oil lump clutched in her hand, leaving them in the darkness to talk of "cross-buttocks" and "levelers" while she inspected the stalls. A soft whinny soon led her to Thunder's side. She put the lamp down and hugged his sleek neck, burying her face in his mane. Thunder held still for a moment only, then turned his head and nipped her smartly in the shoulder.

"All right, all right, you old ruffian! Is it below your dignity to have a mere female shed a few tears on your coat? If that ain't just like a man!"

She hiccoughed in an effort to control her emotions. A large white handkerchief found its way into her hand, and she quickly wiped her eyes before turning to the two men.

"Where is he, Mr. . . . ?"

"Me name's Tuff," muttered the groom. "But I dunno

where Master Tony's gone. He worked here for a sennight, but Mr. Simmons—that be the landlord, miss—he told him he'd earned no more'n what Thunder swallowed up in oats. An' so Master Tony left the horse as . . . as skewerty.''

"Security?" asked Fabian.

Tuff nodded. "An' then he off an' left. To the gamin' dens in Lunnon," he muttered.

Olivia's head reeled. When Fabian's arm stole around her waist, she nestled gratefully against his strong shoulder.

Tony's not here! Only this one thought went round and round in her whirling mind, until she thought she'd drown in the sound.

But as Fabian supported her across the courtyard into the inn, the brisk air helped clear her head, and she was able to sip a dish of tea in Mrs. Simmons's private parlor while Mr. Simmons tried to hoodwink Fabian into paying a king's ransom for Thunder. A haughty stare from under raised black brows soon brought the exorbitant sum down to a figure that covered stabling and feed for the horse more than adequately. Thunder was tied to the curricle, and before long Olivia and Fabian were on their journey home.

She held herself ramrod straight; not a word escaped her compressed lips until they'd reached the mews and Sam unharnessed the grays while Clem took charge of Thunder.

"Clem!" she called after him. "He likes to munch an apple after he's been rubbed down."

They entered Worth House through the back door. All was quiet save for the faint chinking sounds of cutlery and dishes in the servants' hall. Fabian took her pelisse and hung it and his own cloak on hooks behind the narrow door under the stairway.

No thought of retreating to her own suite, or hiding in solitude until she could overcome her disappointment and despair at just having missed Tony yet again, entered her head. Fabian was here to share her anxiety. He would carry some of the heavy load of responsibility that had been her burden alone for so long. Olivia did not even stop to ask herself why she should feel this way. Since her arrival in

London, Fabian had been there during her every moment of need and had provided his aid and support—at times accompanied by a most formidable scolding, but never had he withheld his unstinting assistance.

Olivia's feet led her unhesitatingly into his study, where she sank down on the soft rug before the fireplace and gripped her hands around her knees. Her thin knuckles showed white against the green folds of her merino walking gown, so tightly had she laced her fingers.

"What now?" Her voice sounded toneless, defeated, and she appeared to be addressing the burning logs rather than a person of flesh and blood who might provide an answer.

Fabian settled himself close beside her, one booted foot propped against the hearth and his back supported by the heavy chair behind his desk. He picked up her cold hands and gently pried the tightly clasped fingers apart. Holding them between his own warm hands, he chafed them until Olivia raised her face to his.

His throat tightened when he saw how pale and pinched she looked and how her wide, anxious eyes devoured his own for a glimpse of encouragement. He leaned closer and held her hands against his cheek.

"I won't lie to you, Olivia," he said, hiding his anger at his own inability to work miracles behind a deliberately calm and cool voice. "Our chances of finding Tony now are rather bleak. There are probably four times as many gambling dens in London as there are livery stables, and most of them can only be visited during the night hours."

Olivia looked even more dispirited than before, the corners of her mouth drooping sadly. It was so unlike her to be discouraged that he shook her gently. "Ho! Don't give up yet, Olivia! Charles and I will start the search right after dinner. I think we can save ourselves a visit to the better known clubs such as Watier's, Brooks's, or The Cocoa Tree, etc., where the stakes are beyond Tony's means. Alders, Clem, and Charles's man can also visit some of the less reputable places in—"

"Couldn't I help?" she interrupted urgently, with a spark of interest flashing in her eyes.

Fabian shook his head. No matter how relieved he felt at seeing a return of her liveliness, he'd not have her exposed to such unsavory establishments. He pressed first one, then the other of her hands to his lips, and had the satisfaction of watching a faint blush tint her cheeks. Better and better. She looked almost like herself again.

Suddenly nothing was more desirable than to hold Olivia in his arms and to keep her there, safe and protected and cherished. He could almost taste the sweetness of her lips, feel the soft, pliant body melt against his—

Olivia's heart thudded against her ribs, and her breath came fast and shallow. She tried to pull her hands from his grasp, but he did not let go, and she dared not remove them forcibly.

Fabian's eyes caressed her with compassion and some stronger emotion she feared to identify. His deep voice was like a cloak, enfolding her intimately, quite at variance with the subject matter they were discussing.

He murmured, "I can send some of the footmen to check out the cock pits. For a small bet on the right bird, amazing sums can be won in the course of a few hours."

"No. Cockfighting is one sport Tony will not tolerate."

"I'm glad to hear that he shows some sense occasionally."

Her chest rose and fell rapidly in rhythm with the pounding blood in her ears. Fabian had come so close, or had she moved closer to him? His eyes asked a question, and her lips parted to answer. But it was not necessary to speak. As his mouth claimed hers, she knew that no matter what might happen, she would always love him. His look brought her alive, his touch sent the blood racing in her veins, his kiss drowned her in a whirlpool of sensations she'd never before experienced.

He released her hands, not to let go of her but to pull her closer against him, to set her whole back atingle with his touch. His fingertips aroused shivers of delight as he caressed the nape of her neck, and his lips burned a trail of fire from her mouth to her earlobes, and to her throat, where the small pulsing hollow was exposed by the modest décolletage of her gown.

Carefully Fabian shifted his weight and moved her to lie down on the soft rug. Since she'd clasped her hands around his neck, it was not surprising that he followed suit and lay down beside her. Their lips met again, and her body arched against his in response to his demanding hands. Olivia delighted in running her fingers through his dark hair until the coarse material of the bandage made her gasp.

"Does it hurt?" she whispered against his mouth.

In reply he tightened his hold and sealed her lips with his own. She felt the muscles of his neck and back strain against her palms, and craved closer contact yet. Timidly she slipped her hands under his coat to feel his heartbeat's rapid drumming.

Fabian sighed. Slowly, reluctantly, he pulled away until only their eyes maintained the intimate contact their bodies had shared. But it was not enough. Despite the warmth of the fire, a chill breath of air brushed against her skin.

It was over. She felt hollow and deprived.

"Don't look like that, my love," Fabian murmured and brushed an errant lock of hair off her temple. His charcoal eyes gleamed, and he bent over to nibble her earlobe, then whispered, "Don't you realize that we *must* stop? Unless you wish that I seduce you right here, prey to the curious eyes of anyone who might enter the study."

Hastily Olivia scrambled to her knees, ran her fingers through her disheveled curls, then stood up and tugged at her bodice and skirt. "Of course I don't wish *that*," she said gruffly.

Fabian chuckled softly and got up unhurriedly to help her straighten her sleeves. Olivia darted an incredulous glance at him, then hastily lowered her lashes to hide her confusion and dismay. Fabian was laughing at her! There was no mistaking the glint of his eyes or the quiver of his lips, however quickly he suppressed them.

"What is it you *don't* wish, my sweet delight?" he asked. "Being seduced or getting caught at being seduced?"

Her face flamed with shame and anger even while her eyes smarted from the pain his jesting voice inflicted. How *dare* he destroy the most beautiful and exciting moment of her life! How *could* he regard it merely as a funny little interlude they'd shared like a . . . like a silly joke!

She pushed out her chin and regarded him belligerently. "You misunderstood, Worth. I *don't wish* that you ever touch me again!"

He sobered instantly. With hands outstretched he took a step toward her. "Olivia," he pleaded. "I didn't mean to upset you—"

But her composure and dignity deserted her at last. She could bear no more, not even an apology—especially not an apology for the kisses! She whirled about and fled the study, slamming the door behind her.

Fabian took one step after her, then halted. He stared at his hands. The feel of her soft, warm body was still alive in them. But they were empty now. He pushed them into his coat pockets and paced restlessly. Going after Olivia would be futile. Under all that coldness she'd been hurt . . . and angry. Her smoldering eyes had given her away.

"Damnation!" he muttered. Something had gone wrong. He could have sworn she'd enjoyed their embrace as much as he—in fact, she'd been disappointed when he'd pulled away.

He stopped in his tracks. What a bloody fool he'd been! Olivia had responded to his embrace so naturally and generously that he'd forgotten what an innocent she was—despite her "advanced" two-and-twenty years. She'd not taken him seriously when he'd warned they *must* stop, and then she'd misunderstood when he'd tried to make light of the situation with that cursed jest about seducing her.

Shaking his head at his blunder, he walked to the window and rested his head against the cool glass pane. He should have first assured her of—

Of what? His mind went blank, then his thoughts tumbled so fast he could barely keep up with them.

He loved the chit! He should have assured her of his love!

It was nothing like the calf's love he'd experienced for Melissa, but a deep and burning desire to spend the rest of his life with Olivia. Olivia was charming and exasperating, lovable and maddening. She was soft femininity and unyielding perseverance; she was all he'd ever want in his wife.

But how could he go to her now and ask her to marry him when any moment he might be attacked again? If they married before he could resolve his problem, and should there be a child, he'd only place Olivia and the babe in danger as well.

No. He could not ask Olivia to be his wife . . . yet. But he *could* try to make her see that he loved her.

___ C H A P T E R 1 1 ___

Olivia had spent several hours fretting and worrying. She had berated herself for allowing Fabian to kiss her, and most of all, for enjoying his advances and returning his kisses. She'd also lectured herself sternly for taking his lovemaking as a sign of deep affection when so obviously it had been no more than a whim. And, finally, she'd even questioned her own judgment. Could she possibly have misunderstood? Had he not been poking fun at her?

When the dressing bell sent Lizzy hurrying into her room, Olivia had just decided to act toward Fabian as if nothing at all untoward had happened. If Fabian had behaved as shoddily as she had feared, at least he should not know how much he'd hurt her. And if she'd misunderstood, why, then her neutral manner would provide him an opportunity to make the explanation he'd started when she'd run from the study.

But when she entered the salon and found Fabian already there, she could not help but feel relieved that Lady Worth and her grandmother were also present. Her hand trembled when Fabian handed her a glass of sherry and their fingers touched briefly.

"You look lovely, my dear," he complimented her. "The gold of your gown reflects in your eyes and dances on the tips of your hair."

"Thank you. You're very kind," she murmured and moved away to take a seat beside her grandmother.

The old lady darted a keen look at her. "Kind!" she said with a snort. "What mealymouthed platitudes one has to bear from your generation. You should have rapped his knuckles and nudged him on to be more extravagant in his compliments. There's no spirit in you, child."

"Or you could have flirted with him over your fan, like so," suggested Lady Worth, spreading her silk fan with the pretty ivory sticks open and fluttering it delicately before her face so that only her twinkling blue eyes were visible.

Olivia chuckled. "Alas, I do not carry a fan, and only imagine! Had I rapped Fabian's knuckles, he might have spilled sherry all over my new gown."

"Fiddlesticks!" exclaimed Lady Fenshawe. "In my day only a lady would spill on another's gown; it rid one of an undesirable rival, don't you see? You have a lot to learn yet, Olivia, if you don't know that trick."

"I realize it, Grandmama." Olivia slumped dejectedly. She traced the marquetry work on the arm of her chair first with one fingertip, then with another. Would Fabian attempt to speak to her privately about what had happened in the study? Why was he just standing there by the fire instead of trying to catch her attention? Mayhap she should make the first move—mayhap look at him?

When she raised her eyes, it was to find not only Fabian,

but also the dowager and her grandmother looking at her curiously. Before Olivia could apologize for woolgathering, Robinson entered and announced Lord Charles Baxter.

"Charles, my dear boy!" squealed Lady Worth. "Oh, how dashing you look! Why haven't I seen you lately, you rogue?"

Her bright smile and sparkling eyes left no doubt that the unexpected visitor was extremely welcome to the dowager countess. She introduced him to Lady Fenshawe with all the pride of a mother in a son. "Charles has run tame in my house since Fabian brought him home from Eton once to spend the Easter holidays with us. He is the dearest boy, and if I weren't so selfish to want Olivia for Fabian, I'd be playing matchmaker between her and Charles."

"My dear Lady Worth—" Lord Charles bowed gracefully over her hand. "If Emily give me the congé, you may come to rue your words, for I'd be strongly tempted to court Olivia myself. But pray allow me to apologize for bursting in on you. I won't stay a minute, but, you see, my man tracked me down at the Carringtons' with an urgent message from Fabian. And since I had to pass here on my way to White's, I just popped in to see him."

"I don't know what urgent business my son may have with you, Charles, but surely it can wait until after dinner. You'll stay, of course. I'd be surprised if Robinson had not set another place yet." The dowager frowned, then asked as bitingly as her gentle voice permitted, "That Carrington woman did not see fit to ask you to dine, I suppose?... No? Poor Emily. It's about time she was removed from that woman's clutches. Have you set a date yet, Charles?"

"Come, Mama." Fabian propelled himself off the mantel and strode over to grip his friend's hand in a hearty shake. "Don't put Charles to the blush. Mrs. Carrington may be his mama-in-law one of these days, and after all, she's an invalid; that should account for some of her crotchets."

"There's nothing wrong with Louisa Carrington that a bit of exercise wouldn't cure," said the dowager tartly. "I have it from Sir Whitewater himself."

Lord Charles grinned. "So that's why Mrs. Carrington calls him a quack."

"Who's a quack?" asked Lionel Worthing in his bored, nasal voice from the doorway. "Fabian, I heard you were injured yesterday. Should you be up and about?"

Olivia's hands clenched. A pox on Lionel! The dratted man had a nasty habit of dropping by when he was wanted the least—and unannounced!

"Where did you hear that bit of news, Lionel?" asked Fabian sharply.

Lionel gave a start, then mumbled, "Can't see what difference it makes. Could have been Roxbury, or even Petersham." He minced toward his aunt and bowed deeply over her outstretched hand. "My dearest Aunt Alicia. What a very fetching gown. I wish I could persuade Mama to leave off the puces and browns and wear a confection like this delightful, mauve crepe. You look charming."

"Why, thank you, Lionel. You look quite . . . stunning yourself." Lady Worth's dazzled eyes moved cautiously from his silver and chartreuse striped vest to his cypress-green coat and jade-colored knit pantaloons.

Lady Fenshawe, who'd been studying the exquisite through her lorgnette, suddenly demanded sharply, "Should you be up and about yourself, young man? Looks like someone blackened your eye for you."

And now that it had been pointed out, everyone noticed the dark bruises around Lionel's eyes and on his jaw, insufficiently hidden under a thick layer of face powder.

"What happened to you?" asked Fabian.

Lionel dabbed his forehead with his scented, lace-edged handkerchief. "'Twas nothing!" he said gruffly. "Just some footpads who believed I ought to carry more money than they found on me."

"Careful, Worthing," warned Lord Charles. "Your face is turning green, and it's a shade that clashes with your outfit."

Lionel pivoted around. "Are you calling me a liar, Baxter?"

he sputtered and advanced with raised fists toward Lord Charles.

Quickly Fabian stepped between the two men, but this precaution proved unnecessary, for Lady Fenshawe clapped her hands imperiously, startling Lionel. He dropped his arms to his sides and turned to look at the stern old lady sheepishly.

"That, young man, was not to applaud your manners," said Lady Fenshawe bitingly. "I do not care two raps how you came by your bruises, or whom you fight—so long as it's not in my presence. I, for one, am devilishly sharp-set and I wish to eat my dinner *now*, but I don't wish to do so in the company of belligerent, overgrown schoolboys who yap and snarl at each other like puppies."

There was a moment of stunned silence, then Fabian and Charles caught each other's eye and burst into booming laughter. Charles was the first to recover. "What a splendid set-down, ma'am! And I do beg your pardon for needling Mr. Worthing in front of you ladies." His bow gracefully included Lady Worth and Olivia in the apology.

"Oh, all right. I apologize also," said Lionel. "And speaking of dinner, Aunt Alicia, I've come to beg your hospitality. I . . . ah . . . had to . . . to dismiss my cook, and my valet just don't seem capable of helping out until I can employ a new one."

"Of course, Lionel. You are welcome here anytime." If Lady Worth did not speak her invitation quite as heartily as she'd done when she'd asked Lord Charles to stay, she smiled nevertheless very kindly and asked Lionel to lead her in to dinner.

Olivia had been quite as hungry as her grandmother, but when she found herself seated next to Lionel, her appetite diminished along with the hope of being able to participate in congenial conversation during the meal. Only Fabian's presence at the head of the table to her right aided her in quashing the most cowardly wish to excuse herself from dinner with a headache.

"Olivia!" Fabian's voice startled her. Really! What atrocious manners. Fabian ought to be conversing with Grandmama on his right first.

"Ask Lionel how he came by his bruises," demanded Fabian.

She blinked. Much did she care! But obligingly she turned to Lionel and said, "Fabian wants to know who planted you a facer."

Lionel dropped his soup spoon and blazed angrily first at Olivia, then at Fabian. "Told you, I was set upon by footpads," he spat at his cousin. "Why do you keep harping on it? Anybody can be set upon!"

"Oh, yes," agreed Fabian. "I know that to my detriment. But I was wondering if one of your . . . uh . . . footpads could have been—" Fabian broke off to allow the removal of the soup plates and the serving of the next course. "I wondered if he could have been Frederick," he said when the servants had withdrawn to the sideboard.

"No!" Lionel's voice was sharp—too sharp. He took a bite of the lamb cutlet on his plate and chewed thoroughly, then washed it down with a generous amount of wine.

"I don't know why you should always want to speak of Frederick," he complained. "After all, he's my groom, and I can find no pleasure in talking about him."

"I thought I recognized Frederick yesterday when I was knocked down," explained Fabian. "I just wondered if he had decided that robbery brings more rewards than currying horses."

Lionel snickered. "He'd have known that *my* pockets are to let—haven't paid his wages for months! He'd have waited for a plumper pigeon to pluck."

Olivia laid down her fork and pushed her chair out from the table. Every time Lionel and Fabian addressed each other, she felt obliged to stop eating and lean back in her chair; so she might as well give up eating altogether as long as these two bumpkins insisted on talking across her.

Fabian raised his glass and drank deeply, studying Lionel over the rim of his goblet. "He might have had . . ." he said and carefully replaced his glass on the white damask cloth,

"... a different motivation for attacking you, like your ... inability to bring about a change in your fortune?"

Olivia heard Lionel's sharply indrawn breath and watched him curiously. He had turned very pale under the layer of powder, his bruises standing out starkly, but he ignored Fabian's words and directed his full attention to his food. Now why should Fabian suspect this Frederick of having hit Lionel? After all, if the groom resented that his employer had no fortune, he could leave and take up a post with a nabob. Besides, Lionel would see anyone who dared raise a hand against him in Newgate, wouldn't he?

"And," continued Fabian, "I am asking myself if it was Frederick who told you about my injury yesterday. Neither Roxbury nor Petersham knew about it. In fact, none but the family, Charles, and Bramson knew—not counting my assailants, of course. What say you, coz? Why would Frederick boast to you that he'd attacked me?"

Lionel did not appear to have heard him; he was busy dabbing his moist brow.

Fabian shrugged and turned to Olivia. "You are not eating, my love. Are you not hungry? You really should try the cutlets and some beans, or would you rather have a slice of the roast suckling pig?"

She smiled sweetly. "Are you quite certain that you and Lionel have finished talking across me?" she said. "In that case I shall venture a bite of everything before this course is removed."

The meal dragged on interminably—or so it appeared to Olivia, who worried lest Fabian feel obliged to linger over the port with Charles and Lionel instead of going out to search for Tony. But she need not have fretted. Immediately after the covers were removed, and fruit and nuts had been placed on the table, Fabian pushed back his chair.

"I apologize, Mama, Lady Fenshawe, for rushing off and taking Charles with me. Alas, we have a pressing engagement, and no matter how boring, we are obliged to keep it." He bowed, then took Olivia's hand and kissed it lingeringly.

"My love," he said, "I hate having to leave you, but I promise I'll speak with you first thing in the morning."

She nodded, resolving to wait up for him, no matter how late he'd come in; she'd not be able to wait until morning to hear if he'd found Tony. Besides, she must give Fabian an opportunity to speak of that other matter . . . must let him explain why he'd laughed at her after kissing her.

When Fabian and Lord Charles had left, Lady Worth gave up pretending to enjoy her peach, and rose to lead the ladies from the dining room. "You may bring your port to the salon, Lionel," she said graciously, "unless you prefer to sit by yourself."

Lionel rushed to open the door for the ladies. "Dearest Aunt Alicia. Always so thoughtful. But I must be off as well. If I might just be permitted to have a word with Miss Fenshawe?"

"Of course, dear." The dowager smiled. "There can be no harm in that. It is time you got to know each other better—*Miss Fenshawe,* indeed. Such formality, Lionel!"

When they'd reached the first-floor landing, Lady Worth took Olivia aside. "You and Lionel may have the salon to yourselves, child. I shall invite your grandmama to my sitting room, and you may join us later for tea."

"Thank you, ma'am."

Olivia preceded Lionel into the salon and seated herself primly in one of the upholstered Queen Anne chairs. "Sit down, Mr. Worthing," she invited, agog with curiosity as to why he should have singled her out.

"I won't keep you long, Miss Fenshawe." Tenderly Lionel eased the cloth of his skintight pantaloons off his knees as he sat down and crossed his legs. "But first, my dear Miss Fenshawe, will you not consider my aunt's very just words and give me leave to call you Olivia?"

"Oh, by all means." *Anything* to get him to the point and be rid of him! "Why did you wish to speak with me?"

All of a sudden Lionel looked ghastly again, pale with droplets of sweat glistening on his forehead and his bruises sharply pronounced. But any compassion she might have felt for him was dispelled the instant he opened his mouth and addressed her in his old, derisive sneer.

"Why, to appeal to your better nature, my dear Olivia. If you have one, that is! Have you but considered the harm you are doing Fabian by linking your name to his? Have you forgotten your brother's part in the faro game seven years ago?"

"But what did Richard do?" she asked, puzzled.

"He cheated!"

"No!"

Lionel rose and leveled his quizzing glass at her—a new one on a black silk riband. "Indeed he did, and is therefore banned from all the clubs. *Fenshawe*, my dear, is a tainted name." He made her an exaggerated bow, sinking far back on his bent left leg, then straightened and stalked off, whistling softly to himself.

Olivia listened to the sound until, no matter how much she strained, she could hear no more. Lionel whistling? She wouldn't have believed it possible from that . . . that tulip. He sounded pleased.

But then, however hard she tried to keep her mind on Lionel, other, more painful thoughts forced their way to the foreground. Richard a cheat! A Fenshawe blackballed from the London clubs!

Olivia catapulted off her chair to run to Grandmama, to demand that she deny this outrageous accusation, then sank back again, burying her head in her hands. What if it was true but Grandmama did not know about it? She must speak with Fabian first . . . but how *could* she without being overcome by mortification?

Suddenly Olivia remembered Lady Wanderley's words, how the old lady had tried to tell her that Richard had not spoken the truth about the faro game. And Lady Wanderley had asked her to visit some morning.

Slowly Olivia made her way to Lady Worth's sitting room. Like a puppet she drank tea and responded to whatever remarks were addressed to her by the two ladies, but her mind was busy trying to piece together the puzzle of the faro game—innuendos from Lady Wanderley, a short reference by Charles; nothing made sense, however. Olivia bade the ladies a good night early and escaped to her rooms.

She paced restlessly, on the alert for Fabian's return, but when the watchman in the square called out the first hour of the new day, she crawled into bed. There was no point in waiting up for Fabian. She could not now face him with any of her questions, not about Tony or Richard, nor about his kisses. First she must speak with Lady Wanderley. Yes, that was what she must do.

It was not quite eight o'clock when Olivia stepped out into the crystal-clear morning. A cool breeze ruffled her short curls, and she pulled her shawl closer around her shoulders as she sped toward Mount Street.

All around her the square was alive with persons she'd never encountered before. Scullery maids were busy scrubbing the front steps of the elegant houses; an ale porter ambled alongside a dairy maid carrying pitchers of frothy milk from Green Park while a chimney sweep hurried his band of small helpers across the square; the scent of fresh-baked loaves and buns in the bakery lad's baskets mingled with that of the herb woman's sweet-smelling load, teasing Olivia's nose; and the shrill cries of vendors pushing their rattling carts assailed her ears.

When Olivia climbed the stairs to Lady Wanderley's intricately carved front door, she hesitated, slowing her steps until she hardly moved at all. It did not seem right to appeal to a stranger for information about one's own family—but where else could she go for answers? And then, just as she'd released the big brass knocker to ring against the highly polished plate, a warm flood of color rushed into her cheeks. What if Lady Wanderley was still abed? Lady Wanderley had said to come early, but not every old lady rose at six or seven like Grandmama.

The door opened without delay, however, and a young maid in frilly white mobcap and dainty apron invited her to step inside. "My lady asked to show ye right into the small drawing room. She's seen ye come down the street and ordered fresh coffee, miss.''

''Thank you.''

The maid led Olivia past two of the suits of armor cluttering the huge, marble-floored hall and opened the first door to the left. Rather bemused by her warm reception, Olivia stepped inside and was greeted immediately by Lady Wanderley's loud voice.

''Come, child. Sit down across from me so I can see you. I'm quite proficient at lipreading, and you won't need to shout to speak to me.''

Olivia seated herself in one of the Burgundy plush chairs and smiled at her hostess. ''No wonder I couldn't surprise you with my visit. From this lovely bay window you can spy on everyone traveling in Mount Street.'' She peeked through the lacy curtains, which allowed a good view of all the comings and goings in the street, yet provided privacy to those inside the drawing room.

The old lady nodded vigorously and with a wicked gleam in her pale eyes told Olivia, ''I sit here most mornings—very intriguing. I've had occasion to watch certain ladies and gentlemen slip out of houses where—But that's neither here nor there.''

Lady Wanderley waved away the maid who'd carried in another cup and saucer and a fresh pot of coffee. ''Will you pour, Olivia? The sooner we are private the sooner I can tell you what you want to know.''

Olivia busied herself with the coffeepot and then cream and sugar. Lady Wanderley was sharp; apparently she did not expect to spend time on pleasantries before answering Olivia's questions. ''If you don't mind, ma'am,'' said Olivia hesitantly, ''I should like to hear about that faro game.''

''I'm surprised you waited so long before coming to see me. But then, all you young things are so busy flitting from one ball or rout to the next, it's a marvel you still have a head on your shoulders.''

Olivia smiled politely. Other young ladies might be flitting from ball to ball, but *she* was tumbling from one scrape into the next. "Lady Wanderley, how did you learn about the game?" she asked, trying to steer her hostess back to the main point of her visit.

"Castlereagh told me. You see, when he was much younger he was a protégé of my husband, and he's never forgotten our support. Castlereagh still visits me at least once a fortnight although my dear husband's been dead these past five years."

Lady Wanderley stared blindly at her cup, then shook off the memories of years past and told Olivia, "Castlereagh was there, you see. And it had upset him terribly to witness cheating at Brooks's, and then to have Sir Richard try and pin the blame on Worth! I tell you, my dear, Castlereagh don't like Worth above half—politics, you know—but he said Worth had handled an explosive situation like a born diplomat."

She looked at Olivia and exclaimed, "Here, child! Drink some coffee. You're not going to faint, are you? You're as white as a sheet!"

"I'm all right, ma'am," Olivia whispered as she reached for her cup. The warmth of the drink revived her. She felt the blood return to her head, and the annoying buzz in her ears diminished. "I'm sorry, Lady Wanderley. I suppose I'd hoped to hear it denied that Richard cheated."

"I shouldn't have sprung it on you so suddenly," apologized Lady Wanderley gruffly. She heaved herself out of her deep chair and walked stiffly to a small, carved cabinet on the opposite side of the room. Using both hands, she poured cordial from a heavy crystal decanter into two delicate Waterford glasses.

Olivia rose hastily and joined Lady Wanderley at the credenza. "I'm sorry, ma'am. I should have offered sooner to help you. Please let me carry the glasses for you."

Lady Wanderley chuckled. "Just a touch of arthritis, my dear. A bit of movement does me good, else my joints will soon be creaking louder than Prinny's corsets."

When they'd resumed their seats and sipped some of the

cordial, Olivia asked without looking at her hostess, "Was Richard drunk, ma'am?"

Lady Wanderley snorted. "He'd have to have been drunk to do what he did! Else he was a bloody fool."

A fool Richard was not. But Olivia remembered him—before their parents had died—as a vain, reckless young man who'd constantly demanded money from their father, and the instant he'd received the necessary "blunt," he'd gone off to London again to reappear only when it was spent.

"Olivia—" Lady Wanderley's rasping voice cut into Olivia's thoughts. "I strongly recommend that you get all the particulars from Worth. After all, he was there, while I was not. Castlereagh did not tell me much because he recalled all too soon that this was not for 'a lady's ears.' Ha! I've heard much worse in my time, but I never was one for gabbing, and that's why he mentioned it to me at all. You see, Worth didn't want it bruited about. He'd been rather well acquainted with your papa, and he knew there were younger siblings dependent on Sir Richard. Your parents died just a year prior to the incident, I believe?"

Olivia nodded and raised wide eyes to Lady Wanderley. "Then no one but the gentlemen at Brooks's know about this? You believe Fabian scotched the scandal to protect Tony and me?"

"Yes. And possibly averted a duel as well."

Olivia paled. Taking a deep breath, she rose from her chair, willing her knees not to tremble. "I must go home now. Thank you for telling me, Lady Wanderley."

"I wish I could have had better news for you, child. But you are young; you'll find out that there are worse disasters than having a brother who cheated. Give Alicia my regards, will you? And ask her to bring your grandmother for a visit. Last time I saw your grandmama was at the Misses Praygood's Academy for Young Ladies."

Momentarily diverted, Olivia smiled and exclaimed, "You and Grandmama at school together? My heart bleeds for the

Misses Praygood. But how did you know Grandmama was in town?''

Lady Wanderley cackled with glee. "I wish I could claim omniscience, child. But it's nothing more miraculous than that my maid—Susan, who opened the door for you—is walking out with one of Worth's footmen. Jenkins, that's his name.''

"I will give Lady Worth your message, ma'am.'' Olivia flung her shawl around her shoulders and bent to kiss Lady Wanderley's proffered cheek. "Thank you for setting me straight on that faro game.''

"Good-bye, Olivia.'' Lady Wanderley patted Olivia's hand bracingly. "Do speak to Worth, but I would not mention this to you grandmother if I were you. I doubt that she knows anything about it.''

Thank goodness I did not rush to Grandmama last night, reflected Olivia as she slowly traced her steps back to Worth House. She slipped inside just as the dowager countess and her grandmother came down the stairs.

"Gracious, child!'' Lady Worth gathered the folds of her pale lavender morning gown and rushed down the last few steps. "Don't say you've been walking again—and without a bonnet or gloves! You'll develop chilblains if you don't take care!'' The dowager kissed Olivia fondly, then stepped back and shook her head over the windblown curls and pink cheeks.

Olivia laughed. "It is a lovely morning, with not a bit of a nip in the air. I enjoyed my walk heartily, and you, dear Lady Worth, will be pleased to hear that I'm the bearer of a message from Lady Wanderley.''

"You don't mean Honoria Wanderley née Standish!'' exclaimed her grandmother, who'd stopped on the stairs to regard her granddaughter through her lorgnette. "We attended school together.''

"Yes, indeed, Grandmama.'' Olivia gave a little sigh of relief that her grandmother had been successfully distracted. For a moment it had looked as if Lady Fenshawe were getting ready to demand an explanation for Olivia's early morning walk.

"Hmm," muttered Lady Fenshawe. "Haven't clapped eyes on Honoria these past—well, never mind how long! How does she go on, Olivia, and what does she say?"

"She invited you and Lady Worth for a visit, Grandmama."

"I daresay I could make time to see her."

"Excellent!" Lady Worth beamed happily. "Lady Wanderley is a very special friend of mine. We shall call on her this afternoon, and you can renew your acquaintance at leisure, ma'am."

"It might be rather entertaining, and then again it might not." Lady Fenshawe shook her head doubtfully. "It's often a shock to see one's school friends turned into old harridans—like looking into a mirror." Stiffly she negotiated the last two steps and turned toward the breakfast parlor. "Will you join us for breakfast, Olivia?"

"No, thank you." Olivia's hand disappeared in the folds of her cambric morning gown, successfully shielding her crossed fingers. "I have already eaten, Grandmama."

When the door had closed behind the two ladies, Olivia walked toward the study, her steps dragging and the cowardly part of her mind warning her not to confront Fabian yet.

Rubbish! countered her common sense. *Better now than later when you've drummed up excuses for Richard's behavior and won't listen to Fabian's account any longer.*

With her fingers curled preparatory to knocking, Olivia hesitated yet again. Her hand fell to her side. No, she could not face Fabian. Turning her back on the study, she proceeded down the hall to the library, where she would be able to sit and hide behind a book—and sort out her confused mind.

She hastened her steps to avoid being caught by Fabian, who might at any moment leave his study to go riding or whatever, and whisked into the library, pushing the door shut behind her. Weak with relief, she leaned her shoulders against the solid oaken panel—and looked straight into Fabian's amused eyes.

"Oh," she said helplessly.

"What flattery, my love." Fabian laid down his book and rose from the deep leather chair, and since she appeared unable or unwilling to move, or to elaborate on the one syllable she'd uttered, he guided her to another chair and pressed her gently into it. The amusement faded from his eyes and changed into puzzlement.

"Does the smoke bother you, my dear?" he asked and pointed toward the table where one of the cheroots lay glimmering in an ashtray.

Olivia blinked. As though the tiny movement of her eyelids had broken a spell, she squared her shoulders and said briskly, "Not at all, Fabian. I only hope I'm not intruding."

"Not at all, Olivia." he grinned and sat down, crossing his long legs. "What an unexpected pleasure, my love."

"I daresay it's not altogether unexpected, Fabian. You did say last night you'd speak to me today, did you not? And I'm extremely pleased to find you here, because . . . because I was looking for you!" Might as well get it over with, she decided with bravado.

"Any particular reason?"

"Well . . . yes. But perhaps you'd best tell me about last night first," she suggested.

Fabian made a moue of distaste. "Nothing to tell. I wish I need not even think about it, but I know you're anxious to hear about our exploration. We visited at least two dozen gaming hells—and hell is too mild a description for some of those places. Charles and I even split up part of the night to cover more ground, but found absolutely no trace of Tony. Jenkins, Alders, and Charles's man Bertie had also been out; same result, or rather *no* result."

"Does that mean we won't find Tony?" Her voice rose high in her distress, and she swallowed hard to regain control. "Did you check them all, Fabian?"

"All those that were known to us. Undoubtedly there are many more, but we must have someone to guide us in our search of the lesser-known hells. For instance, I've not ventured into Southwark yet or Seven Dials."

"I've heard of those places," she whispered. "Dangerous slums both of them." Olivia looked up, fear darkening her eyes.

"Tony will be all right," he said gruffly.

She didn't want to say it, didn't want to give him the smallest sign how much she cared about *him*, but she couldn't help herself. "Be careful, Fabian! And for goodness' sake, don't go alone!"

Something leaped in his eyes, a brief flame quickly extinguished. He picked up the cigar, puffed, and blew a perfect smoke ring. "Don't fret," he said, speaking in the offhand manner of one brushing away unsolicited concern. He didn't dare respond as his heart dictated—not until Lionel had been taken care of. He must not risk another misunderstanding. "Now, why were you looking for me, Olivia?"

Nettled, she replied, "I wish to know how Richard cheated you seven years ago!"

Carefully he put out his cigar. "Who told you?"

"Lionel and Lady Wanderley."

"Meddling busybodies both of them. What else did they say?"

"Lady Wanderley hinted at a duel, but she said I should apply to you for a full account of the . . . of the incident."

"Most proper. But I wish she'd stopped to think before she decided to meddle. She shouldn't have told you any of this. It was for Richard or me to decide what you need to know, but since you've learned this much already . . ."

For a moment he stared at his boots, his forehead puckered in a deep frown. "There really is *nothing* to tell," he said finally. "Richard was caught cheating, his membership at Brooks's was revoked, and the other clubs followed suit."

"But where does the duel come in, and how could Richard have tried to pin the blame for cheating on you? I don't know much about faro, but—"

"That was mere bluster!" interrupted Fabian. "He knew well that it was a foolish accusation to make."

"Were you holding the bank?"

"Would that I had!" Fabian rose and strode over to the fireplace to stand in his favorite stance, one booted foot propped on the fender and an elbow on the mantel.

"From what I learned—and you must know that Charles and I did not enter Brooks's until past midnight—Richard had won a vast amount at piquet and had been on the point of leaving the club when Lord Bigsby had to give up the faro bank on account of a commitment to take his fiancée to Almack's."

Fabian glanced at Olivia, who sat white-faced and tense on the edge of her chair, and administered a violent kick to one of the burning logs. What damnable business having to tell his love of her brother's folly and infamy.

"Go on," said Olivia quietly, clasping her hands tighter in her lap.

"Instead of taking his winnings home, your fool brother took over the bank from Bigsby," said Fabian savagely. Frowning, he stared into the leaping flames, then continued in an expressionless voice. "Play was deep and had been going for about an hour, with Richard steadily increasing his winnings, when I entered with Charles."

The men around the faro table had greeted Fabian and Charles cordially. Sir Richard Fenshawe had looked up from his cards. "Care to join in the game?" he called.

Charles shrugged. "Why not," he said, then indicated with a grin the large semicircular indentation at the faro table. "You may have Fox's seat, my dear Fabian. Not that you have the girth to require seating there, but I cannot oblige. I'd feel like I'm sitting in the stocks and wouldn't remember my bets were I to take that chair."

A chuckle went around the table, then young Roxbury got up. "Here, Worth, take my place. The play's getting too deep for me. I shall watch and enjoy the cognac for a change."

"Are we here to exchange pleasantries, gentlemen?" asked Sir Richard with a sneer. "Or are we to play?"

"If you were in our shoes, you wouldn't be in such a

hurry either, Fenshawe," said Lord Castlereagh. "But you have the devil's own luck tonight."

Play was resumed, and except for the chinking of coins as the bets were placed on the green baize, heavy silence lay about the faro table. After about an hour it became painfully obvious that Sir Richard's luck had turned in Fabian's favor. The gaming gentlemen eyed each other and the fast-diminishing pile of gold coins at Sir Richard's elbow warily.

But Sir Richard made no move to give up the bank. "Gentlemen! You will accept my vouchers, I presume," he said peremptorily.

"Perhaps you'd care to relinquish the bank," suggested Fabian.

Sir Richard looked up with a sneer. "To you, no doubt? Damn you, Worth! The bank's supposed to win. And until you joined, the game was going very well, indeed. I'm not about to give up now. Place your bets, gentlemen!"

"May I suggest, Fenshawe," drawled Lord Petersham, "that you write me a voucher for ten thousand yellow Georges. Be simpler than having to write a new voucher each time you must pay off to one or t'other of us."

"I have no intention of paying out much more—my luck *must* change soon. But I'll write a voucher to Worth and take his thirty thousand," snarled Sir Richard.

Fabian looked at the florid-faced young man through narrowed eyes. Drunk, no doubt, and possessed of the gaming fever. Fabian was tempted to get up and leave, but that'd be tantamount to a cut direct, and undoubtedly would inspire the belligerent fop to issue a challenge. How on earth could the late Sir Oswald Fenshawe, always polite and urbane, have sired such a son? But on the other hand, the late Sir Oswald had been an inveterate gambler himself, and had mortgaged his estates to the hilt. How the deuce Richard intended to redeem his voucher, with nothing but inherited debts to back him up, was a mystery to Fabian.

"Very well." Fabian pushed the stacks of coins across the green baize and received Sir Richard's scrawled note in return.

Play continued. Sir Richard was perspiring; he tossed down his wine like water, and the hand that dealt the cards was shaking. Another hour crept by, and still Sir Richard's run of bad luck continued.

Suddenly Lord Castlereagh's hand shot out and pinned Sir Richard's arm to the table just as Sir Richard was about to deal a card to the lose pile.

"I believe those are *two* cards you are holding," said Lord Castlereagh heavily.

Lord Roxbury stepped out from behind Fabian's chair, leaned across the table, and squeezed Sir Richard's wrist until the white fingers opened—two cards spilled onto the green baize, the one hidden behind the face card being the ten of spades, the card Fabian had bet to win.

A tense silence hung in the room; then Sir Richard took a deep, sobbing breath and shook off the hands that held him tied to the spot. His chair fell back with a crash as he rushed around the table to confront Fabian.

"You would accuse me of cheating, would you?" he shouted, although Fabian had not said a word. "Any one of us here must know 'twas *you* who cheated! How else could you have won against the bank?"

Two white lines formed along Fabian's mouth, so hard did he compress his lips in an effort not to give the drunken fellow a much needed set-down.

But young Lord Roxbury, a brand-new member of Brooks's, was painfully conscious of the slur cast on his admired friend Lord Worth.

"How dare you!" he hissed and rushed around the table to slap Sir Richard's face.

Fabian was quicker. He shot out of his chair and grasped Lord Roxbury's arm before the young man could get close enough to touch Sir Richard.

"Let it be, young hothead," drawled Fabian, amused and touched by Roxbury's devotion. "Don't you see he's as drunk as a wheelbarrow?"

Fabian became aware of a commotion behind his back and pivoted around in time to see Charles lunge at Sir

Richard. Charles held Sir Richard's arm much as Fabian was still clasping Roxbury's.

The corners of Fabian's lips twisted upward, but his charcoal eyes bored into Sir Richard with a chilling stare. "You're lucky Lord Baxter prevented your challenge, Fenshawe," said Fabian coldly. "You must be rather more up in the world than I suspected. I advise you to sleep it off, then come and see me at Worth House."

Fabian turned to the other men in the room. "I would appreciate it, gentlemen, if this night's happenings did not come to the ladies' ears. Fenshawe here has a younger brother and sister whose reputations must be protected."

Naturally, the men would want to make certain that Fenshawe never crossed the threshold of any reputable club again and therefore would pass the word from club to club; but Fabian felt certain they'd keep it from their wives' and fiancées' ears on his request, and a scandal could be avoided if only Sir Richard lay low in the country.

"Charles, Roxbury, will you give me the pleasure of your company for an hour or so?" Fabian asked and quit the room without waiting for an answer.

Lord Roxbury and Charles caught up with Fabian before he had retrieved his cloak and hat from the porter. The three men walked slowly toward Piccadilly, and Lord Roxbury filled Charles and Fabian in on the details of Sir Richard's amazing run of luck before they had arrived at Brooks's.

When they reached Half Moon Street, Lord Roxbury begged to be excused. "I have rooms here now, y'know. And I think I'd best call it a night."

Fabian grinned at him. "Being a young blood about town can be wearying, but you'll get used to it. And, Roxbury—" He held out his hand. "Thanks for your championship."

Lord Roxbury blushed to the roots of his sandy hair. He shook Fabian's hand firmly, then departed in a rush.

"Break a bottle with me, Charles?" asked Fabian, yawning hugely.

"Why not."

They hailed a chair and were carried through the deserted

streets to Grosvenor Square, where they were soon ensconced in the comfortable leather chairs in Fabian's library with a bottle of old French cognac and a box of Spanish cigars on the table between them. Fabian had just filled their glasses a second time and was choosing a cigar when a resounding knock on the front door made him drop it back in the box.

"I'd best open up before the whole household is roused."

Charles raised a blond brow. "Where's Robinson, or Alders?"

"Abed, I suppose." Fabian chuckled. "I dare them wait up for me, or place some unfortunate, yawning footman in the hall on the off chance that someone might knock on the door."

He left, but returned moments later with a subdued Sir Richard Fenshawe in tow.

"You!" said Charles with loathing, then turned accusing eyes on Fabian. "Had I known you'd invite this . . . this sharper, I'd have gone with Roxbury."

"Take a damper, Charles. I was hoping Fenshawe would sober up soon and explain to me how he means to redeem his voucher."

Sir Richard ran a finger inside his tight collar. "That's just it, Worth. I can't. And there's no use asking me why I wrote the blasted thing, for I'm damned if I know," he blustered.

"Sit down," said Fabian curtly. "You'll forgive me if I don't offer you a brandy, I'm sure."

"Yes, yes. Don't want any of that stuff in any case." Sir Richard fell heavily into a chair and dabbed his brow. "I daresay you know I wouldn't be able to raise the blunt even if I sold Fenshawe Court; most of it belongs to the bank."

Fabian nodded. "Can you give me one good reason, Fenshawe, why you didn't take off with your winnings when you had the chance?"

"But don't ye see, Worth! I'd never been able to hold the bank at faro before. 'Twas the chance of a lifetime. The bank always wins! I could've won enough of the rhino to clear Fenshawe Court and start on some long overdue improvements.''

"But the bank didn't win," said Fabian coldly.

"You're daft, Fenshawe." Charles looked at Sir Richard with derision. "Don't you know yet that you always lose when you count on winning? You only win when you have so much of the ready that you don't know what to do with it. Look at Worth here; he's a prime example."

"And what do you plan to do now, Fenshawe?" cut in Fabian.

Sir Richard's feverish eyes roamed over the luxurious carpets, the massive furnishings, and the thousands of books lining the library walls. He swallowed. "I'm prepared to pass the deed to Fenshawe Court to you, Worth. It's the best I can do. Mayhap if you put some of your blunt into the land, you'll eventually recover your money. All I'm asking is the fare and a few hundred yellow Georges to give me a new start in America.''

Fabian expelled his breath slowly. His eyes never left Sir Richard's face as he asked, "What about your younger siblings, Fenshawe? Your father once mentioned his *three* offspring to me. Do you require their fare to America as well?''

"No, no," blustered Sir Richard. "Wouldn't dream of asking you for more money. They'll make out. After all, it's about time their grandmother bestirred herself on their account.''

"She is not *your* grandmother as well?" asked Fabian silkily.

"Well, naturally she is, but we've never hit it off. She'd not help me out with a single copper, if that's what you mean. In fact, since the old man—" He coughed. "I mean, since my father wouldn't listen to her sermonizing about gaming, she's more or less cut herself off from the family.''

"So, very likely she'd welcome your brother and sister with open arms.''

Sir Richard's countenance grew even redder, and he

shuffled his feet in embarrassment. His bluster had died, and he stayed silent.

"Tell you what I'm willing to do for you, Fenshawe." Fabian got up and stood towering over Sir Richard. "I shall speak to your bankers and see if they'll let me take over your mortgage. *You* will return to Fenshawe Court and try to get your lands in better shape. I strongly recommend you marry a lady of good sense, with an even better portion, to help you put your affairs in order."

To give Sir Richard a moment during which to recover from his first shock, Fabian picked up his glass and sipped his cognac before stating his conditions. "After two years I shall send my man of business down to Fenshawe Court to determine how much you can afford to pay me annually toward redemption of your debt. But—" stressed Fabian, "*you* will, until they marry, or other suitable arrangements are made for them, provide a home for your siblings."

Sir Richard jumped up and started to protest, but Fabian stayed him with a lift of his hand. "No. I don't wish to hear anything from you now. Sleep on it. I will see you tomorrow—today rather—at five o'clock for your signature on some documents I'll have my solicitor draw up."

Fabian turned on his heel and strode to the fireplace, where he stood with his back toward the room until the click of the door latch had informed him of Sir Richard's departure. Only then had Fabian faced Charles again and offered him another cognac.

___CHAPTER 12___

Fabian propelled himself away from the mantel. With two long strides he stood before Olivia, searching her white face anxiously. His eyes darkened with compassion, but he made no move to touch her; he must comfort with words alone.

"Richard was young then," he said, "a young fool—and probably bewildered by the debts and responsibilities he'd inherited."

"Yes." Olivia looked up, tried to smile, and failed miserably. "But why wasn't I told? If not then, I should have been told when I came of age. And *you*—" her eyes and voice alike accused him, "*you* should not have left me in the belief that you'd enticed Richard into the game and taken Fenshawe Court from him!"

Fabian regarded her steadily. "Would you have believed me had I told you such, Olivia?"

"Well—" She slid farther back in the chair and leaned her head against the cool leather. If only he'd take her into his arms now and hold her tight. But he looked so detached and remote, as if the warm, responsive man he'd been the past few days had never existed.

"Perhaps not at first," she admitted, "but later, when I knew you better . . . yes, later I would have believed you."

"Thank you, my dear." Fabian again searched her face intently. "I'd best leave you to your reflections. When you've had occasion to mull this over, you will realize that it's just so much water under the bridge. What Richard did seven years ago need not affect you, or Tony, at all now."

"Fabian—" Olivia hesitated and bit her lip in confusion, then continued determinedly, "If only a few persons know about the . . . about Richard, why did Charles contend that I cannot cry off from our 'betrothal'? Surely those six or eight gentlemen present at the faro game would not cause my downfall at this time?"

Fabian's eyes were expressionless and dark as the night. "First of all, you may be certain that not just six, but *all* gaming gentlemen in London know. To spread the word in the clubs was the only recourse open to Castlereagh, Petersham, and the others, to ensure that Richard would cheat no one else. They did not spread the word in the ballrooms and salons then, but were you to cause a stir by jilting me, undoubtedly the old story would be rehashed, and since gentlemen love gossip as much as, if not more so, than ladies, both tales would be all over town in no time.''

He bent over the table and placed a marker in Samuel Johnson's *Lives of the Poets*, which he'd been reading before Olivia entered the library. ''Don't fret,'' he recommended. ''If you feel you must end our betrothal, I shall do all I can to help you.'' Without looking at her again, he turned and strode off.

Olivia stared at his retreating back. ''Cheated by Richard, spurned by Tony, and to be jilted by me,'' she murmured softly when the door had closed behind him.

She tapped her fingers against Mr. Johnson's book. She stiffened her resolve to end the sham engagement just as soon as Lionel was seabound. Her whole family was greatly indebted to Fabian; even if he renewed his offer of marriage, she'd not add to that debt by accepting his dutiful proposal.

And if Richard's infamy was to be raked up again, then that would be something with which *Richard* must live. Tony would be in the army, most likely, proving his own honor by fighting that monster Napoleon; Grandmama would be back in Bath, comfortable within the circle of her friends; and she, well, she might be a governess to a parcel of unruly children, perhaps as far away as the wilds of Yorkshire or Northumberland. Merrie would help her find a post away from London, if only she'd return soon.

She shivered and rubbed her arms. The fire was still crackling merrily, but the whole room looked bleak and cold. Deep inside she felt cold. Tears smarted her eyes. Hastily she dashed them away with the back of her hand—someone might enter the library and see her.

Suddenly Olivia longed for the serenity of Merrie's tiny flat. There she could be assured of privacy if she wished to indulge in a good cry, and assured also of the time and opportunity to plan her future. No Lizzy would burst in on her, no Grandmama would study her piercingly through her lorgnette, and no sight of Fabian would make her feel ashamed or set her pulses racing.

She left the library and slowly climbed the two flights of stairs to her luxurious apartment, where she pulled a cloak from the wardrobe and flung it on the four-poster, then hunted for her half-boots and her muff. The boots were soon located; they stood as usual neatly lined up with her other shoes on the floor of the wardrobe. But her muff was neither in the glove drawer nor with her purses.

Tarnation! She'd only worn the muff once. How could she have lost it so soon? Grumpily Olivia donned her cloak, pulled a pair of gloves from a drawer, and selected a large plaid reticule which matched the lining of her hooded cloak. She stuffed a few coins and a handkerchief into her bag, then went to close the gaping wardrobe doors. A bit of light brown fur protruding from behind a hatbox caught her eye. She jumped up and gave the fur a tug, sending the hatbox hurtling down on her. Olivia rubbed her jaw where the box had struck her, but in her hand she held the missing muff.

Her face brightened; something was going right for her. She tossed the muff in the air, keeping her hands outstretched to catch it again, but she quickly took a step backward and swooped her arms over her face to protect it against another missile darting at her, this time from inside the muff. Her heart raced. What on earth had been hidden inside her muff? A thud proclaimed that the object had come to rest on the carpeted floor, and she ventured a cautious peek. A long, dull metal piece lay beside the soft fur.

Olivia bit down a hysterical giggle. 'Twas only the key to the garden in the square which Robinson had given her; and here she'd imagined some murderous instrument designed to do her harm!

She picked it up and took it with her to restore it to its proper place in the closet under the stairs. "Please have the landaulet brought around to take me to Hans Crescent, Jenkins," she told the footman stationed near the front door, and when he'd disappeared through the green baize curtain, she opened the narrow closet door. At first she saw only some dark cloaks such as the footmen and maids wore on cold or rainy days, and several pairs of pattens; then, opposite the door, she noticed the keys hanging from hooks affixed to the wooden wall of the closet.

Squinting, she replaced the key on the hook labeled "Enclosure." There were also keys to the "Harness Room," the "East Attic," "Upper Clothespress," and "Mews," she read before Jenkins returned to inform her that the carriage would be around presently.

"Will there be anything else, miss?" he inquired and watched her curiously as she emerged from the closet.

She laughed softly. "Not unless you wish to tell me where the keys to the dungeons and the gun room are kept, Jenkins."

The footman unbent sufficiently to flash her a quick grin. "When you go to Worthing Court, miss, you'll see the gun room, but I'm sorry to say, miss, we don't have any dungeons."

"Dungeons!" shrieked Lizzy, who came flying into the hall at that moment, her cape flapping wildly behind her and with her bonnet askew on her soft ginger-colored curls. "I should say not! But come now, miss, the carriage be waitin'."

Olivia cast a dark look at Jenkins, then at Lizzy, duly noting the badly concealed apprehension in their eyes. Her lips tightened. This was Fabian's doing. He'd made certain she would not leave without her maid any longer—and that after she'd voluntarily ordered the carriage!

"What kept you so long, Lizzy?" she said crossly and swept outside. At the sight of the dowager's old coachman, Olivia stopped. "Bert! Should you be up and about? How are you feeling?"

Old Bert rewarded her with a pleased smile as he handed her into the landaulet. "Thank 'ee, Miss 'Livia. I'm feelin' quite spritely agin, and 's long as the weather don't turn, this rheumaticky leg o' mine will give me no more trouble."

Lizzy kept up a constant stream of chatter while the open landaulet made its slow way toward Sloane Street, but

Olivia hardly listened. When the carriage had swung into Park Lane, she'd caught a glimpse of a canary-yellow and black phaeton—Lionel's phaeton—and it had turned around, despite the curses of a stagecoach driver and several horsemen, to follow her landaulet. Olivia peeked back again. Yes, those were Lionel's showy chestnuts, and when they followed into Sloane Street, she could see Lionel himself at the reins. The many capes of his silver-gray driving coat billowed behind him, showing an underside of a startling Burgundy shade. Olivia could even make out the fiery carnations in his buttonhole, an arrangement the size of a small cabbage.

She called to old Bert on the box, "I've changed my mind. Don't turn off to Hans Crescent, but drive down Sloane Street all the way and take me to one of the parks before returning home."

"Yes, miss. I could take ye to Ranelagh Street and then Green Park, if that be all right, miss."

Olivia agreed and then settled back against the squabs to give at least the appearance of one enjoying the air and the scenery. There was no point in visiting Merrie's flat. She'd not be able to sit in the wing chair and make plans knowing that Lionel was lurking outside, waiting for her, or perhaps entering number eleven, to knock on doors until he'd found out where she visited. Under no circumstances would she stop and speak with the concierge while Lionel was about, for he'd worm all the information he needed and more out of Mrs. Yates before that good lady had had time to recover from the sight of his awe-inspiring attire.

Not that it mattered a whit if Lionel learned she was only visiting her old governess and not a lover—but the gall of that fop! It was the outside of enough to have him spying on her. He would never learn what she was doing if she could help it.

Somewhere between Green Park and Grosvenor Square, Lionel must have realized that he'd been wasting his time following her about, for when next she turned cautiously to look for him, he'd disappeared. Disgruntled, Olivia jumped from the carriage as soon as it had rolled to a halt before

Worth House and stormed up the wide marble steps, past the butler and a gangly youth in a loud checkered coat whom Robinson had just admitted into the entrance hall. The young man swept off his wide-brimmed hat and bowed deeply. Olivia nodded, but continued to her own rooms without checking her helter-skelter pace.

She had just removed her gloves and cloak when Lizzy rushed in after a very cursory knock. "Miss Olivia—" Panting, Lizzy pressed a hand to her bosom and took a few deep breaths to calm her fluttering heart. "Lud, miss! Ye run off in such a mad dash, I hardly know whether I'm on me head or on me heels," she complained. "I can barely get a word out. But his lordship is askin' for ye. Wants ye to attend him in the study . . . right away, miss."

"Thank you, Lizzy. Please find me the green slippers that match the ribbons on my gown, and then you may leave. Why, you haven't had time to remove your bonnet and cape yet, you poor dear."

Olivia changed her footwear, dragged a comb through her curls, and flung a paisley shawl around her shoulders. The fashionable beret sleeves of her amber cambric dress might be very dashing, but they did not protect her arms against the chill of drafty stairs and hallways.

She hesitated briefly at the study door, listening to the murmur of male voices—Fabian's deep, vibrant baritone, and a second male voice, higher pitched and immature sounding. Well, she'd been summoned; she couldn't help it if she interrupted a meeting.

Fabian responded instantly to her tap on the door and greeted her with a warm smile. "My dear, I want you to meet Mr. Newell Simpson."

The blushing young man—he was the same youth she'd encountered in the hall—bowed awkwardly.

"He is a nephew of Mr. Townsend, one of our feared Bow Street runners," explained Fabian, "and he comes highly recommended by Mr. Townsend himself to help us locate Tony."

"Oh, but I thought—" stammered Olivia. "I thought we didn't want—"

"This is a private arrangement, Olivia. Officially Bow Street is not involved."

She regarded the youth critically. Despite his shyness he met her searching gaze steadily with a pair of shrewd brown eyes several shades lighter than her own. His nose, long and beaklike, cast a shadow over his upper lip, nearly obliterating the first signs of a downy mustache, and his Adam's apple threatened to spike the white cloth of his stock. She still could see no redeeming qualities in his garishly checkered coat and looked in amazement at his old-fashioned knee breeches and short gaiters.

Her eyes met Fabian's questioningly. His lips twitched, but he said gravely, "Master Newell would like nothing better than to be a Bow Street runner, and as you see, he's dressed the part, the spit 'n image of his uncle Mr. Townsend. Alas, he's a trifle young yet to be appointed. He has, however, been following Mr. Townsend about for several years, learning the tricks of the trade."

The young man cleared his throat, and although he was now beet-red in the face, addressed himself to Olivia with creditable clarity. "Ma'am, I knows all the ins and outs of places where a young cove could be 'iding and where you or 'is lordship wouldn't never dream of lookin'. We's instigatin' a search for yer brother, I collect?"

Olivia nodded. She felt his eyes trace her every feature, assess her posture, her stature, and absorb every nuance of color in her eyes and of her hair.

"And he's like a twin to you—" murmured the youth. He was no longer the blushing, embarrassed boy, but a Bow Street runner, certain of his own competence. He squared his thin shoulders and looked at Fabian. "I'll be off then, my lord. If the young cove be alive and in Lunnon, I'll bring 'im to you within five days."

"Here, let me advance you something toward your expenses." Fabian stepped behind his desk and took several bank notes from the top drawer. "Will this be sufficient for now?"

Newell Simpson stuffed the bills into the inner pocket of his atrocious coat. He grinned. "Sure 'nuff, my lord. That'll last more'n five days. Would you be wantin' me to report 'ere every night?"

"Come tomorrow night around seven. I'll let you know then when to report again."

When the door had closed behind the young would-be runner, Olivia sank into the nearest chair. "Do you really believe he can help us, Fabian?"

"One must hope so." Fabian perched on the edge of his desk. "I'm at my wit's end, Olivia. I do not know my way about the stews and slums of London, and neither does Charles. Short of going to Bow Street with an official request to search for Tony, we have no choice but to put our trust in this young sprig. Newell Simpson may be only sixteen, but for five years he's been Townsend's faithful shadow; he also assists one or two of the other runners who have a soft spot for him. Newell knows London like the back of his hand."

"How ever did you find him?"

"I asked Mr. Townsend for advice this morning." Fabian grinned. "If any good comes of this, I'll give Charles a dozen bottles of my best claret, for he reminded me that Townsend owed me for a favor I'd done him in '02. That's when I met the runner for the first time, and mind you, the favor was more in the nature of an accident, but he felt obliged nevertheless."

"What did you do?" prodded Olivia when Fabian did not continue but sat chuckling to himself.

"Ah, well—" He shrugged. "Townsend had been assigned to accompany Prinny to Drury Lane, but despite the runner's diligence a light-fingered little ladybird had weaseled herself close to Prinny's side and snatched the Order of the Garter right off his chest. The baggage would have got away, too, had I not been such a clumsy young fop then. Upon hearing the commotion behind me, I had whirled around so rashly that my smallsword swung out in an arc and knocked against the hussy's knees as she was fleeing past me, and it sent her sprawling.''

"Gracious, Fabian," said Olivia with a teasing smile. "Carrying your sword at the theater! Did you also wear your hair powdered? Oh, how I wish I had been there to see it."

"You, my dear, were still sewing samplers in the school-room." The laugher died from Fabian's eyes. *Gad,* he was eleven years older than Olivia. She'd been a child of twelve when he'd been drinking and gambling with the Prince of Wales and his fast set and had been enjoying the favors of opera dancers and other high flyers. But he was *not* too old for Olivia. After all, he'd witnessed marriages between young debutantes and men who could have been their grandfathers.

Fabian slid off his perch. "Come here." He took her hand, pulling her off the chair and behind the desk. Keeping a firm grip on her wrist—he wasn't about to let go of her at this important moment—Fabian rummaged with his free hand in the middle right-hand drawer.

"You and Mama are taking your grandmother to Lady Sefton's rout, I believe?" He deposited the long, slender case containing the silver-mounted dueling pistols his father had purchased in Venice on the desktop, then searched the drawer again.

"Yes, that was the plan for tonight. Are you not attending?"

"No. Bathurst sent for me." The two pistols he'd bought from Manton a couple of months ago clattered onto the desk. He felt Olivia's startled jerk and smiled reassuringly. "Don't worry, love. They're not cocked."

"But they're loaded."

"Of course." He looked at her in surprise. "Of what possible use would an unloaded pistol be if I found myself suddenly in the position of having to fend off an intruder?" Then his hand closed around the small box he'd hidden at the back of the drawer. He took it out and led Olivia back to her chair. "Sit down, please."

Her eyes widened in sudden apprehension. "What is it, Fabian?"

"I would have done this sooner, but there was never an appropriate moment—or, if there was, it was cut short through some misunderstanding or other." He opened the slim box and displayed a diamond necklace and ring.

"The Worthing betrothal set," he said quietly.

He sensed her stiffening. Olivia glanced briefly at the glittering gems as they nestled on a strip of soft blue velvet. "Very beautiful," she said and started to rise.

Fabian's hand clamped down on her shoulder, pressing her back into the chair. Would the girl never stay still long enough to give him a chance to explain? She was always dashing off just when he thought he'd gotten close to her—almost as if she were afraid.

"Listen to me, Olivia," he commanded. "I wish I could accompany you tonight, but an urgent matter has come up at the ministry, and Lord Bathurst requires my help."

"I feel certain Lady Worth and Grandmama will understand, Fabian."

"And you?" he asked quickly, searching her face for a sign of her feelings. Her expressive hazel eyes were veiled by long, curving lashes, but the absence of a dimple showed him clearly that all was not well.

"Oh, I understand perfectly," she said and added musingly, "It may prove a blessing in disguise—your absence will provide me an opportunity to get acquainted with some of the eligible bachelors."

Olivia laughed, but it was not the usual, irrepressible chuckle and did not sound too happy. "If I remember correctly, Charles recommended that we should *both* find someone else to become engaged to."

His eyes narrowed. Did she believe he was flaunting the diamonds as a signal that he was ready to enter into a betrothal to another woman? "Don't you understand, Olivia? I want you to wear the ring and necklace tonight."

She drew in her breath sharply. "I shan't."

"Why not?" In exasperation he shook her shoulder and

glared at her. "Like it or not, you are presently betrothed to me, and you shall wear my ring."

She raised her face to his, and now the storm clouds gathering in her eyes were only too evident. Fabian experienced a stab of remorse when he saw tears forming as well.

"Unhand me!"

When he did not comply immediately, Olivia slapped his hand away and rose hastily. "What makes you think, my lord, that our tenuous relationship gives you the right to force your will on me? Perhaps you would also dictate which gown I should wear?"

"The gold satin shot with emerald," he replied promptly.

Her mouth opened, but no sound issued forth.

"Only make certain you carry a hatpin in your reticule. I would not wish for you to be mauled about by the eligible bachelors."

Olivia tossed her head and whirled about. She flounced from the study with her chin in the air and her back as straight as though she'd swallowed a poker.

Slowly Fabian closed the jewelry box and slipped it into his coat pocket. She had been close to tears, *yes*, but instinct told him he'd reacted in just the right way. With her dander up, Olivia would be able to tackle her emotions; she'd not be tempted to run out on him, thereby depriving him of the precious time he needed to court her.

But it had been a mistake to bring out the diamonds now. He should have waited, as he'd intended, until he was prepared to follow up with the declaration of his love. But suddenly he'd been afraid of losing her, afraid she might feel attracted to someone young—like Roxbury, or even stammering Mr. Wilburton.... *Ridiculous!* She'd never looked at them twice.

Fabian patted his pocket gently. Well, he was not above a bit of trickery. He'd see to it that Olivia accepted his ring tonight, before he left for his meeting with Bathurst. What a curst nuisance that today of all days they must discover a weak link in the Horse Guards. Bramson would be none too pleased either—one of his fellow officers was suspected of spying for Bonaparte!

By the time the dressing bell sounded, Olivia felt sufficiently composed to direct her concentration to her toilette. In any case, she must hurry now since there was no time left to worry and wonder over and over again whether Fabian had meant that she wear the betrothal set temporarily, or whether his gesture had been an oblique renewal of his proposal. Lady Worth had indicated they'd be leaving for Lady Sefton's rout immediately after dinner, and although Olivia wouldn't dream of donning the gold satin, she did not wish to look a dowd either.

Time flew as Olivia chose and discarded first the ecru muslin, then a silver gauze gown, and finallly settled on Madame Bertin's latest creation. She allowed Lizzy to help her into the pale blue satin underdress, cut to cling snugly to her figure but with a deep slash on either side of the skirt to allow her freedom of movement. It left her arms and shoulders bare, but all expanse of creamy skin was then covered demurely by the overdress of midnight-blue silk, so sheer as to appear diaphanous. The full skirt of the over-dress, open in front to reveal the pale blue satin, was gathered under her bosom and hung in graceful folds down her back, ending in a demitrain.

Olivia stared into the mirror. What a perfect foil the gown would have made for the diamond necklace. Annoyed, she compressed her lips and swept from the room. It was too late now to change again.

Robinson hovered anxiously in the hall, waiting for her descent before announcing dinner. Fabian was polite but cool and devoted most of his attention to Lady Fenshawe while Olivia listened to Lady Worth's prattle of famous routs and balls given by Maria Sefton in the past. Finally the covers were removed, and she looked to the dowager count-ess for the signal to withdraw.

"One moment please, Mama," said Fabian. "I have finally remembered to have the betrothal set cleaned, and I simply cannot let Olivia go out tonight without the diamonds, not when she is dressed to show them off to perfection.''

"Splendid!" Lady Worth clapped her hands. "I did not wish to appear prying so I never said anything, but I did wonder why Olivia never wore the diamonds. I didn't realize they needed cleaning.''

Fabian's eyes twinkled. "Neither did I, Mama.''

He rose and came to stand behind Olivia's chair. "Permit me, my love.''

Deftly he fastened the necklace, his warm fingers setting her skin ablaze where they brushed against the nape of her neck. Then he picked up her hand, and since he did not move to stand beside her, Olivia had perforce to turn in her chair or have her fingers twisted at a most awkward angle. With Grandmama's lorgnette and Lady Worth's shining eyes trained upon her, she could not very well create a fuss and snatch her hand away.

Fabian slipped the large, diamond-shaped ring with its multitude of sparkling stones onto her finger, then raised her hand to his lips. "You are beautiful," he whispered and kissed the inside of her wrist and her fingertips.

"Thank you, Worth." Hastily Olivia withdrew her trembling hand.

When Fabian had left, she sat as though turned to stone, the blood pulsing rapidly through her veins and undoubtedly staining her cheeks a bright crimson. What a dastardly trick to play on her! Why, she'd . . . she'd . . .

Olivia couldn't think what she'd do, what with Grandmama and Lady Worth complimenting her on her looks and urging her to get her wrap. Maria Sefton was one of Almack's powerful patronesses—it wouldn't do to set up her back by arriving late.

Well, there was nothing she *could* do, not until Lionel had been sent off.

___CHAPTER 13___

Five days after Lady Sefton's rout—as dreadful a squeeze as any hostess could have wished—Olivia let herself into Miss Merriweather's flat. She'd arrived in Hans Crescent very properly with carriage and maid, but without Lionel to spy on her. Olivia had refused point-blank to let Lizzy come inside with her; instead she'd enjoined the old coachman not to keep the horses standing. He was to take Lizzy for a drive and return to Hans Crescent in about a half hour.

A look around the tiny entrance hall dashed Olivia's hopes that Tony might have pushed a note under Merrie's door, for nothing but dust lay on the parquet flooring. In the sitting room Olivia deposited her cloak and muff on a ladder-back chair by the door, then busied herself with opening the window and dragging the wing chair closer to the refreshing, cool breeze.

This was the fifth day of Newell Simpson's search for Tony, the day he'd given as the limit for finding her brother. It was three o'clock in the afternoon, and they hadn't heard from him. In fact, they had not seen young Simpson since he'd made his third report on Wednesday—he'd not shown up at Worth House last night at ten as he and Fabian had arranged. The only person with news to impart had been Lieutenant Bramson. Briefings of the new officers and subalterns had commenced; could Tony *please* show his face by Monday?

Fear tightened her stomach. Where on earth could her troublesome little brother be? "If the young cove be alive..."

Newell Simpson's words rang clear and terrifying in her head, but were dismissed instantly. Tony must be alive.

Her head hurt after a long, sleepless night spent tossing and turning until her sheets had been in such disarray that she'd been forced to remake her bed. Olivia rubbed her throbbing temples, but the pounding in her head became more insistent. It was *not* in her head! Olivia jumped up, rushed to the door, and came to a halt with her hand poised to turn the knob. She listened intently.

The knocking had ceased, but someone stood outside, breathing in short, ragged gasps. *Tony?* Olivia could not control the tremors that shook her whole body; she had to clasp both hands around the knob to open the flimsy door.

"Ah, there you are, dearie," huffed Mrs. Yates.

Olivia, breathing just as hard as the fat concierge, let her arms drop to her sides. "Won't you come in, Mrs. Yates?" she invited in an unsteady voice. How foolish to have expected Tony at the door.

"Nay, dearie. I've only come to tell you about this here note. I saw you step out of that fancy carriage and tried to catch you, but—"

"You have a message?" interrupted Olivia. She pressed a shaking hand to her bosom. "For me, Mrs. Yates? Where is it?"

The concierge fumbled in the pocket of her voluminous puce round gown and extracted her quizzing glass along with a stained, torn piece of folded paper. With the glass held to her eye, she peered at the dirty scrap. "Yes, here it is. It came last night, oh, about nine of the clock."

"Was it my brother?"

"Well, I don't rightly know. I think it was just an urchin who brung it, but he was already running off when I came to the door and he didn't turn back, call as I might. He must have gone upstairs first, and when he found Miss Merriweather from home—you see, it's addressed to her."

Olivia snatched the note from Mrs. Yates's hand and unfolded the paper carefully.

"Anyways, I think he stuffed it under my door because Miss Merriweather didn't answer his knock," concluded the concierge, undaunted. "Is it from your brother, miss?"

"Yes." Her eyes riveted on Tony's signature, Olivia could barely contain her impatience. "Excuse me, please." She started to shut the door, hesitated, then ran into the sitting room to grab her muff. She dug two coins from the small pocket sewn into the muff's lining and handed them to the concierge with a smile. "Please buy yourself a pound of your favorite tea. And thank you so very much, Mrs. Yates."

Finally she was alone. She stepped closer to the open sitting room window to take advantage of the light while studying Tony's atrocious pencil scrawl, made none easier to decipher by the splotches of grease and the frayed edges of the cheap paper.

Dearest Merrie, she read. *Am in a dreadful scrape— please send thirty guineas immediately!* "Immediately" was heavily underscored, a sure sign of the urgency of Tony's request. He had continued, *Ask Richard or Grandmama for five hundred guineas. Imperative I get them by October 18! Send money to Golden Rooster, Spittle Market off Crispin Street. Desperately, Tony*

The note fluttered from her nerveless fingers. Five hundred guineas! How could Tony have spent so much money!

Olivia gave herself a mental shake. Even if Tony had gambled it away, the how and why were immaterial now. First she must fetch Tony home, and to do that she needed Fabian. Fabian would know how to get to the Golden Rooster.

With her cloak tossed carelessly around her shoulders and the muff clutched under one arm, Olivia hurried off, but came to a sudden halt halfway down the first flight of stairs. The note! She'd left the note in Merrie's flat. When she returned to the sitting room, however, she found not a trace of the scrap of crumpled paper she'd dropped on the floor.

Frantically she looked about her. She must find Tony's message. What had he written? He was at the Golden Rooster. . . . Spitalfields? No, that did not sound right.

Small beads of perspiration gathered on her forehead as fear once again clutched at her insides. With a sob she swung around to the window to let the breeze fan her heated face. Then, as the significance of the coolness penetrated her numbed mind, she gasped. She'd left the window open! Galvanized into action, Olivia first slammed the window shut, then turned her attention to the approximate area where the draft might have blown the piece of paper. On hands and knees she searched under the wing chair, under Merrie's sewing basket, even under the credenza, and finally located the elusive scrap behind the coal shuttle.

Hastily she flattened it out and committed Tony's location to memory: Golden Rooster, Spittle Market off Crispin Street. Heaving a sigh of relief, she left the flat again, conscientiously locking the door behind her, then descended to the street.

There was no sign of the carriage. Olivia looked up and down the street, tapping her foot impatiently. Surely she'd been inside the building more than thirty minutes. Well, perhaps old Bert was just driving around the block to keep the horses warm. Barely had this rational thought flitted through her mind when impatience flared up in her again. Would nothing go right? Olivia stuffed Tony's note into her muff and started walking toward Sloane Street.

She had proceeded no farther than the next building when she was jostled roughly by a young man who'd come bounding up the area steps and vaulted over the iron fence before the tall house. The impact of his body crashing against hers sent her reeling, and she would have fallen had she not clung to the man's arm for support. His was a familiar if unwelcome face.

"Lionel!" she cried indignantly. "Watch what you're about!"

Her eyes widened as she took in his attire. There was no sign of the dandy now, for he wore a faded corduroy riding jacket with an awkwardly sewn patch on each elbow, stained breeches, and scuffed jockey boots. Olivia stared at the filthy cap on his black locks and drew back a few steps.

"What kind of masquerade are you playing at, Lionel?" Apprehensively she looked about her, but the street, save for a skinny gray cat, was deserted.

He merely grinned wolfishly and pressed closer until the retreating Olivia was trapped against the fence. His arms shot out, and before Olivia had time to take breath for a scream, she was imprisoned in a viselike grip. One hard, callused hand covered her mouth, crushing her lips cruelly against her teeth, the other clamped around her waist, pinning her left arm and the muff between them.

Furious, and not a little frightened, she struck and clawed at his face with her free hand. Once her fingernails hit a target and dug in sharply. Lionel grunted in pain, but then he chuckled and murmured close to her ear, "Wildcat! What sport I'll have taming you." His voice, quite unlike his usual, nasal tones, held a deep, sinister note, making her blood run cold with fear. Then he started dragging her toward the gate in the fence. Panic-stricken, Olivia gave up swinging her fist at him, and instead held on with all her strength to one of the iron bars.

As from a far distance, she heard the rattle of carriage wheels and the crack of a whip urging a fast team to an even wilder pace. *Dear God, let it be old Bert,* she prayed and dug in her heels although her arm was in imminent danger of being pulled from its socket by the powerful yanks Lionel exercised on her resisting body.

Suddenly he let go. Olivia went flying against the fence, her hipbone crashing against the unyielding metal. She fell heavily to her knees just as Lizzy erupted from the coach and old Bert shouted to the maid to go to the horses' heads.

Lionel swooped down and grabbed Olivia's muff. Holding it like a trophy, he fled toward Sloane Street, leaving old Bert, who'd finally clambered off the box, to shake his whip after him in an empty threat.

"Oh, stop yer useless gawking, Bert," screamed Lizzy,

deserting the perfectly calm horses. She ran past him with her skirts hitched up to her knees. "Get back to the coach so's I can help Miss Olivia!"

Gently Lizzy pried Olivia's stiff white hand off the iron bar and chafed it gently until Olivia felt the circulation return with a rush of tingling blood. Olivia wriggled her stinging fingers and was surprised to see them obey her command. The whole hand had felt so numb earlier, she'd been half afraid she'd lost the use of it.

"Miss, can ye stand? Are ye all right?"

"He got my muff," whispered Olivia.

"Ah, miss. If that be all! Ye can always buy a new one. Up ye go now. Must take ye home, miss."

Yes, she must go home to Fabian before Lionel had time to plan mischief with Tony's message. Supported by Lizzy's strong arms, Olivia exerted every ounce of her strength to drag herself upright and negotiate the few steps to the carriage on knees that threatened to buckle under her. It was a trifle more difficult to climb in, but finally she slumped into a corner of the upholstered seat.

The coach rocked gently as Lizzy bounded in and old Bert pulled up the steps after her. Despite a smarting hipbone and rib cage that hurt as if she'd been kicked by a horse, Olivia sat up stiffly. "Spring 'em, Bert!" she commanded.

Bert muttered under his breath and slammed the door shut, but when he cracked his whip, the horses took off at a pace that sent Olivia hurtling back against the squabs. She clenched her teeth and concentrated on Tony's note, repeating the message over and over in her mind until they'd reached Grosvenor Square. With more haste than grace, Olivia scrambled from the coach and rushed into the house.

"Where is Lord Worth?" she demanded of Jenkins, who'd jumped up from his chair when she burst into the entrance hall.

"Upstairs, miss. I believe his lordship is getting ready to go out. He's—"

"Please ask him to see me in the study," she interrupted.

"Oh, never mind, Jenkins. Here—" Olivia tore the cape off her shoulders and tossed it to him. "Give this to Lizzy. Ah, there she is. Lizzy, stay in my rooms! I may need you to help me change in a hurry," she called over her shoulder, already halfway up the first flight of stairs. She took the second flight at a more sedate pace. It wouldn't do to arrive at Fabian's door out of breath and unable to relay her important news.

Olivia rapped on Fabian's sitting room door and waited impatiently.

"Yes, miss?" Surprise and barely concealed reproof were mirrored on Alders's craggy features.

"I must see Lord Worth!"

"Best wait in the small drawing room or in the salon, Miss Olivia. I'll tell 'is lordship ye're wishful of 'aving a word with 'im."

Olivia took a deep breath. She didn't have time now for silly restrictive conventions which forbade that she see a gentleman in his private apartments. Besides, hadn't she been alone with Fabian in his sitting room before, when he'd been knocked on the head? No one had raised a ruckus then.

"I want to see him now, Alders." Quickly she pushed the door open and brushed past him into the room. What now? Should she call Fabian?

Before she or Alders was called upon to decide on the next step, Fabian's voice rang out, coming closer with every word. "Alders! Where the deuce is my blue—" He broke off when he saw Olivia facing him through the connecting door, his dark eyes narrowing as they searched her face. He nodded to his valet. "I'll ring for you, Alders."

"I'm sorry, Fabian, I—" Embarassed, she took a step backward as Fabian came toward her. He'd obviously been dressing; he was wearing boots and breeches, but no coat, and his lawn shirt was still unbuttoned at the neck. Hastily she averted her eyes from the sight of his pulse beating at his throat. If only she didn't blush so easily, she fretted not for the first time in her life, and hung her head, hoping to make her burning cheeks less visible.

"What is it, my love?" Fabian's deep voice was full of laughter. In two quick strides he stood before her. "Don't tell me the intrepid Miss Fenshawe has second thoughts about invading my sitting room."

Her head came up. "What fustian!" she snapped.

"There, that's much better," he said with approval. "Now sit down and tell me what this is all about."

"I know where Tony is!"

Fabian, in the act of taking a seat across from her, hovered motionless for an instant before sitting back in the deep armchair and crossing his legs. He listened attentively while Olivia told him about her visit to Miss Merriweather's flat, the words tumbling from her lips, and her breathless pace not even slowing down when his brows shot up in disbelief while she related the part Lionel had played, and how he'd snatched her muff.

". . . and now he has Tony's note," she concluded.

"Lionel?" said Fabian, incredulous. *No,* he thought, *Lionel was at White's at that time, playing a rubber of whist with Charles, Roxbury, and me.*

"I'm positive! He may have been dressed like a groom and spoken like a libertine, but there was no mistaking him—his black locks, his eyes, and . . . yes, and the mole on his temple! I know Lionel will try to get to Tony and do mischief. We must hurry, Fabian!"

"We?" Fabian's brow shot up. "My dear girl," he drawled. "The Golden Rooster is located in the Spitalfields area—not a safe place for a young lady."

"*That's* inconsequential. Of course I'm going with you. Tony has a need of me, and . . ."

"No!"

The one word was uttered with such finality that Olivia fell silent, only her glowering eyes and the mutinous set of her jaw still conveying her rebellious thoughts.

"Tony is a man," said Fabian quietly. "He must learn to fight his battles without your help. I don't mind at all giving him a hand this once and making certain he presents himself at Bramson's office on time, but then he must fend for himself. He cannot stay tied to your apron strings forever.''

If looks could maim, he thought ruefully. He understood very well that his dictum must go against the grain with her, but there was no help for it. "I shall take Alders with me, and I'll send a note to Charles asking him to meet me at the Golden Rooster. That should be sufficient reinforcement to face Lionel and even a brace of Mohocks. . . .''

Olivia took a deep breath and opened her mouth to speak.

". . . but I shall *not* take you," he continued smoothly, "and subject you to the dangers of Cheapside and Spitalfields. Now, if you will excuse me, I'll get on with dressing and be on my way.''

She nodded stiffly and left the room, but the memory of her huge eyes, overbright from tears hastily blinked back, and her white, set face stayed with him while he donned his coat, ordered Alders to be ready to accompany him, and penned a terse, concise message for Lord Charles.

When Alders joined him in the study, Fabian had just completed loading his dueling pistols. "Here, you'd best carry these," he said to the valet. "I'll have my hands full with the grays.''

Jenkins was then dispatched with the note for Lord Charles, and a few minutes later Fabian and Alders sped off in the racing curricle.

Alders was briefed in a few well-chosen words, and all Fabian could do until he'd reached the Golden Rooster was to stew in his own impatience and hope that Horwood's map of London had indeed supplied him with the best route. Even his grays, having enjoyed a several-mile run—protesting the presence of other quadrupeds or threatening to stampede over the slower pushcart vendors—were no distraction any longer; they'd settled willingly into the fast pace he prescribed for them.

Fabian's thoughts turned to Tony Fenshawe. Olivia's little brother was in desperate need of five hundred guineas before October 18, which could only mean he'd incurred *gambling* debts.

Devil a bit! Was the young cawker obsessed by the same fever that had ruined his father and his brother? Fabian berated himself for not having considered sooner that gambling and the laying of wagers on the outcome of the most ludicrous events were major pastimes of the officers in Wellington's army while they awaited their orders—and at times one might be stuck for several weeks in the most damnably boring surroundings until new orders came down. He'd best have a talk with young Tony before Olivia got to her brother; she couldn't be expected to show the necessary degree of severity.

As though Alders had divined that Fabian was now thinking of his fiancée, the valet broke into his musings. "What surprises me, milor', is that Miss Olivia didn't want ter come along."

Fabian shot a quick glance at Alders's carefully expressionless face. "Well, she did; but I told her no."

Alders turned around on the narrow box seat and studied the teeming Cheapside traffic behind them. "Can't see 'er as yet," he muttered and directed his gaze straight ahead again.

Fabian grinned. "Miss Olivia *is* a rare handful," he acknowledged.

Perhaps just this once she would listen to reason and remain safely at Worth House. If not—well, he'd alerted Clem to be on the lookout for her and either accompany or follow her if she so much as set foot outside the door. In any case, he could not now worry over something he had no power to prevent; else he should've locked the chit in Lady Fenshawe's parakeet cage and thrown away the key.

Reluctantly Fabian dragged his thoughts away from Olivia to pay attention to his surroundings. They'd been traveling on Bishopsgate for a while, and it was time to watch for his turnoff. Yes, there it was. Fabian swung into Union Street, and from there followed Crispin Street into Spittle Market. He found the Golden Rooster without trouble, the garish sign with its gold-colored bird and incredibly green, violet, red, and blue tailfeathers shouting its location to all and sundry. But Charles and his elegant tilbury were nowhere in sight.

In the cobbled yard of the two-story brick building, Fabian tossed the reins to a groom. "Look after them," he ordered before he disappeared with Alders in the Golden Rooster, where the proprietor, a tall, cadaverous fellow covered from neck to knees with a stinking, ale-splattered apron, met them with many obsequious bows.

Alders shouldered him aside. "'Is lordship's come ter speak with one Tony Fenshawe. Where in this 'ere 'ostelry did ye put the young gent?"

Upon learning that he was not to have the elegant and obviously highborn gentleman for his customer, the inn-keeper's face clouded over with discontent. "First there's not a soul ter see the young cove, and 'im bein' at death's door with a nasty fever; and now *four* gents in the space of as many minutes 'ave come ter pay their respects," he grumbled. "Top o' the stairs, first door to yer left. But mind ye, I won't 'ave 'im leave without payin' the shot. Thirty guineas, my lord!"

Fabian tossed him some gold pieces and started up the stairs. As soon as he and Alders had rounded the bend in the stairway, he halted and motioned to the slender box Alders was carrying. The valet raised the lid, and Fabian removed first one of the deadly weapons, cocked it, and then the other. If the landlord was correct and two men were already with Tony, then he'd best be prepared to face Lionel and Frederick up there.

Without a sound, they crept up the remaining steps and positioned themselves before the door indicated by the landlord. The wiry little valet needed no one to tell him what to do. He knew that Fabian, with a pistol in each hand, could not kick the door open for fear of jarring the triggers of the sensitive, Italian-made weapons. Eyes narrowed and shoulders hunched in concentration, Alders thrust a booted foot against the door handle, propelling the door wide open.

Immediately he ducked and launched himself out of Fabian's way.

In an instant Fabian stood on the threshold, facing a grimy, uncurtained window with a small, round table and two ladder-back chairs below it; to his left he could see half of a wardrobe, the other half being hidden behind the open door; and to his right—

Fabian lowered his pistols, for they were of no use under the circumstances, and stepped into the room.

"Good evening, Lionel."

"Welcome, cousin." From the right-hand corner of the small chamber Lionel smirked at him, the muzzle of his pistol cutting into Tony Fenshawe's temple.

Tony's pale face blanched even more, and he shrank into the lumpy pillows on his rickety bedstead, his feverish hazel eyes darting from one man to the other. Then he stared with burning intensity at the door behind Fabian.

Correctly interpreting the silent warning, Fabian called, "Watch out, Alders!" But it was too late.

Lionel's groom Frederick charged from behind the door and felled Alders with a cruel blow of his cudgel. He shoved Alders's inert form into the corner by the wardrobe, then kicked the door shut and positioned himself squarely in front of it with his club at the ready.

"That's better," said Lionel. "Now we can be comfortable. You may wish to sit down for a spell, my dear Fabian." He indicated one of the chairs, his eyes glinting maliciously. "And you may as well put away your pistols. You can't shoot me without getting Olivia's precious brother killed as well."

"Stow your jabbering, Lionel!" commanded Frederick.

Placing his pistols carefully on the wobbly table, Fabian watched the half brothers curiously. Seen apart from each other, Frederick and Lionel might have been taken for identical twins, but in the same room together as now, it was obvious that Frederick was the more powerfully built of the two, and that his voice was much deeper.

"Get on with the business afore someone else comes

blasting into this lice-riddled hole.'' Frederick crossed the room quickly and stood beside Lionel. "Here, let me have your barking iron so's I can keep this foolish cawker in check. Just look at him," he said, pointing to Tony. "Shaking all over he is, as if he had the ague.''

Lionel took three hasty steps away from the bed. "The ague? But he told us 'twas nothing but a mild bout of stomach disorder; that he'd only made it sound worse so the innkeeper wouldn't kick him out!"

"You're a damned fool, Lionel." Frederick darted after his half brother and took the pistol from his unsteady hand. "Now get out your sabers and start that blasted duel," he ordered. "So far I've had to do all the dirty work, and though 'twas a good thing I did, it's *your* turn now. Just think if I hadn't decided to go after that hoity-toity Miss Olivia again after you'd given up, we still wouldn't have been any closer to Worth than we were last week. Now we have him right where we want him.''

"I've done my share," protested Lionel. "Didn't I find that place in Hans Crescent in the first place? And didn't I try to warn the girl off Fabian?''

Frederick spat on the floor. '' 'Cause I darkened your daylights for you! And even then you messed up the affair, 'cause she's still just as betrothed to Worth as she was afore you 'warned' her off.''

Tony Fenshawe raised himself on one elbow and stared at Fabian. "*You* betrothed to Olivia, Worth?" he croaked. "Thunder and turf! If I'd only known.''

"I daresay you'd have come to Worth House instead of skulking around in gambling dens," said Fabian. "Too bad you didn't read the notices in the papers, Fenshawe.''

Frederick nudged Lionel with his foot. "Get a move on!" he hissed. "I want to get out of here and start living!''

Lionel cautiously approached the bed again and pulled two swords from under it, dislodging thick wads of dust in the process. "Damn you, Frederick! Couldn't you have hidden my dueling swords on top of the wardrobe? This infernal dust has ruined my new boots! Hoby finished them only yesterday."

Frederick's reply was a well-aimed stream of spittle, landing alarmingly close to the tips of Lionel's gleaming white Hessians.

Lionel narrowed his eyes to slits but said nothing. He bent and pulled off his boots, then set them tenderly out of harm's way behind the nightstand.

"Sorry you carried your dueling pistols for nothing, coz." He motioned to Fabian to pick one of the rapiers. "Always been an ambition of mine to prove that there's one thing I'm better at than you. Mind you, I'm not saying I couldn't best you with pistols as well, but they're so damned noisy."

Fabian weighed the sword in his hand, then tested the blade. "But can you go through with it, Lionel? Can you kill your own kin?"

Lionel blanched. "Who's talking about killing? No, I'll pink you cleanly through the arm, then we'll tie you up and ship you out to *Hejaz* or *Asir* as a slave—why, Olivia might be on the boat with you, you lucky dog! If we catch her in time, that is."

Fabian gritted his teeth as bile rose bitterly in his throat. He must remain calm while speaking with Lionel.

"You can't possibly get away with it, you know," he said conversationally. "Do you wish to end up on the gallows?" Fabian watched Lionel closely and, detecting a flicker of uncertainty in his eyes, pressed on. "You have a nice little property, and if you wouldn't throw away your money on gambling and . . . lightskirts, is it? Well, then you'd have a tidy fortune to spend on your raiment and whatever else it is that gives you pleasure."

Lionel's hand tightened on the hilt of his sword. "I *had* a profitable estate—it's mortgaged now. I've been in dun territory for years, barely outrunning the constable. But when you were wounded at Fuentes de Oñoro, and it looked quite as if you'd succumb to the fever, all of a sudden the cent-per-centers, the tradesmen, and tailors offered me unlimited credit. Of course, after your recovery they tightened the purse strings again,'' he said bitterly. "And then, when your announcement appeared in *The Times*—"

Lionel shrugged and struggled out of his tight, pale blue velvet coat and removed his brocaded vest. Snatching up his rapier, he slashed it through the air. "Enough of the talk now. Let's see who's master of the sword.''

"At least let's remove the table and chairs over to the foot end of the bed. This chamber is narrow enough without obstacles to hamper us as well. But tell me, Lionel, where does Frederick come in on this?''

Before Lionel could open his mouth, Frederick spoke, his voice surly. " 'Twas my idea in the first place to do away with you—and I'm not talking of shipping you east and having you pop up again in a few years!'' he said viciously.

He turned to Lionel, who'd gasped in stupefaction, and said with venom, "I'll personally finish him off if you don't have the gumption, or better still, I'll shoot *you* if you draw back. Do you believe I want to be a groom always—I, the grandson of an earl? The family should've done more for me. Well, now that you're in River Tick, I'm seeing to it that I get my share through Worth. You'll kill him in a duel fair and square and be the next Earl of Worth, but *I* shall make certain you don't squander your inheritance on anyone but me.''

Fabian shrugged out of his coat. He had not a chance in the world to fight them both without endangering the hapless Alders and Tony as well, but once the fencing was under way, there might be an occasion for a daring feint; he might be able to run Frederick through, especially if Frederick kept his pistol aimed at Lionel instead of Tony.

Fabian cast a quick glance at Alders, but his valet had not moved; his skin looked pasty, and his iron-gray hair was matted with blood. Alders would be out for a while yet, but there was still Charles to reckon with.

If only he could prolong the duel! But he could *not* delay the start. Frederick's pistol was moving from Lionel's to

Fabian's head—and his black Worthing eyes glinted maliciously.

Slowly Fabian raised his rapier. *"En garde!"*

___ CHAPTER 14 ___

Olivia stormed into her bedchamber and slammed the door behind her. Fabian's high-handedness was not to be borne! How dare he refuse to take her to Tony!

"Miss Olivia—" Lizzy rose from a dainty, chintz-covered chair by the window where she'd been mending the lace on one of Olivia's petticoats. She regarded her mistress's scowling face with curiosity. "Which gown would ye want me to lay out, miss?"

"What?" Distracted, Olivia ran her fingers through her short curls. "Oh! You may go, Lizzy. I shan't be changing after all."

"Yes, miss." Hastily Lizzy gathered her sewing materials and scurried from the room, directing a last, puzzled look at Olivia drumming her fingertips against the window, before softly closing the door.

Olivia stared down into the small garden behind Worth House. Her eyes traveled the flagstone walk leading from the house to the iron gate in the wall, the same path she and Fabian were wont to use as a shortcut from the stables.

Fabian is on his way to the Golden Rooster, where Lionel is waiting—

The drumbeat of her fingertips became more urgent as her thoughts tumbled faster. She must get to the Golden Rooster. Tony needed her . . . but also . . . also to be near the maddeningly, infuriatingly autocratic Earl of Worth. Fabian had not believed that Lionel possessed the note now—he'd walk straight into Lionel's trap.

Again her eyes flew to the gate in the garden wall. Beyond lay the stables—and Firebrand.

She whirled around and ran to the wardrobe, but even an extensive search of assorted boxes on the upper shelf did not bring Tony's clothes to light. They were not in the bedroom she'd occupied as Tony; she remembered distinctly Lizzy's telling her that she'd packed up "all them britches and pantaloons" and that she'd take them . . . Where the dickens had Lizzy taken them? The upper clothespress!

Furtively she crept out of her room and down the stairs. There was no one in the entrance hall, no one to say her nay when she removed a key from its hook in the closet under the stairs, and no one to raise a brow when she stole into the study to test the middle drawer on the right-hand side of Fabian's desk.

Olivia's eyes widened in fleeting surprise. The drawer was not locked! She'd been prepared to attack the lock with a penknife if necessary. Gingerly she removed the two pistols, making certain they were not cocked; it wouldn't do to shoot herself in the leg or, worse, hurt Firebrand. She was about to close the drawer when she noticed the absence of the dueling pistols. Her breath caught sharply in her throat. Much as she wanted Fabian to be armed, "dueling pistols" had such an ominous ring—

The top of Fabian's desk looked more cluttered than ever with a large map spread over his papers and stacks of ledgers, and with a pen still resting in the inkwell. Leaning closer, she squinted at the fine lettering inside a circle drawn in bold, black ink on the map: *Spittle Market*. With a hiss of elation she snatched up the map. Now to retrieve Tony's breeches and riding coat!

A scant half hour later Olivia, astride Firebrand, was clattering toward Oxford Street with the pistols safely stowed in saddlebags and Horwood's map of London in her coat pocket. The black cape she'd snatched on impulse from the closet under the stairs bellowed out behind her as she pressed her mount past slower moving carriages and pedestrians.

She tried to think of her destination only, and the twisted lanes and alleys that would take her there once she'd passed Holborn Hill, yet the thought of Fabian and his dueling pistols preyed on her mind. She should be thinking of Tony, but invariably Fabian's dark, chiseled features would eclipse Tony's softer, immature face.

Olivia couldn't help but notice the lengthening shadows also. She hadn't checked the time before she left Worth House but estimated it must be nigh on six o'clock. There wasn't much daylight left—

Touching her heels to Firebrand's side, she uged him to dodge between a dray and an oncoming stagecoach—still so far to go; she was only in High Street now—when she heard the sound of hoofbeats even faster than Firebrand's and the whinny of a horse behind her. Firebrand tossed his glossy black head and answered proudly.

A cautious look over her shoulder confirmed her fears. Firebrand had recognized one of his stablemates. There was no mistaking the gleaming chestnut coat of Sultan or the diminutive figure perched on his back. Her first, instinctive reaction was to try to outdistance Clem, but on second, more rational thought, she pulled up and allowed him to catch up with her. It lay not within Clem's power to order her back to Worth House, but he might be willing to accompany her to Spittle Market.

As soon as he'd fallen in beside her, she nudged Firebrand on to a faster pace again. Clem appeared perfectly content with this, and so, with a sidelong glance at him, she said, "I almost gave you the slip, didn't I?"

He flushed crimson. "'Twas only 'cause the guvnor believed you'd come out the front door, lookin' for a hackney as you's always done afore. But I'd Sultan 'ere ready an' waitin', and when I saw ye go 'ell for leather toward Oxford Street, 'twas none too 'ard ter catch up with ye."

Olivia swallowed. So her hunch that Fabian had set the tiger to spy on her had proven correct. Strangely, this did not annoy her as much as it would have a few days earlier.

Was she learning to accept Fabian's high-handed manner? She shook her head in irritation. Of course not; she was merely preoccupied with her urgency to get to the Golden Rooster, and besides, it wouldn't make any difference if she was growing used to him—her "betrothal" to Fabian must end soon.

They rode in silence, Clem taking the lead and Olivia accepting his role as guide unquestioningly. When they pulled up in the yard of the Golden Rooster, the sun was touching down on the rooftops in the west. Olivia slid off the saddle, tossed the reins to Clem, and then, with a pistol in each hand, darted across the yard. The door of the inn stood open, but there was no one about, and even after she'd called for the landlord, the inside doors remained stubbornly closed. Olivia hesitated uncertainly, eyeing the dark, winding staircase ahead of her with misgiving.

"Best give me one of them barkin' irons, miss." Clem, who'd slipped into the hall behind her, gestured toward the pistols.

Without a word Olivia complied. Keeping her left hand firmly on the baluster for guidance, she ventured up the stairs, listening intently. But no raised voices or the crash of furniture overturned in a fight guided her steps. Only a faint, metallic sound—

Swords!

Olivia's foot missed the next step. Clem's firm hand pushing against the small of her back saved her from a fall, but when he would have taken the second pistol from her hand, she tightened her grip around the butt and shook her head at him. She was all right, her hand as steady and still as the sentries standing guard in Whitehall. Only she must hurry!

She raced upstairs, Clem hard on her heels, until the clash of steel resounded loud and menacing in her ears. Cautioning Clem to silence, Olivia tiptoed to the door. They must not break the fencers' concentration lest Fabian falter and— Carefully Clem inched the door open, and then they both stood gaping into the gloomy chamber.

Fabian and Lionel in their white shirts and with their gleaming swords flicking back and forth were easily discernible. They were fighting fiercely, never taking their eyes off each other. Sweat glistened on their foreheads, and the harsh gasps of their breathing rang as loud as the clash of the steel blades.

Lionel thrust wildly. Fabian parried, forcing the blade aside, and instead of his heart, the point only pierced the fullness of his shirt.

Thank God!

Then she saw the third man. He stood in the far right corner of the room, a large horse pistol dangling from his hand. Olivia drew in her breath sharply. Even in the dusky light she could see that he looked as much like Lionel as she looked like Tony. She recognized the corduroy riding jacket. *He* had stolen her muff.

As if her angry scrutiny had drawn his attention, he moved his head and looked straight at Olivia. His lips twisted in a grin. He raised the pistol in a salute, then slowly pointed it at Fabian—Fabian, who was concentrating on Lionel and unaware of this new source of danger to him.

Stifling a cry of outrage, she sprang farther into the chamber. She leveled her pistol with both hands, taking careful aim—and stared petrified at the living, breathing man, her target.

The palms of her hands grew clammy; a tremor raced along her outstretched arms, and droplets of ice-cold perspiration pearled on her brow. She saw his smirk widen; then he shifted his gun away from Fabian until the evil eye of the barrel focused on her forehead.

Olivia could neither pull the trigger nor break from the hypnotic spell of his gun. She had frozen like a rabbit before the hunter.

Fear for her life gave Fabian added strength and agility. Quick as lightning, his blade whirled, struck with violent force against Lionel's sword, knocking it from his hand, then, like a silver arrow, pierced Frederick's wrist a breath before he pulled the trigger. The bullet whistled past Olivia's head and smacked into the plaster of the wall behind her.

Sudden silence hung in the air. Olivia blinked and looked at the men standing frozen into immobility, caught in midmotion as if posing for a tableau. Fabian, with his sword poised for yet another thrust, had his eyes fixed on Olivia's face; Lionel stood with mouth agape in stupefaction; and Lionel's look-alike was staring at his bleeding wrist in utter disbelief.

She saw his hand open and the pistol drop to the floor. He still held his arm outstretched before him, and she could see the dark blotch on the inside of his wrist widen until it overflowed and dripped onto the warped oaken floorboards.

Tarnation! She spun around on her heel, her stomach heaving alarmingly. Throwing her forearms across her face to block out the sight of the wounded man, Olivia leaned against the wall.

Someone pried the pistol from her trembling fingers; strong arms wrapped around her and led her to the window. *Fabian.* She leaned into his embrace, murmured a soft protest when he removed one hand to press the window open, and fell silent when his arm once again closed the circle around her.

Olivia breathed in deep gulps of the cool evening air and was beginning to feel better when a voice, achingly familiar yet rendered strange by the feeble, plaintive note in it, startled her.

"Dash it, Olivia," said Tony from somewhere across the room. "You can't go soft on us. Pluck up, gal!"

"Clem, go pick up Frederick's pistol—" Fabian's voice was barely audible, but it reached the tiger, who was hovering in the doorway, his pistol wavering between Lionel and Frederick.

Instantly he darted across the room and snatched it off the floor, but with this act Clem broke the spell that had kept Lionel and Frederick motionless.

Lionel, face distorted with rage, drove his fists into Fabian, who still held Olivia within the protective circle of his arms, while Frederick launched himself at the diminutive tiger, bringing him down easily. With great presence of mind, Clem sent the pistols skidding across the floor and hung on to the much larger man by sheer force of will when Lord Charles burst through the open doorway.

For an instant he stood poised on the threshold, surveying the room anxiously, then a wide smile split his boyish features. "By George!" he roared, tossing his cloak off his shoulders. "What a great turn-up. I'd half feared I might be too late." With a shout of joy he plunged into the melee, dragging Lionel along with him.

Fabian chuckled and, knowing that Charles's enthusiasm would more than make up for Clem's lack in stature, gave his undivided attention to Olivia.

"Crazy little fool," he murmured and kissed her forehead tenderly. "Just wait until we get home. . . . I'll blister your backside. . . . I'll lock you in the cellars with the mice and spiders. . . . I'll never let you out of my sight again," he warned, punctuating each threat with a strategically placed kiss until her face felt tingly all over.

"Pardon me, Fabian." Charles's apologetic voice drew them apart. "Thought you might wish to know that Alders has come around. I've put him on the bed for now. And what the devil am I to do with your Bedlamite cousin and his groom now?"

Slowly Fabian released her. Olivia blinked. Someone had lit three stubby candles on the nightstand, and in their flickering light she saw Tony, thin and pale, shivering on the edge of the bed and Alders stretched out behind him. With a guilty start, she rushed over to her brother. While she'd stood in Fabian's embrace, there had been no room for thought of anyone save Fabian in her whirling mind.

"Oh, Tony!" She sat down beside him and threw her arms around his neck. "What a scare you gave me! Don't you ever, ever run off like this again."

Tony grinned a little sheepishly, but his mind was on other matters. "I hear you're betrothed to Worth. Well— I mean, you'd better be after the way you let him kiss you just now.''

Olivia drew back a little and regarded Tony frowningly. Had he no word to say of his own escapade? ''I'll explain later,'' she said. ''How are you, dear? You don't look too—''

''You'll *explain* to me?'' he interrupted. ''Great scot! As though I'd voice any objections. You've caught yourself quite a fish, my girl!''

She rose, cheeks flaming angrily, and looked down at her brother. ''I shall explain it to you later, Anthony, and until then I'll thank you to keep your opinions on the subject to yourself.''

With a toss of her head, she went to join Fabian and Charles, who were trussing Lionel and Frederick with the strips of linen Clem tore from the threadbare sheets of Tony's bed. Olivia stared curiously at Lionel's groom. The likeness was astounding.

Catching her puzzled look, Fabian winked at her. ''Wondering about the likeness, love? You shouldn't, you know. Happens in the best of families.''

She blushed crimson, but before she could say anything, the young would-be runner Newel Simpson charged into the room.

''My fifth day—'' He huffed, his face crumpling with disappointment when he saw Fabian. ''But you beat me to it. How'd ye trace him afore I did?''

''Never mind now.'' Fabian sprang up from his crouching position and pointed at the two trussed men. ''I still have work for you. Dangerous work, Newell.'' Turning to Lord Charles, he asked, ''Do you have the money, my friend?''

''Why else would it have taken me so long to get here?'' Charles cocked a brow at him and grinned. ''Best transfer your funds while you can. Had to run your banker down at the Cocoa Tree, and it took some persuading to get him to leave in the middle of a rubber. Barely made it to Hoare's before they closed.''

Lord Charles stalked over to his cloak, extracted two

leather pouches from pockets hidden in the side seams, and tossed them to Fabian. "Dash it all," he muttered, shaking the heavy folds of his garment. "Wouldn't be surprised if my new cape had lost its shape with all this weight tugging at it."

Fabian skimmed a handful of gold coins off the top of each purse and handed them to Newell. "These are for you, my lad." He gave him time to count and deliver his stammered thanks before passing the two bags of gold to the would-be runner as well. "The purses will remain in your safekeeping until these two . . . uh . . . gentlemen are aboard a ship that is about to lift anchor. Then and only then, you may hand a purse to each."

"What ship?" asked Newell in confusion.

"Good question, my lad. Let's see—" Fabian narrowed his eyes and propped his clefted chin onto his hand while Newell stared at him in rapt attention.

A smile lit up Fabian's harsh features. "I've heard tell," he said, "that on the Irish coast one can still embark on a journey to America. Newell, my lad, take these two gentlemen to Ireland and make certain they'll never darken the shores of England again. If you require an assistant, just skim an additional fee off the top of their purses."

"America!" Lionel lifted his head and blazed angrily at Fabian. "Do you want to see me killed? We're at *war* with America!"

Fabian grinned. "Only consider, Lionel. In America you may become a Republican and need never worry about a title again. And Frederick will envy you no longer; you and he both will have the same amount of capital to set you up. You'll not find me ungenerous, I promise you. Deposited at the bottom of your purse you'll each find a draft on my bank, which—after the war—any American bank will be glad to honor."

Then followed the most tedious half hour Olivia would ever wish to live through. While Newell Simpson was off somewhere looking for two of his friends who happened to own a coach, Fabian engaged Tony in conversation—although, truth to tell, it looked more like a lecture delivered by Fabian, with Tony giving an occasional nod or shake of his head, as the case might be. Olivia had wanted a word with Tony herself regarding the matter of five hundred guineas, but decided that her homily could wait after all.

Clem had left to take Firebrand and Sultan to Grosvenor Square, and Charles had dragged the table and chairs back to the window. "For heaven's sake, sit down, Alders," he admonished when the valet heaved himself off the bed and tottered about. "You look like death warmed over. Wouldn't wish to drop in a faint at Miss Olivia's feet, would you? You'd best sit down as well, Olivia. Makes me nervous to watch you pace."

He himself strode back and forth in the narrow chamber, every once in a while inquiring of Alders and Olivia how they felt, or telling Lionel and Frederick that the gallows were too good for them and that Fabian was out of his mind to let them off so easily.

The two miscreants sat propped against the wall near the door, and whenever Olivia looked up, she encountered Frederick's bold, black eyes roaming over her breeches-clad figure. Her skin crawled. If only Fabian had blindfolded the lecher; if only... if only she were wearing a gown so that she might stand up and turn her back on Frederick with a most disdainful swish of her skirts.

Finally, even this ordeal had passed. Newell and his burly friends led Frederick and Lionel to a traveling chaise that must have been built several decades ago when springs had been unheard of, and Fabian handed Tony and Alders into Charles's care.

"The tilbury will be much more comfortable for our two invalids," he said with a grin, pulling Olivia into his curricle.

Suddenly, remembering his gentle kisses, his threats—or had they been promises?—Olivia felt vulnerable. They'd found Tony, and Lionel had been dispatched to a distant land. Now was her time to depart from Worth House, to disappear out of Fabian's life. But Fabian had said, "I'll never let you out of my sight again."

Once before he had showered her with kisses, set her aflame with his touch. She'd come to believe that he cared for her, only to be jolted from that dream by his jests and laughter. Was this another occasion when she was reading too much into his words, his kisses?

"A penny for your thoughts."

Hastily she gathered her scattered wits. "They aren't even worth a groat. I was wondering when you'd begin scolding me. After all, I've shown conduct quite unbefitting a lady of quality. I have"—she ticked off on her fingers— "dressed in breeches and ridden astride, run off without an escort for 'twas none of *my* doing that Clem accompanied me part of the way. I have . . ."

"Enough! Give over, Olivia." He chuckled, but caught himself instantly. His deep voice held a thread of menace when he said, "If Lizzy aided and abetted you in your harebrained scheme—dressing up as Tony again, by George! —she need not look to me for a reference!"

"Oh, you mustn't blame Lizzy! She had no notion! I found Tony's breeches in the upper clothespress—there was this key under the stairs, you see, and I . . . I slipped out the back door with none the wiser. Well, except for Clem, of course—"

She threw him a sidelong glance, but it was too dark to see the expression on his face; there was not much evidence of streetlights this far east in the city. "About Clem—" she said. "You set him to *spy* on me. For shame!"

"And didn't I have reason?"

"How could you think he'd be able to prevent my coming to the Golden Rooster?"

Fabian sighed and eased his back against the squabs. "I did not ask him to keep you at home. I merely requested that he make sure you'd come to no harm, for I'd realized already when I told you *not* to come that you wouldn't heed me at all."

"Then why the deuce didn't you take me?"

There was a minute pause before he replied, "If I could be assured you wouldn't swear in company, I could feel more relaxed about it, my dear."

"I never! It just seems to slip out when I'm either very comfortable with someone or very angry."

"That is exactly what I feared."

"Well, why didn't you take me if you knew I'd follow?" she persisted.

"Because one should never give up hope."

"Oh." She mulled this over for a while, her heart steadily sinking. She had disappointed him again.

"Don't take it to heart, love. No one's perfect."

Even in the dark she knew he was laughing at her. There was that unmistakable lilt in his voice. "No. And that goes particularly for you. You apparently...forgot?...or neglected to mention quite a few interesting facts to me. Why didn't you explain the relationship between Lionel and Frederick to me?"

"What? And sully a maiden's ears with such tales?"

"Fiddlesticks."

He was silent for so long that Olivia was beginning to feel acutely uncomfortable. "I . . . I haven't thanked you yet for coming to Tony's rescue."

"No, you haven't. Are you going to?"

"Well, of course!" She drew herself up and stared at him. Here, in Oxford Street, she could make out his features whenever they passed under one of the new gas lights, but his impassive face told her nothing.

"Good," he said, "for I was beginning to wonder if you really wanted him found. You didn't say much to him. I expected you'd be bubbling over with joy; instead you were pensive and very quiet at the Golden Rooster."

Olivia chewed her lip. Her reunion with Tony *had* been sadly flat. When she'd first heard his voice in the dim chamber of the inn, she'd been in Fabian's arms—reason enough to forget about a mere brother, she thought, no matter how beloved, and no matter how lost he'd been. Then, when she'd hugged Tony, he had commended her for "catching" such a warm man as Fabian. As if she'd care anything for his fortune! She felt deflated by Tony's shallow reaction.

These were not matters she cared to divulge to Fabian. With a weary sigh she said, "I *am* happy that Tony is found. But suddenly I was impatient with him and angry, and I'm not even certain whether I was angry with myself for having kept him tied to my apron strings"—she saw his impudent grin and sniffed—"or with him for not having cut them. Besides, he said something. . . ."

"Something like having landed yourself a great catch?"

"Ohh! You heard!" Her face burned with mortification. Not because she felt guilty of that kind of mercenary thinking, but because she'd indulged in daydreams lately whenever Fabian had been tender toward her or had called her his love. And since they were pulling up under the bright lantern before his home just then, she felt quite certain that he'd witnessed her embarrassment, and promptly became tongue-tied.

The great front door of Worth House opened, disgorging Jenkins, who ran to the horses' heads, Robinson, Lizzy, and—hanging back genteelly—Lady Worth and Lady Fenshawe.

Fabian jumped down from the box and held out his hand to Olivia. She took it and allowed herself to be handed down, but when she would have hurried ahead of him, Fabian slid an arm around her waist, holding her easily his prisoner.

"Good evening!" he called to the assembled company. "I know you must have been anxious about us, but I beg you to contain your curiosity a few moments longer. Charles will be along presently with your grandson, ma'am . . ." He bowed exquisitely to Lady Fenshawe. ". . . and with Alders. Mama, please look after them. Fenshawe will require no more than a bath, some hot food, and perhaps a tonic, for he's just gone through a mild bout of influenza. But Alders has been hurt. Please have someone fetch Sir Whitewater to him."

Still holding Olivia firmly encircled with his arm, he pushed past the crowd on the stairs into the entrance hall. "Charles will tell you everything you'll want to know," he called over his shoulder as he steered Olivia into the study.

"And now," he said, closing the door behind him, "we have some unfinished business to attend."

A firm hand in the small of her back propelled her toward the fireplace. "Please take a seat, my lady." With a flourish he indicated the soft rug before the hearth; then, when she'd sat down with her legs tucked under her, he knelt beside Olivia.

"You'll be too warm in your cape. Let me help you." Already his fingers touched her chin, lifting it gently. He unbuttoned her cape and slipped it off her shoulders.

His eyes caressed her slender figure. "As charming a boy as you make, I wish you were sitting here in your gold and emerald satin," he murmured, "so that I might kiss your shoulder just here."

He pushed away her riding jacket and traced the spot with his fingers, setting her skin atingle even through the material of her shirt. "But then, there's always a next time—"

She drew herself up. "There will be no 'next time,' Worth! Tomorrow I shall be leaving with Grandmama. My role in this house ended at the Golden Rooster."

"What? And desert Tony? Without you I'll never have him fit by Monday to start his career in the army. Besides, I believe your grandmother is promised to Lady Wanderley for dinner tomorrow. Surely you'd not deprive her of that pleasure?"

"Then I shall leave by myself! Now, if there is aught you particularly wished to say to me, you'd best do it this instant for I'm about to retire."

Trying to hide her trembling hands in her coat pocket, Olivia looked at him defiantly. That proved her undoing; Fabian was smiling at her, not only with his lips but with his eyes, their charcoal depth warmed by an inner fire. Even had she wished to rise and leave the study, she would not have been able to budge—her knees were a gelatinous mass of uselessness while, to her dismay, she felt her mouth curve in a responding smile.

His face came closer. "There is indeed something I particularly wish to say to you, something I neglected to say when we last sat tête-à-tête before the fire here." Folding his arms securely around her, he pulled her toward him.

"I love you, Olivia."

Then his mouth covered hers, and her protests and arguments died before she could rally sufficiently to organize her thoughts. Besides, if he loved her, there was no need to argue, she thought fuzzily. Unbidden, her hands slipped from her pockets to clasp behind his neck, drawing him even closer.

Again the magic of his lips awakened her deepest feelings, and his hands set a flame burning within her. When he drew back, Olivia sat stock-still. He'd said he loved her. Why did he stop kissing her? She *knew* he wouldn't laugh at her, yet the shadow of that other time lingered.

Fabian read her uncertainty, the question darkening her hazel eyes. He wanted nothing so much as to kiss her again, reassure her of his love, but he must hear from her own lips as well that she loved him.

"I cannot guess your feelings, my sweet delight," he said reproachfully. "You must tell me."

She blushed adorably—would that she never lost that endearing trait. Her apprehension had gone—amber flecks of mischief danced in her eyes, making him feel drunk with desire.

"What must I tell you?" she asked demurely.

His fingers tightened on her shoulders, shaking her gently. "That you love me, delicious torment!"

"I love you, Fabian."

Joy exploded in his chest in great, painful bursts. He drew a shuddering breath. "Good. Then we'll marry so that the portrait of my youthful counterpart may be restored to its proper place—outside your bedroom. I do not intend to give you time to miss me at night."

"Devil a bit! You knew?"

His kiss was the only answer she received to that stormy query, but it proved eminently satisfactory. She made no demur when he shifted his position and pulled her onto his lap. Her head fit just right between his shoulders and his chin when he leaned back to rest against the chair behind his desk, and he only needed to tilt his head a fraction to kiss the lips offered so temptingly.

"How on earth could Tony have spent all that money?" she murmured once.

"Dicing," he replied and continued with the more pressing business of tasting her dimple and the tiny beauty spot at the corner of her mouth. Then his lips must explore her ear, her slender neck, and the fluttering pulse at the base of her throat.

Suddenly, when her shirt and riding coat proved too much of an obstacle in his quest, he sat up and looked at her sternly. "Tarnation! If you ever wear breeches again, I'll—"

Fabian decided against a foolish commitment, but crushed her against his chest instead and knew the satisfaction of her unconditional surrender.

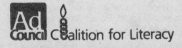